THE BUTCHER'S WIFE

A DARK MAFIA ROMANCE

SACRED VOWS
BOOK 2

EVE CIRIC

To my parents,

For your constant love and support, thank you.

(No, you still aren't allowed to read this.)

Glossary

Alici - Anchovies
Arancini - Deep-fried balls of rice
Bella - Beautiful
Buon Appetito! - Enjoy your meal!
Consigliere - Advisor to the don
Cornetti - Croissants
Crostata - Tart
Fiorellina - Little flower
Fottuta puttana - Fucking bitch
Gracias - Thank you
Minchia - Fuck! (Lit. Penis)
Miseria - Misery
Nyet - No
Pulotti - Offensive word for cops. (Lit. Pig)
Signora - Ma'am
Signore - Sir
Sottocapo - Underboss (second in command after the don)

PROLOGUE

ANNETTA

My husband is dead.

My hands stopped shaking an hour ago, but my heartbeat stutters every time I glance in the rearview mirror. I don't recognize the black sedan that's been following me for the past hundred miles.

I thought I had more time.

I should have known better.

Tall, formless trees loom over me, and rain beats on my windshield as I navigate over the stretch of dark, slick road barely visible past my headlights. My heart urges me to drive faster, to scream down the highway, but I can't afford to. If a deer jumps out, I'll crash.

Another glance in the mirror shows the black sedan pulling off on the exit I just passed.

I'm alone.

I'm free.

Something between a sob and a laugh burst out of me, and I clap my hand over my mouth.

I can't cry, not yet. I have to get home first. I have to look my parents in the eye, tell them what I did, and crawl into my sister's bed to sleep, just like when we had nightmares as kids.

My wedding ring glints in the darkness, and I submit to a wild urge as I balance the steering wheel with my knee and tug at the ring, grinding it briefly against my knuckle until I cast it off. I lower the window and fling it into the forest.

My husband is dead, and I'm going home.

1

ANNETTA

Three Days Later

"You look good," Mom says.

Her clear, steady voice is nothing short of a miracle after so much wine, but the slight droop in her left eyelid gives her away, despite having injected enough Botox over the years to kill a horse. A half-empty bottle of Pinot Grigio sits within arm's reach on the bathroom counter, surrounded by a spray of sparkling droplets.

The face that looks back at me in the mirror isn't my own. This woman has long, dark eyelashes glued to her eyes. Her lips are raw and puffy from a last-minute exfoliation. Self-tanner smears her skin with a false glow.

Serafina gazes back at me.

Except that isn't right.

Serafina is gone.

I don't move when Mom touches the ends of the new hair extensions that fall below my breasts.

"You look just like her," she says.

I only look like Serafina if you're drunk.

Her comment should annoy me, but instead, I'm numb.

The doorbell rings downstairs, and Mom startles. She turns to the mirror, plucks a tissue from a marble container, and dabs at her eyes.

"Leave this." She takes what's left of the pansy out of my hand and tosses it into the sink.

Bruise-colored petals circle my feet. My fingertips are wet and stained.

I follow her from the bathroom, and my sister's shape in the mirror trails behind.

The sticky-sweet scent of flowers suffocates me as we pass Serafina's workbench. She'd been crafting an arrangement for Aunt Francesca's birthday. It's unfinished.

I don't look at her bed, where the gossamer canopy drapes over the top like a shroud.

A deep laugh seeps up through the floorboards from downstairs, and my stomach twists.

"Sweetheart." Mom looks back at me expectantly. That's what she calls Serafina.

I look down at my feet, surprised that I've stopped.

"I don't want to go." My voice croaks. I've barely spoken a word in the past three days.

I was supposed to be done with all of this.

Mom's brows pinch together. She's usually more careful about letting that happen. Gives you wrinkles.

"It's too late for that. Don't keep him waiting." She twists her hands together. "He'll send Junior."

I wait for fear to whisper in my ear, to curl around my muscles and bones like it does whenever Junior's name is spoken, but my grief sinks me into a deep, dark well. Nothing can touch me here.

Mom sucks in a breath and rolls her shoulders back.

"Don't be difficult. It's one dinner. You go, you sit, you look pretty. Do you want Dad getting in trouble?"

"No."

"No, we don't." Mom looks lost for a moment. "We'd better go now."

I jerk my legs forward like a clumsy marionette puppet. If I'm Serafina, then she would listen. She always obeyed.

Mom smiles wearily and loops her arm through mine.

As she tows me through the house, the bleached hallway runner bleeds into dark wood underneath my feet. She tugs me to a halt next to Dad's worn loafers. I stop. The tops of my high heels shine like two black beetles against the marble flooring of my parents' foyer.

"We were getting worried about you! Thought I'd have to send up the cavalry."

It's Aldo who speaks, but it's his son Junior who I look at first.

Junior draws my attention the way an arm sticking out of a dumpster would. You want so badly to be wrong about what you're witnessing, but the longer you stare and the closer you get, the more sharply horror claws into your throat, until eventually, you turn and walk away. You don't engage with men like Junior. You avoid eye contact and pray he doesn't notice you. At family events, if he looked at me or Serafina for more than a few seconds, it would plant a seed of terror in my heart that would grow for days after.

Today, though, I'm only mildly interested in the new eyepatch covering his left eye.

He grins at me, too much white circling his single eye and too many teeth flashing like a dog baring its fangs. When I don't react, his brow crashes down in visible rage. Mom's hand on my arm tightens.

Grief feels like a superpower in this moment. Junior

could shove a gun into my mouth, and I wouldn't blink an eye. He seethes as I turn to his dad—my future husband.

It has been a little over a year since I last saw Aldo, but he looks a decade older. His cobweb hair clings to his scalp, and his skin hangs loosely over his face like melted candlewax.

"Serafina," he says.

I nearly gag. I don't want to hear his voice croaking out my sister's name with that pathetic imitation of compassion. If he had a single shred of honor or kindness, he wouldn't be forcing my sister into a marriage in the first place.

But what I want doesn't matter anymore.

The don needs a wife.

Mom releases me to Aldo, who gropes into the open air until I'm squeezed against his side. I accept his touch. Serafina didn't deserve this, but I do. This is my penance.

Outside in the dying sunlight, I float by Aldo's side along the length of the walkway where Serafina had once planted a river of billowy golden bushes. Did she tell me their names? I can't remember.

Aldo stops me next to his pitch-black SUV, where Dad and Junior are already sitting inside. Through the driver's side glass, Junior's gaze cuts to mine, and his eyes narrow.

Dad is already settling into the backseat for a nap. He always pretends not to see the way men treat Serafina and me. Mom says he loves us in his way, but she's too afraid to acknowledge the truth.

Aldo poses me so I'm facing him. Serafina's fawn-colored wool coat does little against the chill that cuts through to my bones.

"I'm sorry about your sister," Aldo says, caging my biceps in his hands. His thumbs lightly graze my breasts and then press into the flesh there intentionally, stroking back and forth. "A fucking hit-and-run? Don't worry about a thing. When we find the bastard who did it, he's gonna pay."

I try not to breathe as he presses a withered kiss to my lips, but when he draws back, snatching a handful of my ass, I choke on his awful scent—like sour milk. Flakes of dry skin litter his face.

When he smiles, his veneers are blinding.

Aldo releases me, leaving me stumbling into the car. Dad is snoring against the far window.

"Seat belt, Serafina," Aldo calls from the passenger's seat as the car pulls away.

I buckle myself with mechanical movements and face the window without seeing a thing.

The golden plants in the walkway shimmer in my mind. What did Serafina call them? I remember flicking through old photos on my DSLR on her bed, and her voice, soft and sweet from years of practice, excited to share a new perennial that turns gold in the fall. She called it *Amsonia*. She said it would last forever.

"Break open the cigars!" Aldo's voice snaps me out of my reverie.

I blink away unexpected tears. Outside my window, gravel leads to Turi's mansion in the center of manicured hedges and a field of dark, rippling grass. I haven't been here in years.

Serafina told me Turi had recently gotten married. She said it was a scandal, but I had just gotten into a fight with my husband, and I was snippy with her. I ended the call early.

It was our last phone call.

A huge, familiar figure outside my window startles me. Everyone else has left, and I've been sitting in the empty car with my hands in my lap. The door swings open as I unbuckle myself, smoke and pine needle scent coiling through my senses before I turn. A crisp black button-down wrapped around a tall, heavyset build fills my vision until the man lowers his face to study me with espresso-colored eyes. A strand of dark hair slips from his bun to brush against his thick, tattooed neck.

For the first time in three days, I feel a spark, a flicker, of *something* as I say his name.

"Dom."

2

DOM

Something is wrong.

I fold my arms and lean against the wall of Turi's formal dining room as Aldo forces laughter and pretends we're all good buddies. He's not the issue, not at this moment. He's doing what I've known him to do for roughly the last twenty years—he arrives in a bad scene, blusters and bluffs his way through until he can get his feet under him, and attacks when people least expect it.

Tonight, his usual tactics are failing him.

Turi sits at the head of the dining room table with his wife Marisol at his side. Ignoring Aldo completely, he's only got eyes for Junior, Aldo's malevolent monster of a son. That's not what's wrong either.

Junior attacked Marisol, and now Turi's going to kill him. Simple.

Barbara is immune to the tension in the room, his wrinkled hands clasped on his belly and his eyelids half-closed. He's more dangerous than the doddering old man act he puts on, but even knowing that, his little nap routine is damn effective at lulling you into a false sense of security.

I rest my thumb on the waistband of my pants—a silent threat to Junior that he better behave. One sudden movement from him, and he's eating a bullet.

Half of the people here tonight, pushing food around on their plates and pretending to drink wine, I need to protect. If I let myself get distracted, one of them could die.

So why am I so focused on the woman sitting in the chair?

I blame it on how she was acting when she got out of the car. She looked up at me with her big brown eyes, and her cheeks were wet with tears.

It's no mystery *why*—she's the twenty-year-old fiancée to sixty-year-old Aldo, whose past five wives have all mysteriously disappeared, Henry the Eighth-style. Hell, if I was in her shoes, I'd be crying too. Junior makes sure his stepmoms don't last long.

But Serafina doesn't cry. It's part of why I like her. She bottles up all her feelings like a good Catholic, stuffs them in a prayer box once a week, and goes about her day, no one the wiser. The last time I saw her cry, she was seven, and even then, a sharp look from her mom had her shutting down in seconds.

Serafina's twin sister, on the other hand? Polar opposites. If Serafina feels nothing, Annetta feels *everything*. That woman will cry at a sad puppy commercial or news of some estranged family member's divorce, no matter how many dirty looks their mom throws her.

So if Serafina is crying, something is really fucking wrong.

I already scanned her over as we walked up to the house. No bruises or cuts, which tracks. Aldo's been too lazy to hit his wives after his second wife started fighting back.

I'd chalk it up to her finally snapping—Serafina's wound tighter than a clock—except that she caught Junior's eye too. For all of that sick fuck's many flaws, he's perceptive. If he thinks there's something worth watching Serafina for, then it could be the difference between life and death that I figure it out first.

Serafina jolts in her seat when Aldo drops his fork to his plate with a clatter. He pats his belly and pushes his chair back. "Let's go check out your bar in the kitchen. I want to talk shop. Let the ladies catch up."

Fuck yeah.

Just a little longer, then all hell breaks loose. Years of practice have me glued motionlessly to the wall instead of shaking my limbs around like a baseball player about to walk up to the pitch. Better to be like Barbara and have no one pay attention to you until it's the perfect moment.

Turi and Junior maintain eye contact as they rise, their tense animosity only breaking when Turi bends down to whisper in Marisol's ear.

Barbara jerks up with a snore and funnels out with everyone else, leaving behind Serafina, Marisol, and me.

Barely visible in the cradle of the formal dining chair, Serafina's thin shoulders slump forward, and she chokes out a sob. Even if I don't know what's going on with her yet, I'm already pissed off that Aldo ignored her—or, worse, he saw his fiancée's tears and still brought her to his stupid celebratory dinner. If Turi doesn't shoot him tonight, I will.

At the head of the table, Marisol shifts in her chair. "I... uh, need to go to the bathroom."

Goddamn, she annoys the piss out of me. She's always got some scheme or another up her sleeve when all she needs to do is follow orders. While I guard over her and

Serafina in here, Turi takes Aldo and Junior and shoots them out there.

"No," I say, without pulling my gaze away from Serafina's back. "Stay here."

Serafina spins around in her chair, her eyes wide. "Dom?"

She's normally more observant than this. Her eyes are rimmed with tears, and her face is all puffy like she's been crying for a while. Hours, probably.

"It's okay." I use the same tone I would use with my brothers and sisters when I wasn't fast enough and Dad hit them.

That's what it is—she's acting like she's been hurt. Just because I didn't see any injuries earlier doesn't mean there weren't any.

I clench my hands into fists. Aldo was supposed to wait until the wedding to consummate his unholy union. Did he force himself on her early?

Or—fuck—I think of Junior's attention on her. Did *Junior* touch her?

I nearly forget Marisol's in the room with us, and tell her in a hard voice, "You need to stay here until Turi says otherwise."

She pauses. "I need to check my phone."

She can't help herself, Turi's little hacker wife. She's just like him—always has to know what's going on.

"You want to watch the cams? Go ahead."

She glances deliberately at Serafina, who's following our exchange with wide, doe eyes. Marisol thinks we can't show Serafina what's going on? If Junior fucking touched her, she deserves to see him shot in the face more than anyone.

I jerk my chin toward Serafina. "She's good. She can see too."

"Fine." Marisol scowls, pulling her phone out of her pocket and jabbing at the screen.

Serafina turns to look up at me with an unfamiliar, meek expression that has my stomach souring.

I extend a hand to her, murmuring, "Come on."

She takes my hand and lifts from her chair, putting extra weight into my palm like she needs me to keep her upright. Dread settles into my bones. So much has been going on lately—I haven't been watching over her like I should. I thought she'd be free of Aldo and Junior tonight, but I might already be too late.

I arrange her so I'm supporting her upper back and gripping her forearm. She slumps into me like a house on a bad foundation, and I guide her to stand behind Marisol's chair so we can watch over her shoulder.

The kitchen camera is displayed on Marisol's phone. A miniature Turi and Junior glare at each other from either end of the kitchen bar while Aldo drinks from a glass of wine and gestures between them. I'm almost impressed to see how quickly Barbara is dozing off on one of the barstools.

As Aldo talks, his desperation oozes through the screen. Good. He starts making wild promises—promising to promote Turi to underboss and help him kill his dad if only he agrees to give his wife to Junior. Fat chance. I've seen the covetous, obsessive gleam in Turi's eye when he looks at his new wife. He's not giving her up for anything.

Serafina whispers, "He's talking about killing Ottavio?"

"Fucking idiot," I mutter in Italian and scrub my hand over my beard. Aldo's not getting anywhere near Ottavio, especially not to kill him. If it were that easy, Turi would have done it years ago.

I can't figure out why Turi's stalling as he asks how Aldo

plans on killing his dad, but even as Marisol's breathing speeds toward hyperventilation, I'm not stressed. Turi's got things under control. He always does.

Aldo lays out a harebrained scheme, outlining how he's going to take down *Ottavio*, the head of the Commission—the five ultra-powerful Mob families in New York. The old man is completely oblivious to how deranged he sounds.

Serafina makes a choked noise next to me when Aldo waxes poetic about taking her to a beach somewhere after this is all over.

I squeeze her hand.

"What do you think, Turi?" Aldo asks.

Turi watches Aldo in that unnerving, too-intense way of his, lifting a hand to the gun at his waist—hidden to the others by the kitchen counter. As he moves, so does Junior.

Turi needs a distraction.

"I think we have ourselves a deal," Turi says, clearly lying through his teeth.

Marisol sucks in a breath.

Aldo falls for it hook, line, and sinker. He claps Turi on the shoulder and praises his loyalty as Turi asks Barbara to escort Marisol to the basement.

The phone screen turns dark. Marisol starts to stand, but I drop a hand on her shoulder and push her back down.

Serafina jerks her head toward me. "Dom! Don't."

I can't tell if I'm impressed or amused that Serafina is daring enough to clutch her slender pianist fingers around my arm and try to pull me off Marisol.

"Trust Turi," I say. "He has a plan."

"His plan is to sacrifice Marisol," Serafina hisses, yanking on my wrist. Where's that meek little girl from a few moments ago? What am I still missing?

I lean toward Serafina, peering into her face, and she

rears back, her eyes growing wide like she's been caught red-handed doing something she shouldn't.

A ridiculous thought enters my head, but before I can act on it, Barbara strolls around the corner, not looking the slightest bit surprised to see me wrangling both women at the end of the dining room.

"Dom," he calls out. "Take Serafina home. Now."

About fucking time.

I snatch her up by the waist, my fingers biting into her ribs, and cross the room.

She kicks me hard in the shin—which fucking hurts—but I only grunt and throw her over my shoulder like a bag of flour.

"Dad," she screams as she pounds her fists against my back. "Dad, please. He's giving her up! She'll die!"

Barbara doesn't even spare his daughter a glance, locked in a silent standoff with Marisol.

Serafina thrashes against me like a kitten in a burlap sack as I carry her out the front door, my boots crunching across the gravel toward one of Turi's SUVs.

She's all skin and bones, practically weightless on my shoulder, but her squirming and fighting make it hard to keep her from hurting herself. She rains her fists down on my back like she thinks her little tantrum will have any effect.

Then, right next to the car, she twists toward me and sucks on my neck. Her hot, wet tongue flicks out, shooting an unexpected jolt of heat through me.

I stumble. "Serafina, what the fu—"

She bites down. *Hard.*

"What the fuck!"

I jerk and tear her off me like I'm pulling a bulldog from a rope and toss her against the passenger door. She bangs into it with a grunt.

I'd feel a lot worse about hurting her if she weren't bearing a mouthful of my blood at me like a crazed cannibal.

Her eyes flick from me to the house as I tilt my head to the side and touch a fingertip to the bite mark she left. Shit stings, and I know it's going to leave a scar.

I ought to yell at her, but that uncertainty from earlier stops me.

I've always known Serafina to play by the rules and to do as she's told. She'd never dirty herself with violence, and even though she's a good person, she wouldn't put herself in danger for a near-stranger like Marisol. Either there's a brain-eating parasite in that head of hers, making her act all crazy, or she's not Serafina.

"What's going on, Serafina? This isn't you." I test to see if maybe she'll just come out with the truth.

Her eyelashes flutter, and my suspicions grow.

For what fucking reason would I have Annetta here, dressed up as her twin sister and biting me?

She sucks in a breath and stands tall.

"They're going to kill her," she says, voice steady. "You need to go back. Save her. Don't let her die."

Warm blood slithers down my neck into my shirt collar, but I make no move to clean it.

I fall forward toward her, catching myself with my palm on the window next to her head. She flinches at the dull thud but doesn't back down.

I grin.

This close, I can smell blood on every ragged breath spilling from her mouth. She must be terrified, but she's facing me with everything she's got, even though I'm nearly twice her size. Most men would have already pissed their pants by now. Maybe she's foolishly certain I won't hurt her.

"Do you remember what I told you in the stadium?" I ask.

Her eyes flash wide, and her breath catches.

Yeah. I got her.

Weeks ago, Serafina and I had a little chat at Wrigley Field. If I'm wrong, she'll pass my little test, and I can figure out what's actually going on with her. But she's gonna fail, because I'm pretty damn sure this isn't Serafina.

She wipes the blood off her mouth with the back of her hand and traces her fingers down my forearm before they fall to her side. If she thinks flirting with me is gonna make me back down, she'll find out that it will take a lot more than a pretty face to sway me.

"Please don't let her die, Dom," she whispers.

My chest gives a light squeeze. How can she be so worried about Marisol when she's got blood on her tongue and a man like me breathing down her neck? Annetta has always been like this—too much of a martyr for her own damn good.

"Listen to me," I say, our faces inches apart. Gunshots ring off from inside the house, and she flinches. I don't. "Do you trust me?"

More gunshots. Her gaze flickers back and forth between me and the house.

She hasn't answered my question, but I continue, "You don't need to worry about Marisol. Salvatore would sooner saw off his right hand than let harm come to that woman. If he's sending her to the basement, it's because she'll be the safest there."

I glance down at her blood-kissed mouth once, then

drop my hand away from the window. "Get in the car. I'm taking you home."

I swing the passenger door open and shove her inside.

Rolling my shoulders, I touch the bite mark. Fucking woman tore a goddamn chunk out of my neck. I may need stitches.

I stride to the driver's side, get in, and drive us away from the chaos, barely sparing Turi a thought. Whatever is happening, he can handle it. As much as I hate to admit it, his wife's a tough bitch too. They'll be fine.

In the passenger seat, *Serafina* looks frail as a bird, clutching the seatbelt and squeezing herself into the smallest shape possible against the passenger seat. She has transformed from a she-wolf back to a scared little bunny, casting doubt over my suspicions yet again. I've always prided myself on my intuition in any situation, but in the span of a few minutes, the woman next to me has my internal compass spinning in circles.

I drive us down the long, dark road from Turi's house back to her parents' house in Oak Brook.

After several minutes of complete silence, I ask again, "Do you remember what I told you in the stadium?"

I'm not the kind of man who can let something go. Used to drive my dad nuts.

"Remind me," she says in a dull voice.

I nearly laugh. Still playing coy, then. "I told you I wouldn't let any harm come to you. Ever."

She snaps her head toward me, her hands still strangling that seatbelt.

"You mean that?" she asks me in an oddly hopeful voice.

I break my attention away from the road to hold her gaze for a fraction of a second.

"Of course," I say slowly, feeling like I'm missing something really fucking important. "You're like a little sister to me. I won't let anyone touch you."

Her gaze burns into the side of my face as she twists the seatbelt in her hands. She doesn't say anything else for a long moment, until my patience finally frays and snaps.

I ask the question that's been stirring at the back of my mind since she got out of the car.

"Where is your sister?"

3

ANNETTA

My hands drop to my lap.

The words catch in my throat as I say them aloud for the first time.

"She's dead."

Dom swerves violently, swinging the car toward a copse of trees. I squeeze my eyes shut.

"That's not fucking funny," he says.

I open my eyes. We're in our lane again.

Did I imagine that?

The muscles in his jaw shift under his thick beard as he works to unclench his teeth.

"Car crash." My voice is hoarse. I don't miss the irony as I add, "Three days ago. Hit-and-run."

I'm already fading, my consciousness falling away from me like sand between my fingers. There's nothing I can do to stop it, and I don't want to. I don't want to feel anything. Better this fog than that pointless rage. I clasp my hands on my lap, the meat of my palms aching from how hard I hit Dom.

"Who knows?" he grits out.

"Mom and Dad. My brothers. Aldo and Junior."

He strangles the steering wheel. "Aldo knew, and he still took you to Turi's?"

"Yes."

A few hours ago, I felt the same sense of injustice. Now, I just feel like a hollowed-out eggshell. I've barely eaten in the past few days, and all that exertion sapped away the little energy I had. A headache throbs against my temples. I press my cheek against the cool glass of the car window and my eyelids flutter closed.

Dom's voice drifts to me like a dream. "I thought you were... never mind."

I MUST'VE DOZED off because when I open my eyes again, night has fallen. The outdoor lights illuminate my parents' walkway, casting long pockets of black shadows in Serafina's *Amsonia*. Dom kills the engine, and we both sit in silence— well, almost silence. At some point, he turned the radio on to a low volume. Now it's just us sitting together and a woman singing *let go, let go, let go*.

I should be worried about Dad being stuck in that house with the rest of those men, and I am, but it's distant. I can't touch it behind the glass.

For the second time today, Dom startles me as he opens my car door. He gives me a pitying smile. "Come on, *fiorellina*."

His nickname for Serafina. *Little flower*.

I swallow around the lump in my throat, and the secret I've been guarding deep inside my heart like a live coal, letting it burn me over and over again, spews out. "It's my fault."

I didn't think—I just ran, but why, *why* did I come back home? I could've gone anywhere in the world, taken my curse with me, corrupted a town of strangers, and not my family. Not my sister.

Instead, I was too stupid and scared. I left in a blind panic, looking only behind me, without considering the future consequences. They came anyway, just not to me—to Serafina, when she was mistakenly murdered in my place.

My headache hammers every thought into my brain, driving them into place.

Selfish.

Foolish.

Useless.

The grief swells inside me, pressing against the underside of my skin until it breaks, and I bury my head in my hands with a sob.

I barely notice Dom unbuckling me as I hide my face and my shame from him.

"It's not your fault," he declares, like he could say anything less to a grieving woman.

I sob harder.

He's wrong. It *is* my fault, and I don't even have the decency to weep for the loss of the bright, innocent soul that was my sister. I grieve for myself, for the guilt that coats me like a layer of black tar.

Only my parents know. They blame me. And they're right to.

I curl up in a ball and sob in the passenger seat for a long time while Dom, one of the few good men I know, bears witness to the lowest point in my life.

Never have I been so ugly and worthless.

After a long time, I'm spent again. I crumple against myself like a used tissue paper. Even grief has its limits.

"Serafina?"

Something halfway between a laugh and a sob bubbles out of me. Every single time I hear her name directed at me, it's a knife to the chest. It's the least I deserve.

Dom takes my boneless hand in his. I rotate my limbs to the right and tumble out of the car, expecting to fall onto the concrete, but he catches me with an effortless athletic grace. Everything's so easy for him.

I don't allow myself the chance to enjoy the sensation of being carried in his arms. I lie in his grasp with all the emotion of a wooden log and close my eyes against the sight of his handsome face. I don't deserve this.

"What happened?" Mom asks with a slurred edge.

"She's okay. Barbara's still at the house."

Mom scrapes her shoe against the marble before my hand is clutched in hers and I'm buried in a cloud of Pinot Grigio. She squeezes me, but she doesn't ask any painful questions. That's not how our relationship works.

Dom carries me upstairs with steady, sure-footed steps to Serafina's room. Even in private, I must pretend to be her.

For your safety, Mom had said, but her eyes were hard and condemning.

I might've lost my sister, but Mom lost her favorite daughter.

Dom brushes aside the canopy to lay me on Serafina's bed and steps back to let Mom take off my shoes. The mattress envelops me like tepid bathwater. I wish they'd let the canopy fall into place and let me sleep for a hundred years.

"I'll bring you some broth," Mom says.

A weight tips the mattress, and I open my eyes, turning toward Dom. He's kneeling on the floor with his arms on the edge of the bed like he's about to pray.

There's no one up there to listen, I want to tell him. I tried.

My prayers, my reaching for the smallest scrap of my sister's... what? Her soul? Her consciousness? My clawing against the void for the most minute assurance she's somewhere peaceful was met with a resounding, yawning nothingness.

Dom covers my hand with his. A week ago, his hand on mine and his massive body kneeling at my bed would've shot pleasure into my veins, but right now, it makes me nauseous.

His dark eyebrows pulled up in the center and the soft line of his lips forming a pitying expression doesn't suit him at all, but the dried blood on his neck, strangely, does.

"It's going to be okay," he says in a low rumble as his thumb strokes against mine. Shame and desire spiral through my body.

I turn to hide the way he's affecting me, but even that's a lie I tell myself, because I leave my hand tucked under his. I can't admit how badly I want him here, sitting at my bedside, tending to me, stoking my stupid little crush on the older man who's always been like a part of my family.

"You won't have to marry Aldo," he says.

Too tired to lift my head, I roll my face back toward him and wait.

The rough pad of his thumb scratches lightly against my knuckle as he strokes my hand in long movements. A vicious flash of jealousy toward my sister shocks me.

Did he touch her like this?

It doesn't matter.

It doesn't matter. I don't get to be jealous of a dead girl.

"Turi's going to take care of him."

I want to smile, but the connection between my brain

and muscles is so weak that my face doesn't even twitch. Dom is naïve for a man in his late thirties.

What does it matter if Aldo dies? I'll just be married to Junior or any one of my dad's associates. My parents didn't send us to ballet and pilates and piano classes, pay for our nose jobs, and fly us out to Venice and Florence and Tuscany in the summers so we could be single.

Dom may promise me the world now, but he'll fade away from my life again like he's done for the past three years. His loyalty isn't to me—it's to Dad, to the Family.

"Did you really mean what you said?" It surprises me to hear my own voice, raspy from my screaming.

"Mean what?"

Even though I know better, part of me wants to believe the lie he'll tell me, to give myself one thing in my life I can hold on to. "That you'd protect me?"

He fixes me with a focused stare, the dark brown of his eyes glowing from the light of the bedside lamp. "With my last breath."

I exhale and turn to stare at the ceiling.

I can tell by the staggered steps on the carpet that Mom's returned. She takes Dom's place at the edge of the bed, and he walks away.

"You have to drink something," she says.

As she pushes me into a sitting position, I catch Carlo just outside my door. I haven't seen him since I returned home, but the record of his grieving is written all over his face. His tired, bloodshot eyes meet mine for a moment before he turns his gaze to Dom. My lanky, tattooed, leather-jacketed older brother looks like a child in a Halloween costume next to the other man. They measure each other for a moment.

Dom takes one step forward and wraps him in a bear

hug, and my devil-may-care brother, who I haven't seen cry since he was a little boy, hugs Dom back and sobs.

I WAKE up in the darkness, my heart pounding.

The gauzy canopy surrounding me reminds me where I am, why I'm here, and not in my bedroom in Tampa.

Why Serafina is in the ground at Graceland Cemetery and not in her bed.

I clutch the blankets at my neck. The house is completely silent. No—I can hear noise downstairs.

Is Dad back? A split in the canopy shows the softly glowing display of the wall clock reading almost three in the morning.

Something's buzzing in the room. I squeeze my eyes shut, fear wrapping around me like a python.

The noise stops.

I relax into my mattress a little. Then it starts again, and I recognize it. I want to let it die, like a wasp under a glass cup, but the moment the buzzing stops, it starts back up again.

It's a monstrous effort to move my body, shift it until I've rolled off my sister's bed, even to look in the direction of the sound.

Too exhausted to stand, I slide against the nearest wall until I can open the top drawer of Serafina's vanity. My phone was destroyed days ago. It's Serafina's phone I find inside.

Unknown number.

I slide my thumb across the screen and press the cool piece of glass against my ear.

At first, silence.

A woman exhales on the other side.

I swallow. "Hello?"

"I know what you did."

The caller hangs up.

The phone falls from my hand.

I sprint through the hallway to Rafa's room.

"What's wrong?" Rafa asks sharply when I crash inside, throwing the door shut behind me. He's already reaching for the gun he keeps in his desk drawer and rising from his chair.

My throat doesn't work for a moment.

Then—Rafa doesn't need to know. I can't have him risking himself for me.

The words all seem to tumble out at once. "A nightmare. A bad dream."

His hand falls away from the hidden gun in his drawer. He scrubs his face as he lets out a sigh.

"You know..." He pulls off his glasses, folding and setting them on his desk. He's wearing grey sweatpants and a T-shirt, and he's got a bunch of papers strewn along the top of his desk. The computer screen is filled with lines of numbers. "It's fine. Did you want to stay in here for a while?"

I exhale a short laugh, the nightmare already fading in the soft light of Rafa's bedroom. Nearly three years later, and I'm still a little girl running to his room whenever I get scared. I straighten up, tugging at the tight black sheath dress I never changed out of after the dinner.

Rafa glances back at his computer, as if it physically pains him to be away from his work. He'd probably hand me a spreadsheet and have me check for errors if I asked to stay in his room, telling me how much math helps *him* relax.

He's gotten so skinny since I've moved out. All of his

baby fat is gone, and he looks so much older than I remember.

"Where's Carlo?" I ask.

Rafa makes a dismissive noise and waves his hand around as if to say *who the fuck knows*? He pulls a stack of papers from the desk onto his lap.

I bite my lip. "Do you know what happened? At Turi's house?"

Anyone else would admonish me for such a brazen question, but Rafa only ignores me for a few moments. He's not so much older than me and Serafina, but unlike us girls, he's always been expected to play a more active part in the Family. Since Carlo's interests lie with drinking and women, Rafa had to step up. All of that responsibility has turned him into a distant stranger. I can't remember the last time I've seen him smile.

"Please, Rafa," I say.

My brothers, for all their faults, have always tried to do their best for their sisters.

He sighs. His hands still over the papers. "I guess you'll know soon enough. Aldo's dead."

My heart stutters.

Rafa's dark eyes meet mine. "They're saying Dad shot him. Turi has Junior in his basement now."

Aldo's dead. If Junior's in Turi's basement, he's as good as dead. Something fragile flutters in my chest. I almost can't breathe.

"And Marisol?" I ask.

Rafa raises an eyebrow. "Turi's wife? Yeah, she's fine."

I exhale a long, shuddering breath.

"Okay," I say as I turn to leave. "Thanks."

"Wait. Uh, I know... do you want to talk about what happened?"

I turn. Rafa looks vaguely pained. He's never been good at this sort of thing.

I paste a smile onto my face. "No, Rafa."

The answer doesn't seem to surprise him. "I miss her too."

My smile melts into something a little more genuine. "I know."

I leave my brother to his work.

As I pass through the house, a deep undercurrent of emotions swims through my limbs, pushing me forward with each step. Dom kept his word. Aldo and Junior are dead, and Marisol is safe.

How could Dom have been so sure of what would happen?

He's always been like that—unwavering and invincible. Capable of the impossible.

I find myself just outside Mom and Dad's door, fighting the rising tide of exhaustion that threatens to tow me under. A whisper curls around the back of my mind.

Why am I doing this? What's the point?

A rush of guilt and longing for Serafina surges over me. There's only one person in the world I want to talk to about this, and she's gone.

I half-turn to walk back to Serafina's room, but the fear of what's lurking there stops me. That was Giulia's voice, on the phone. My late husband's family were always bound to come after me, but I thought when they took Serafina, that'd be enough.

I inhale deeply. Rafa, Carlo, Mom, Dad—I can't lose anyone else.

I lean toward the door, listening for noise inside. Mom's talking in a low voice.

"Mom?" I call through the door, suddenly feeling eight years old again.

"Come in."

When I step inside, I'm struck by how old my parents look. Everyone's aged so much since I've been gone. Mom's hair is tucked inside a pink satin bonnet, and she's wearing a matching pink nightgown. She has a face full of makeup—in case of an emergency, she always says, but Serafina and I are pretty sure it's because Dad's never seen her without it. Dad's shirtless. His hairy belly juts out over his lap, his hands clasped on top. His CPAP mask lies next to his thigh.

"What is it?" Mom asks.

The ridiculous thought of asking to sleep in their room crosses my mind, and I cast it aside just as quickly.

"Are you okay?" I ask Dad.

"Anne—Serafina!" Mom scolds.

We never talk aloud about Dad's stuff. He's whole. There's no blood or broken bones. If I have concerns, I keep them to myself.

Dad grunts. "What do you want?"

"Rafa told me what happened," I say. "Who am I going to marry now?"

Mom gives an exhausted sigh. "It is three in the morning. Let's save this for breakfast. Your father had a long day, and he needs to sleep."

"I want..." I say, and for a moment, I fight against the wild thrashing of indecision, until—*this is how I keep my family safe*. It's the same way I've always kept my family safe, with my beauty and my body. "I want to marry Dom."

Mom sputters, choking on her shock like a fish on a riverbank. "Annetta!"

"Serafina," I correct, and she snaps her mouth shut. I turn to Dad. "Can you do it? Make Dom marry me?"

"That man is twenty years your senior," Mom says.

Aldo had forty years on Serafina. Dad has eight on Mom. Since when do they care about what's appropriate?

"He could protect me," I say simply.

He could protect all of us. If anyone can do the impossible, it's Dom.

Dad blows out a long stream of air. Mom looks over at him sharply.

He'll think about it. It's as good an answer as I'll get tonight.

"Thanks," I say, feeling like I've left a slip of paper in the prayer box. "I'm glad you're okay, Dad. I love you both."

4

ANNETTA

MY FIRST WEDDING had fallen straight out of a fairytale. The joining of the Barbaras and the Chiarellis could be nothing short of perfection.

I'd ridden on a horse-drawn carriage through arches of pink roses and lavender wisteria, dusted with tiny, delicate baby's breath. When I stepped out in my hand-embroidered gown, which had been flown in from London and cost more than a house, everyone turned to admire me. I'd spent weeks starving myself to squeeze into the dress, but the corset top still made me a bit breathless as I walked down the aisle. If you looked very closely, my skin was visible beneath the faintly sheer white of the fabric.

The men I'd grown up around, my uncles, cousins, and family friends, leered as I walked past, but I didn't cringe. I didn't hide. I held my head high, like a good daughter. I was there to show power, and the way a woman in our family shows power is by being skinny, beautiful, and pure.

The sight of Frederico at the end of the aisle, watching me with adoration and looking like a prince with his perfectly coiffed hair and his tailored tuxedo, made guilt tug at me. The Chiarellis had asked for Serafina—the accomplished, pretty, elegant twin—to be his bride. When Serafina cried herself sick each night for weeks, I asked to meet Frederico privately and gave him a clumsy, enthusiastic blowjob so he'd pick me instead.

It hadn't felt like such a hardship. Frederico was charming and young. He was a better choice than any other match I would have had.

Maybe I would learn to love him.

Serafina was grateful I'd given her a few more years of freedom, so much so that I had to make her stop bringing me tea and bouquets. As I walked down an aisle strewn with softly wilting rose petals to a handsome, kind-faced husband, I thought, *maybe I should've let her do this*. Frederico would be a good husband. He would make his future wife happy.

I was wrong.

Now, at Saint Roch Catholic Church, where dust bunnies and wafer crumbs collect along the edges of the pews, and the faint smell of mold permeates the air, I make myself a different bet. This won't be the husband who makes me happy, but maybe he can keep me safe.

The priest thumbs through the Bible on his lectern, glancing with watery blue eyes over his glasses between me and the double doors to the nave. Now and then, he dry coughs into a worn handkerchief.

My wedding dress is cheap and paired with the tallest pair of white heels I could find online. I'm so short that even with these stripper heels, the dress still drags on the ground. I adjust one of the uneven sleeves and force myself to stay still, but the itchy lace makes me want to crawl out of my skin. The sleeve slips down again.

Mom didn't want to bring our usual seamstress over to

the house. She thought the clever woman might recognize the difference between me and who I should be. Dad made me wait a month for his answer, and had only given me a day's notice that he'd arranged the wedding.

I can only imagine what the rest of the family will say about this.

Every time I shift to lift my dress sleeve, a few dried petals flutter to the ground, and the priest gives me a dirty look. I wanted the last bouquet Serafina was working on—the one from her bedroom. Besides Dom, it was the only thing I asked for.

There's no clock, and my toes are slowly going numb from standing for so long. I lift one leg to roll my ankle.

"Serafina," Mom hisses.

I drop my foot back down. Instead of a massive crowd of people to witness my union, it's just Mom, Rafa, and Carlo. Carlo is wearing sunglasses and looks like he might be napping through an all-day hangover. Next to him, Rafa types away at his phone, which he pulled out after two minutes of waiting. Dad is out there in the rain somewhere, hunting down my future husband.

Is Dom coming? Doubt blooms and with it, a touch of panic. He's my last resort. I haven't been brave enough to turn my phone back on after the call, but it doesn't matter—the message had been sent.

My hands are so sweaty that I have to keep shifting the bouquet to wipe one palm along the side of my dress.

"Serafina," Mom says again.

A faint pinkish stain streaks the sides of my dress.

I glance toward Mom, who's pinching the bridge of her nose.

"Sorry," I whisper, the sound magnified in the empty

church. The bouquet in my hand shivers, and a few more petals shake down. "Sorry," I say again, crouching to pick them up.

"Serafina, stand up," Mom pleads.

"Sorry." I launch up, holding the bouquet in one hand and a few dried petals in the other.

Ahead of me is a stained-glass image of Mary Magdalene calmly washing Jesus's feet with her long hair.

I close my eyes and wait.

Maybe I'll find myself waiting the entire night. I'll stand here in the darkness like a marble statue at an art auction until another man comes up to claim me. With any luck, he'll be strong enough to weather the danger I bring with me.

I wrinkle my nose so I don't sneeze from the mildew surrounding me. I glance at the priest. Is it him I'm smelling? He looks up from the Bible and scrutinizes me.

I resist the urge to apologize, bowing my head to avoid his gaze.

The other reason I'd been looking forward to this wedding with the smallest scrap of anticipation is that I thought, I *hoped,* that in this church, I would feel something —a powerful assurance at the presence of God around me, or a whisper to let me know everything is going according to plan. I'd light a candle, and I'd feel the weight of my sister's cheek pressed against mine one final time, hear her voice in the wind, or God himself would plant peace in my heart.

There's only emptiness.

Her soul is supposed to go somewhere. Isn't that a law of nature? Energy isn't created or destroyed.

But I can't feel her, and I can't make myself pretend otherwise, though I wish I could.

Tears prick my eyes. Even if she were only a prayer away, I wouldn't ask for her. I don't want her here in this rotting church. I don't want her anywhere near me. My soul will corrupt hers and weigh it down with my sins like a yoke around her neck until she sinks to the bottom of hell.

A breath ghosts over the back of my neck, and my eyes fly open. The church doors burst open with two heavy thuds.

Licking his dry lips, the priest opens his Bible to a marked page. Mom points to her sleeve.

I pull up my dress collar, and a few more petals float down. My chest heaves as I inhale, and heavy footsteps thunder around the corner to the nave. Whatever happens now, I asked for this. I turn toward the newcomer, and my heart stops, the seconds unfurling into infinity. The man striding toward me doesn't look like a husband.

He looks like a warlord. Somewhere outside, thunder cracks.

Dom is soaked, dressed in his usual dark jeans, black boots, and a brown leather jacket with fur trim. Most of his hair has been pulled loose from his ponytail and hangs around his face in an unruly mane. He storms toward me like he has the intention to tear me from the altar and sling me over his shoulder as his spoils of war.

I lick my lips. *This* will be my new husband?

He stomps to a halt in front of me, not meeting my gaze.

Dad strolls around the bend with his hands in his pockets and joins the pew where Mom and my brothers are sitting.

My future husband gives the priest a dark look.

The holy man clears his throat. "Well. Okay. Friends, family. We are gathered here today under God's watchful eye to witness the joining of two souls..."

As the priest drones on, Dom rolls his head to one side, then the other, the muscles in his neck and jaw flexing as he looks everywhere but at me. The fur trim of his jacket hides that private joining between his neck and shoulder where I bit him. I run my tongue over my teeth.

For a month, I'd held on to a certainty that Dom, like any other man, would accept a marriage with Serafina, but I'd also clutched at a secret hope that I'd made a mistake at Turi's house and had revealed my identity to Dom in a way that only a person intimately familiar with me could know. How he'd looked at me—I thought maybe he'd known who I really was. That the kiss I'd stolen from him when I was eighteen, next to the rosebush at the foot of my bedroom window, had carved out a tiny little *What if* in his heart for him the same way it had in mine.

But I see the truth now. Dom, who's been a bachelor for almost as long as I've known him, who just has to snap his fingers for a woman to throw herself at him, fought this union tooth and nail. Dad only won out with threats or bribes.

I swallow a lump in my throat and glance at my parents. Mom has her head bowed. Rafa looks like an overgrown high schooler with his phone tucked against the side of his thigh, tapping against the screen. Carlo snores until Mom elbows him sharply, and he jerks up. Dad meets my eye. One of his eyebrows twitches up.

Well?

I look back at Dom, forming a fist over the dried petals in my palm.

So, he doesn't want to get married? Tough. We all have to do things we don't want to.

His eyes are lined with dark circles, and a tendon in his neck jumps as he glares at some far-off spot in the church.

He shifts, throwing another menacing look at the priest, who stutters in his reading.

I stand as tall as I can, shifting my weight between my heels, and burn my gaze into the side of Dom's face. He *will* look at me.

Right as I'm considering reaching forward to tug at his hand or clear my throat, the priest saves him.

"Do you have the rings?" the priest asks Dom.

"No," Dom rumbles.

The older man blinks a few times. He scratches behind his ear and turns to me. "Serafina?"

For the briefest moment, I fight the urge to look for my sister. But he's talking to me.

Instead of answering, I stare back.

The priest casts a pleading look at my parents.

"Here," Mom calls. She steps forward and drops a set of rings into the priest's outstretched hands. A little spark of surprise skitters through me. Did Dom get those? Maybe I've misread him, maybe some small part of him wants to make this work.

If he gives me a chance, I can make myself a good wife for him.

"Right." The priest clears his throat and turns to us. "Please face each other and hold hands."

I turn to Dom, and he turns to me, but he's staring at a point right above my head. I frown. He's killed people on his boss's orders, he laughs as he faces down other dangerous men, but he can't look one woman in the eye?

"Dom," I whisper harshly.

Then, on an exhale, he finally looks at me.

The look in his gentle, dark eyes is one of pure *hate*.

All of the air sucks out of my lungs, and the bouquet quivers in my hand.

Mom appears behind me.

"I'll take those," she says as she slips the flowers from my hand.

Dried petals spray onto the ground.

I deserve this.

I don't look at Dom's face anymore. I fix my gaze on his hands, which rise to meet mine. My right hand is still clutching a handful of dried, crumbling petals, and he simply wraps his hand—rough and covered in tattoos— around my loose fist. The word *miseria* is tattooed across his fingers.

Misery.

Is that dried blood on his knuckles?

Dom recites his vows in a gravelly voice, ending on *till death do us part.*

The priest has to cue me several times as I stumble through my vows. Mom mutters under her breath behind me. Oddly, I don't feel embarrassed like I normally would. Even if he hates me, this is Dom. I've seen him pretend to scream for mercy while he let a teenage Carlo pin him to the ground. He's performed the viral dances my cousins have taught him in the living room while my parents laughed. He's not a man shame sticks to.

But when the priest passes me Dom's ring, my heart crumbles. I recognize this ring, an old gold scratched-up thing with the initials *D + F* inscribed on the inside.

This is Dad's.

Dom didn't get these rings. Mom harvested her and Dad's wedding bands just to save face.

I let the petals drop to the carpet. Humiliation burns my cheeks, and tears blur my vision as I take Dom's left hand, massive and unyielding as a bear's paw. Two of his fingers twitch as I work the ring onto his third finger, forcing it to fit.

I swallow back tears at *that* implication. My mind's racing, stumbling to latch onto anything that might comfort me.

I'm forcing him to marry me just like Aldo would've forced me.

Oh God. He really does hate me.

I clamp my mouth shut to keep an apology from spilling out. There's no one else I know with Dom's power and resources who can protect me and my family like he can. I can't back out of this—I'll have to make it up to him in another way.

Bowing my face to hide the tears in my eyes, I raise my hand so he can slide my ring on. It's my Mom's thin, gold wedding band, dented on the left side from washing dishes. A tear slips down my cheek and drops to the frayed blue carpet.

With some difficulty, I swallow. I'll make this work. I have to. It's life or death, and I have to at least try, because...

I glance at my family on the pew, just the four of them now.

I can't take another loss.

"You may now kiss the bride," the priest says.

My heart rate explodes. *What did he say?*

I shoot my head up. Dom's already watching me, disgust curling his lips. My mouth goes dry. I'd be lying if I said I've never imagined what it'd be like to kiss Dom again, or to run my fingers through his beard and long hair.

Dom tracks the movement of my tongue, which darts out to lick my lower lip. It's too late to back out of this. I have to make this work.

Even with my stripper heels, he's so tall that the top of my head only comes up to his mouth. He'll have to lean down to kiss me, but he's not moving closer. Instead, I see it

—when he decides he's going to leave me here, without a kiss.

His mouth firms, and he shakes his head imperceptibly, shifting like he's going to walk away—the warlord leaving his bride in the cold, dark forest to freeze and starve.

I crush my hands into fists. He has to do it. I need him. He can't leave me here.

Before he moves, I reach for his forearm and seize it in my grip. My hand doesn't even come close to circling the muscle there, but I jerk him toward me all the same.

"Kiss me," I say in a soft, urgent voice.

At least one truth I've always known doesn't betray me. I'm not at all shocked when Dom the Butcher, Salvatore Luporini's most loyal dog, bows his head without thought. Acquiescence is written into his bones. His breath, warm and minty, washes over me. Did he brush his teeth for this? Maybe there's a small chip in his armor of hate.

I circle my arm around his neck, pulling him toward me as he brushes his lips against mine—no, that's not enough, he's going to leave. Before he can stand, I flex my arm with all of my strength and lunge onto my tiptoes to press a hard kiss to his lips and lick along the seam of his mouth.

I hear it.

A grunt—no, a *moan*.

I release him just as quickly, and when he stands, his expression is wild—pupils blown out and the whites of his eyes visible—like he's processing what just happened.

"Congratulations," the old priest says.

The spell breaks. Dom blinks a few times before turning from me and storming out of the church, slamming the doors shut as he leaves.

I turn back to my family to see Rafa watching me with a

raised eyebrow, looking just like Dad, though he'd hate to hear it. Mom's on the verge of breaking into tears, and not the happy kind. Dad watches me with a twist to his mouth, and I can practically hear his thoughts.

You asked for this, daughter.

Only Carlo's grinning. He throws me a thumbs-up.

As we're shuffling out of the church, I look out across the parking lot into the street for another glimpse of my new husband, but his car's already gone.

It's the shape of a different man that catches my eye. He's built like a knife—tall, thin, and dressed in black. I can't quite make out his face from here, but it doesn't matter. I'd recognize him anywhere.

He's haunted every dream I've had since I came back to Chicago.

The same white shirt he wore that night winks at me from the split in his black coat like a flash of bone in torn muscle. His hair is just as I remember—dark and perfectly gelled into place.

He's staring right at me.

I'm frozen. My heart pounds in my throat. My mind races.

That couldn't be. There's no possible explanation. Frederico's dead. His brother—it has to be his brother, Marco.

As I watch, he turns and walks down the sidewalk, disappearing behind a building, while I waver on my heels.

Frederico's supposed to be dead.

I saw him die.

"Serafina," Mom calls, shocking me into reality like a bucket of icy lake water.

I turn. Rafa and Carlo are on their phones, and Dad's napping in the passenger seat.

Tears prick my eyes.

Where is Dom? He said he'd protect me. He gave me his word.

My mind folds in on itself, rejecting conscious thought and forcing my legs to move forward like an automaton until I reach the car.

A week later, I move into Dom's penthouse.

5

DOM

I STINK.

The ungodly smell wafting from me into the open windows would rival a pig fresh from rolling around in mud and cow shit. And while I won't be admitting this to Turi anytime soon, I feel great.

After that disastrous wedding with Serafina—the poor woman was nervous and on the verge of tears the entire time—my presence was demanded at Aldo's funeral. It passed in a dark haze, and when Turi took me aside to order me to fuck off to the woods for a week, I left without a fight. I packed just enough shit not to die and disappeared to Devil's Lake, perfectly timed for open hunting season—maybe a coincidence, but over the years, I've learned not to underestimate Turi.

For one week of bliss, I hunted deer with my compound bow, drank pine needle tea, harvested cattail roots only a little past their prime, and slept shivering in my tent on the hard-ass ground. My back hurts, I'd kill a man for warm bread, and I smell god-awful, but no one could contact me, so I'm more at peace than I've been in years.

At least until I spot the beat-up silver Toyota Matrix across the street from my parking deck. Instead of pulling in, I let out a long sigh and drive to the end of the street to circle back.

Yeah, just what I thought. Fucking Mauro's watching my place. Or, he should be anyway, seeing as how he's looking at his phone and hasn't noticed me driving past. I park and drum on the steering wheel, deep in thought.

I should probably go see what Caterpillar Brows thinks he's doing watching my penthouse, but I haven't showered in a week, and I'm about to choke on my own ball stench, so... *fuck it.*

I gotta haul all this shit to my place first and shower. I'll just set an alarm for the middle of the night and scare the shit out of him later. Even if Turi sent him to watch my empty penthouse, he should know better than to be staring at his phone.

I pull out my phones from the glove compartment. The second my work phone boots up, the damn thing floods my notifications with a hundred and thirteen texts and forty missed calls. I drag a hand over my beard. There goes all that precious relaxation. I don't see anything from Turi or any of his pet nerds from his cyber team, so at least nobody started World War III while I was out.

On my personal phone, I browse my family chat. Looks like my youngest sister Allegra finally popped out her baby —a fat little boy with a shock of dark hair. I mark all the photos with a heart and consider calling her until my stomach growls pitifully.

I pat my belly. *Soon, buddy.*

I jump out of my truck, the thud of my boots echoing off the concrete walls of the parking garage, and the impact knocks about five pounds of caked mud off. I haul my massive ice chest to the ground. The thing's packed to the gills with fresh deer meat, and I still had to give the extras to a couple of overjoyed teen hunters I came across on the trail.

I strap my backpack and bow to my back, brace myself, and lift. "Oof."

Fuck, this thing's heavy as shit. I'm half-tempted to see if the concierge will drag it in, but I've worked hard to make sure the employees here like me. I'm not about to fuck that up because I'm feeling a little tired.

I spend the long elevator ride up daydreaming about my plans for the night. First, obviously, a steaming hot shower. And you know what? *Fuck it*, a jerk-off session. Then, I'll stuff myself with six entrees from the apartment's in-house restaurant and pass out on the couch with a half-eaten pizza on my belly before I scare Mauro.

The moment the doors ding and open to my penthouse, all my plans fly out the window.

My place smells *delicious*. The sweet, tart smell of roasted tomatoes spikes a gush of saliva in my mouth.

What the fuck is this? None of my exes have access to my penthouse, and Turi's overbearing, but he wouldn't send someone ahead to cook me dinner for the moment I arrived. Did his head chef Conchetta let herself in so I wouldn't starve?

From the elevator foyer, I glance around the living room. None of the furniture has been touched. If this is some kind of Dom-themed ambush, first off, *kudos* to the attacker because this has easily got to be the cleverest approach to lowering my defenses. Second, they should already know I'm here from the elevator doors opening.

Exhaustion snaps out of me, and I set the cooler down as softly as I can just inside the foyer. Straining my ears for odd sounds, I shuck off my backpack and grab my compound bow. I pull an arrow out of the quiver, notching it in my bow in silent, fluid movements.

The oven beeps from around the length of the foyer, and something shuffles along the floor. Whoever it is, they aren't trying very hard to disguise their presence. Lulling me into a false sense of security, maybe?

I check my phone again. Nothing from Turi or his head of cybersecurity, Worm. Maybe it's one of my brothers— Bertino thinks it's a fucking gag to drop by unannounced, and I keep forgetting to put him on the "Call First" list with the concierge. Probably not him, though—he'd sooner chop off his left nut than cook for me.

I inhale and step forward, aiming my bow toward the kitchen.

It's *her*.

I lower my weapon.

All the grief I'd bottled up and ignored for a week comes back to drown me. No—*fuck*—no. I smother it with anger. Why the *fuck* is Serafina here, like I need any reminder of her dead sister?

Why is she in my penthouse? Why is she *cooking*?

Her back is to me as she chops a leafy green vegetable on the counter. The top of her hair is tied back, but the rest flows freely over her delicate shoulder blades.

She turns to me and shrieks, lifting the knife as the cutting board clatters to the floor. Even though I can't see from here, I know whatever she's been preparing has been sprayed all over the floor.

"Dom," she exclaims. "You're back!"

My new wife is wielding a knife at me. Her face is bare, and her whole body is on display in those tight clothes— pink bicycle shorts and a matching tank top that shows a tantalizing strip of tanned belly—as she slowly lowers the knife to the counter. Even though I've seen Serafina in plenty of bikinis over the years, this is the first time her slim figure has stirred interest in me.

I snap my gaze to her rueful face, annoyance settling into mine. Why is she surprised to see me? Could someone just sneak up on her like this?

"Who let you in?" I ask roughly, ignoring the blood rushing to my cock.

Women like Serafina have never been my taste—I like big, opinionated, bad bitches, not soft-spoken princess-types.

Serafina gulps, glances down at the bow and arrow in my hands, and smiles nervously. "Dad let me in."

Whatever she's got cooking in the oven smells like cheese and tomatoes. Pizza?

I swallow around a mouthful of saliva. "You need to go back."

Her face crumples with devastation. *Fuck me.* Is she going to cry?

It doesn't matter. My penthouse isn't a place for a young woman. I'm never here, I have loaded guns all over the place, and there's basically no protection besides the cyber-security Turi had set up.

"This is for the best," I say, knowing it's as much for me as it is for her—I don't need another fucking responsibility.

The oven beeps behind her, and a change passes over her face. *Goddammit.* She calms herself with a deep breath.

While looking me dead in the eye, she picks up the knife from the kitchen counter. I remember the flower petals in her hand, how she made me smell like roses after our wedding, and how I scrubbed my hands under a gas station bathroom sink to rid myself of her scent.

"We are *married*." It's impossible not to see Annetta in her face. Of the two, Annetta was always the strong one.

The old doubt that had crawled into my brain back at Turi's house returns with a force. Her parents had me convinced Annetta was dead, and I'd chalked up her strange behavior to her sudden loss, but now?

My gut says something is off again.

"I'm not going back," she says.

Then, like she's dismissing her lowest employee, she turns to set the knife next to the oven and uses a dish towel —I don't even own dish towels, especially not ones with blue butterflies on them—to pull out whatever she's cooking and proceeds to ignore me like I'm a door-to-door salesman and not a stinky, six-foot-five bearded man with a compound bow in the kitchen.

I bite back a string of swears. The tray in her hand that she's sliding on top of the stove? It's got my favorite focaccia with escarole and tomatoes. Even from here, I can see she's added extra anchovy, just how I like.

There are a thousand things I should do, but I finally settle on the most mature option—I throw a big, man-baby tantrum.

I chuck my bow onto the nearest couch, stomping back to the elevator to grab my backpack and cooler. I drop the cooler in front of the refrigerator with a heavy thud that earns a startled jump from her as she sweeps green leaves off the kitchen floor. That makes me feel like an even bigger asshole, but instead of apologizing, I stomp upstairs to my bedroom.

I have to take a shower before I can deal with the half-naked woman in my kitchen.

Tonight's surprises are endless. My bedroom, my oasis, has been transformed. A suitcase filled with robin's egg blue, bright lemon, and cream clothes spills onto my bed like an overturned vase. I glance at my closet—more of her Easter-egg clothes peek out from between my shirts.

"Nope." I'm not dealing with this right now. I march to the bathroom and nearly crack a tooth from how hard I grit my teeth. "Motherfucker!"

Crystal bottles, jars of creams, and a sparkling glass case of makeup litter my bathroom counter—well, not *litter*, exactly, because they're neatly lined up like they're afraid to take up too much space, but it's still fucking annoying. A glance at the shower tells me nothing is safe from the invasion.

"Fuck this."

I swipe clean clothes from my closet and take my ass to the next room over. In here, at least, nothing has been touched. My housekeeper keeps it from getting dusty, and my brother keeps his favorite bottle of all-in-one hair-beard-body-ass wash in the shower for his rare visits.

I throw my backpack onto the ground and lock myself in the bathroom to take a nice, hot shower—sans jerking off. When I'm done, I pull on clean jeans and a T-shirt and drop into the armchair in front of the bed. I feel clean and less shitty, but I'm still pissed.

Who does this woman think she is? She can't just waltz into my place, infect all my things with her *woman* shit, and take over. That's... that's squatting.

For the first time in a week, I glance down at my empty ring finger. After our wedding, Barbara made me return his wedding ring, which I had to use soap to remove, and told me I needed to get my own.

I don't have to do shit. I didn't fucking agree to this wedding. Barbara and Turi set it up like backstabbing bastards, and Turi used his new Don status to force me into it. Well, I'm the *sottocapo* now, and I don't have to take this lying down. They can make us get married, but we don't have to live together, and Turi's about to hear an earful about it when I drive over to his house tonight.

Not like I can stay here anyway, not when I can see the soft curve of my young, grieving wife's vulva through her bicycle shorts. I scowl, throwing myself forward to pull on socks and tie up my boots.

Once I'm downstairs, I turn the corner to the kitchen. She's bent over my ice cooler, the spandex of her shorts stretching so thin it's almost transparent across her ass and pussy. I bite down hard enough to crack a tooth.

Minchia!

A few chunks of deer meat have already been packed in parchment paper—*where is she getting this shit?*—and the sight of that thoughtful action pisses me off even more.

At the end of the kitchen bar sits a plate loaded with a steaming serving of focaccia and a sizzling steak. A drop of condensation slithers down the tall glass cup of amber beer placed next to the food.

She stands, a hunk of raw meat in her bloody little hands. Before I can suppress it, my brain notices how the meat seems to dwarf her tiny frame and how small she'd look in comparison to other—

"Are you hungry?" she asks sweetly.

It takes all my decades of training not to look back at the trap she left on the counter. But apparently, my body doesn't catch the memo because my stomach lets out a growl so long and pathetic, I'd be surprised if it's not audible from outer fucking space.

She and I stare at each other for a long moment. Her rosy lips twitch like she's fighting off a giggle.

"No," I grit out. If I express anything other than anger, I'm gonna laugh.

She raises her eyebrow in a way that looks *exactly* like Annetta, and I don't give a shit what her parents told me.

Serafina would never laugh at a man who didn't want to be laughed at, and she'd never give him the look she's giving me now. But Annetta? She loved to laugh.

"You don't like focaccia? I put extra *alici* on it," she says, putting a little Italian accent on the words. Cute, given that she can barely speak the language.

I glance back at the plate once before snapping my eyes to her.

No. I'm getting to the bottom of this twin mix-up, and then I'm kicking her out. This isn't my shit to deal with. My stomach growls again, the traitorous bastard.

Her smile lights up her face, and she drops the deer flank on top of a sheet of parchment paper on the counter. "Sit down. You must be tired and hungry. I almost have this cleaned up."

I don't say a damn thing. I don't trust myself right now, and my mouth's too fucking full of saliva—drooling like I'm a goddamn dog. I walk across the kitchen, past all the temptation.

"Where are you going?" she calls after me.

Without stopping, I answer, "Out."

"When are you coming back?" Her voice is so soft and vulnerable—it pierces my heart like a needle.

"Later." I turn the corner and jam the elevator button to escape my own fucking house.

MOMENTS LATER, I pull out onto the street in my SUV—still starving, I might add—and when I spot Mauro again, I make a snap decision. I park down the street, far away from him, and jump out of the car. My blood boils as I stroll up to his driver's side window without him once looking up from his phone.

I rap sharply on the window, and he jumps, throwing his phone up in the air and scrambling for his gun. His terror transforms into a wide-eyed *oh-shit* face, his stupid caterpillar eyebrows eating up his entire forehead.

I grin at him and motion for him to lower the window, leaning a forearm against the roof of the car.

"Mauro!" I say, the moment the window's rolled down.

He swallows dryly. "*Signore.*"

"How's the family doing?" I ask in Italian. He barely understands English past the word "shoot". "Six kids, is that right? Palermo? They doing good?"

Mauro nods, sweat already breaking out along his hairline. "Yes, sir. Thank you for asking, sir."

Some guys eat up the kowtowing and the bootlicking, but that's never been my style. I couldn't care less if they respect me, so long as they do their fucking jobs. Right now, though, that attitude is the only thing keeping me from reaching into Mauro's car and strangling him with my bare hands.

My grin widens, and I drum along the roof of the car. "Who sent you here, Mauro?"

I don't bother with threatening him to tell me the truth. He knows who I work for. I'll find out if he's lying.

"Uh... the don, sir. He wanted me to help keep an eye on the *signora.*"

"That it?" I exhale a chuckle, and Mauro relaxes a little. "Tell me, Mauro, you got eyes on the back of your head?"

"N-no, sir."

I strike into the car, clamp my hand around his neck, and squeeze.

"Then how the fuck you gonna watch my wife with your fucking nose in your phone?"

Mauro tolerates it for all of two seconds before he's scrambling at my fingers, but even with his life literally in my hands, he's not so stupid as to reach for his gun. When purple blotches start to color his face and the *real* panic sets in, I toss his body to the side.

He hunches over, gasping for air.

"Next time I see you on that phone while you're supposed to be watching my wife, I'll shove it up your ass," I say, without dropping my grin, and adding loud enough that he can hear me over his heaving. "And I mean that *literally*."

Mauro catches his breath enough to choke out a "yes, sir."

I leave the man to his job.

As I walk back to my car, I exhale, waiting for that familiar feeling of satisfaction to wash over me. Instead, I'm more pissed off than ever as I slam my car door shut.

6

DOM

I HAD to stop for fast food, and after a week of eating dirt and gnawing on half-cooked venison, it's doing a number on my intestines. The drive to Turi's house is long enough that if I didn't grab *something*, I'd complete my transformation into a giant, hungry, hairy man-beast. No one wants that.

Most of the usual vehicles are missing as I pull into the lot next to Turi's house, which doesn't bode well for the amount of work waiting for me. My boots crunch across the gravel as I approach the front door, and I wave at Eduardo, who has an AR-15 strapped to his back as he patrols the house perimeter.

"Hey, Dom! Where's my deer? I've been going hungry over here," he calls out over the dark lawn.

The image of my new wife with that hunk of raw venison in her bare hands flashes in my mind.

"Better not let Conchetta hear you say that!" I let out a slightly forced laugh and grab my dick, thrusting in his direction. "But don't worry, buddy, I got a mouthful for you right here."

Eduardo bursts into laughter as I enter the house.

I like Eduardo. He's a simple, reliable man. If a joke involves farts or dicks, he's going to laugh.

I follow my nose into the kitchen for a quick detour before I check in with Turi.

Conchetta, the tiny, ancient grandma Turi employs as his head chef, drops a ladle into a big soup pot with a splash when she sees me. Tonight, it's just her and the other cook, Nola, which means the rest of the men must be out on the streets. Nola gives me a beaming smile and a friendly wave before returning to the huge bowl of garlic in front of her. Conchetta scurries down from the step stool she uses to reach the stove and darts over to me.

"Little Dom!" she says in Italian, even though she comes up to my nipples.

I lean over so she can pull me into a hug, and as I stand back up, she snipes a sharp pinch on my belly fat.

"You've lost weight," she says in the same tone a parent would use to admonish their kid for getting a tattoo.

"Yeah, Mother Nature's a cruel bitch sometimes."

Conchetta swats me. "Language!"

I gesture to one of her huge pearl earrings. "You got a man, Conchetta? Or just one of your many admirers?"

She touches one of the earrings fondly. "A gift from Marisol. She's a sweet girl."

I glance over at Nola, who's also sporting a new set of diamond earrings. Figures Turi's foodie wife would set herself to bribing the kitchen staff. I can't tell if I'm impressed or pissed I didn't think of it first.

Conchetta waves me to the stools at the kitchen bar. After all that shit at dinner, my soul rests a little lighter knowing Aldo died in this very kitchen. Junior died in Turi's basement, but sometimes in life, you gotta accept compromises.

"I made your favorite, fava bean soup," she says, although she literally says that about every meal she cooks for me, and she's never wrong. "Sit down, I'll bring you a bowl."

I know better than to disobey her, so I pull out a stool and balance on top. Conchetta's only supposed to be getting me a single bowl, but I don't argue as she loads a big plate with cut meats, bread, and cheese to snack on first. She reminds me so much of my own mom that way—using food as a love language.

"Eduardo said you were bringing us back fresh venison," Nola calls to me without looking up from the delicate garlic skins she's peeling away.

Thankfully, Conchetta brings over my plate at that moment to distract me from thoughts of the woman and the deer at my house. I just ate, but my stomach growls again at the sight.

"I bet that wife of his is hoarding it all," Conchetta says without malice.

I choke on my first bite and have to cough to clear my throat.

"That's what I'd be doing. Is she a good cook, Little Dom? I'm a little worried you're so hungry after coming back. If she needs to learn, bring her here, and I'll teach her. That's what happens when you marry for looks—empty bellies."

Nola nods solemnly behind Conchetta's back, even though she's also stunningly beautiful and recently got engaged to one of Turi's soldiers, Camillo, and I know that bastard will never go hungry with her around.

I think of the focaccia and steak steaming off my plate back home and that cold, cold beer dripping with condensation. I fix on a grin and point it at Conchetta.

"She's a great cook, but you know I always save room for you, *bella*."

Conchetta rolls her eyes, but a blush colors her wrinkled cheeks as she turns back to her cooking.

Once I have a belly full of good food, I head upstairs to Turi, with a huge bowl of perfectly cut strawberries in hand, "for that sweet angel wife of Turi." I don't bother knocking as I key the code into the door of the nerd lair he calls his watchtower.

Inside, the room is cool, and a couple of skinny lamps light the corners. Most of the light comes from the thirty computer monitors hanging over Turi's huge desk. From the opposite side of the room, about a dozen monitors hang over his wife's desk—no, thirteen. She adds a new one every time I visit. On the last wall, instead of windows or anything that could remind you that you weren't stuck in a dark cave, a huge network of beige interconnected cat towers threads together against the wall. Marisol's asshole orange cat Buck narrows his eyes as I enter. I shoot him the middle finger.

Marisol hunches at her computer chair like a gargoyle, reaching past her legs to move her mouse around. Instead of the usual sixteen bags of candy littering the top of her desk, she's got a few bowls of fresh fruit that she occasionally stabs at with a single chopstick. I will never understand why Turi obsessed over her so hard—she's such a little freak. She raises her hand in greeting without turning to me as I drop the bowl of fruit at her desk.

She still suspects I'm a rat for following Turi's orders at that dinner and letting Barbara take her to the basement while I saved his daughter, even though she was never in any real danger. Leave it to a woman to hold a grudge over something you haven't done. She'll get over it eventually.

In contrast to his wife, Turi stands in a perfectly straight military posture as he stares at his computer monitors. He must have come back from a meeting because his black tie is tossed on his desk. The shape is suspiciously noose-shaped. I glance at Marisol, whose hair is messed up, and there are a few overturned trinkets on her desk.

Ugh.

"Is there a single square inch in this room that's safe from a black light?" I ask as a greeting.

"No," Marisol calls over her shoulder.

Turi doesn't even blink. "How was the trip?"

"Good, I only got diarrhea twice."

Turi's jaw twitches, which is as close as I'll get to a laugh from him. "I wasn't expecting to see you today."

"Yeah, well, turns out there's a whole home invasion situation going on. Why the fuck is Serafina in my house?"

"She's your wife."

"She's a little girl."

Turi's untouched. "Barbara said she wanted to live with you, and you said you'd protect her."

I throw my hands up in the air. "Yeah, from Junior and Aldo! But they're dead now, so why the fuck is she with me? Her sister's dead. She needs therapy, not another old man pawing at her."

"You're not that old."

"I'm pushing forty. She's *twenty*."

Turi does that stupid, annoying thing he likes to do when he wants to distance himself from an argument and turns away from me to change the images on a few of his computer monitors. I recognize the inside of Red's bedroom, the Capital, the street outside my house, and the camera that shows my own penthouse interior—the entrance to the elevators, the one I installed myself. I wouldn't admit under torture that I'm a little disappointed not to see Serafina.

"I imagine she was scared," he says. "The Family deals with instability through marriage, and the beautiful, virginal daughter of an established *consigliere* is a powerful bargaining chip. She knows you, and better for me to strengthen the Family from within than look to outsiders. Unless you'd prefer we marry her to one of the New York *capi*? Nico?" A flash of annoyance crosses Turi's face at the mention of his younger half-brother, and I have to admit I do get a little sick bubble of amusement from that. "Better for her to marry a known factor than a strange man who might disrespect her." Turi turns and makes eye contact with me. "Where's your wedding ring?"

"I don't have one."

"You can cheat—with an outsider. You can put Serafina in a new apartment, you can keep her and find her a hobby, you can do whatever you'd like, but wear the damn ring. That's an order."

Goddammit.

I exhale. "Yes, boss."

"You doing your rounds today? You should rest after your trip."

"Yeah, well, if I don't get a heavy dose of cigar smoke and cheap whiskey, I risk going feral."

Turi shrugs, turning back to his monitors and changing a few more images. "I'll fill you in."

As he talks, my gaze drifts back to the camera in my penthouse, searching for a glimpse of the woman inside. Turi's suggestion of finding her a hobby chafes. She's not my kid. Why do I have to find her a fucking hobby? If I'm wrong and it really is Serafina, I don't even know what she likes to do. Serafina was always into flower arrangements, piano, and ballet. Everything in favor of looking beautiful—not that I can blame her, really. She's been training to be someone's trophy wife since she was a kid.

It was Annetta I could understand. She did piano and ballet, too, but she also cooked. She could sew. She babysat. She liked photography.

When Annetta was sixteen, I'd come over to her house for dinner with her family. I'd thought nothing of her absence through the entire meal until I stepped outside for a smoke with Barbara, and I spotted her. She was lying perfectly still on her stomach on a blanket across the lawn, a big camera in hand, and peering through the lens without moving an inch. I remember being impressed that a kid could be so patient and thinking it was a shame she hadn't been born a man. She'd make a great hunting partner.

It was also then that I decided I'd stay away from her. Nothing good came from a man wanting to befriend a girl, and besides my lapse of judgment on her eighteenth birthday, I'd held to that.

"You get that?" Turi asks, one eyebrow raised.

I nod. He thinks the old-guard capos are conspiring against him—which, of course, they are. They're not going to appreciate our quick, violent change of power, and the only reason Turi isn't on the chopping block is because he had the full support of his dad and the rest of the Commission in New York.

"Some of Aceto's men are meeting for drinks," I say, which is hardly intel. They meet for drinks almost every night. Aceto was the most vocal in favor of Turi's promotion to don, so I'm curious to hear if he had anyone try to sway his vote behind the scenes. "I'll go see about that."

"Thanks."

I glance back at the cameras.

"Can you send someone to trade shifts with Mauro? He's

old as fuck, and I'll have to kill him if he can't keep his eyes open."

"I have two guards cycling to watch her, but I'll add a third to the rotation," Turi says with a stupid, private look of amusement.

I resist the urge to ask for more. We don't need to waste resources to watch one girl cook dinner in a penthouse. I do voice my other concern, the one that's been nagging at me since... since that dinner at Turi's house when Serafina bit me. She left a crescent-shaped wound, too. I resist the urge to pick at the still-healing skin.

"Turi, how closely have you been following Serafina in the past few weeks?"

"Seeing as how she seems to have little intention to overthrow me, not very."

"What're the odds the girls have switched?"

Turi throws me an annoyed look. "The odds that my *consigliere* has been lying to me and instead of marrying his virgin daughter, you've been tricked into marrying Chiarelli's widow?"

A widow, huh? I didn't realize her spineless husband had kicked the bucket. "Let's say I got a gut feeling."

7

ANNETTA

At twenty years old, I've never really been alone.

At my parents' house, I had Serafina, and at Frederico's, I had expectations. If I wasn't with him, I was with his mom, Giulia, or one of the other wives from the family. It was hard to pick who I liked least. The wives were a bad influence, always asking me to get day drunk or to go shopping and gossip about our husbands. When I came home, Giulia would be there, judging my expensive new handbag, the happy flush to my cheeks, my lack of caution.

"A wife should never embarrass her husband," she'd say, patting my warm cheek.

When I would tell Frederico, he'd blow me off.

"She tells you that stuff out of love, you know?"

"She's from a different generation."

"Not now, Annetta, I've had a long day."

So he was a mama's boy. He never forced me in bed. When he had time, he took me on dates. He bought me fancy jewelry. I'd gotten luckier than I ever could've imagined. For a long time, I distanced myself from Serafina, poisoned by the guilt that I'd tried to shape destiny and inadvertently ruined hers. She was the princess of the family. It was she who deserved the Prince Charming husband.

And then I saw what Prince Charming did behind closed doors, and I thanked God every night after that I had taken her place.

Now, lying in Dom's California king-size bed, I'm completely alone. If he came to the penthouse last night, I didn't see him. Outside the bedroom window, silver and rust skyscrapers jut out of the ground, piercing a blanket of grey clouds so dense it looks like someone forgot to paint the sky. I've been working up the courage all morning to drag myself out of my burrow of warm blankets and search for Dom in his ice chest of a penthouse—seriously, I need to layer up just to get a cup of water—but with no one demanding my presence, sleep eventually sucks me back under until noon.

When I wake up again, I stand in Dom's closet like I have every day this week and sift through his shirts. He used to give everyone in the family a hug when he'd come over for dinner. The familiar pine and smoke scent of his cologne brings a rush of memories—Serafina and I rolling our eyes at Carlo and Dom arguing over some baseball game, the brief sensation of Dom's rough fingertips brushing against mine as I passed the salt, heat plunging through me when he stretched long after a big meal, his button-up straining across his broad chest. Of all the men Dad has worked with over the years, Dom's one of the few I have happy memories with.

I pull a light blue button-up off the hanger and slip it on, rubbing my arms through the thin fabric to keep warm.

Dom didn't tell me any of his expectations for me when he stopped by the penthouse yesterday, not that I had high hopes after the loathing way he looked at me on our wedding day. Maybe he thinks he doesn't want a wife, or that I'm too young for him, or he resents being told what to do—it doesn't matter. We're married now. If I can convince him I'd be a good wife for him, whatever that might mean, I can prove to him that this marriage can serve us both.

Unless he wants kids? My mouth goes dry.

He's thirty-eight and never even been married as far as I know. He won't want that. Probably.

Twisting the hem of his shirt in my fingers, I walk downstairs in search of him.

While Dom's been over to my parents' house hundreds of times, we've never had dinner at his place, and I've always held the idea that it would look something like a medieval tavern. There'd be a big bearskin rug in front of the fireplace with caskets of beer strewn about. Or maybe it'd look like Cousin Tito's place, with a massive television always tuned to soccer and a single brown recliner in the center of the living room, and an ice chest of beer within arm's reach.

Instead, I was bewildered to find a long, wide fish tank stocked with ghostly silver angelfish and swarms of tiny glittering fish darting through gently waving green plant fronds. In all the time I've known Dom, I'd never heard any mention of him keeping fish, and I'd never seen him reading a book, definitely not any of the elegant-looking Italian classics lining his modest bookcase.

His place is modern and airy, with framed portraits of tall, smiling women, bearded men, and mop-headed children all over the walls and countertops. Pictures of a little boy and girl with dark eyes and wide smiles in soccer uniforms and multiple sets of family Christmas photos are stuck to his refrigerator door with magnets. I didn't even know he had siblings, and now I'm finding out he gets dressed up as Santa for his family's Christmas photos. I couldn't find any photos of his parents, which supports my long-held belief that the only explanation for Dom's huge appetite is that he was raised in the woods by a pack of wolves.

The inside of his fridge is the only part of his house that makes sense. It's completely empty, save for a few bottles of condiments and a half-pack of Guinness. When Mom brought me here a few days ago, she took one look at the kitchen, muttered a string of criticisms under her breath, and came back hours later with a full stock of groceries and kitchenware. She wasn't about to send me off to battle without my weapons.

Without any sign of him, I make my way upstairs to crawl back into Dom's bed and stare up at the ceiling, spreading my arms and legs like a starfish under the comforter. I haven't shaved my legs. I haven't done my makeup. The nail polish on my left pointer finger has a chip in it. I should get back up and fix those things, but if Dom isn't going to come home anytime soon, what's the point? No one's here to see me, and it's at once as intriguing and terrifying as the bottom of the ocean.

Thanksgiving is in a few days. Mom said she's going to find someone trustworthy to deliver groceries for me. Once that's settled, I could take the day and practice cooking all of the dishes Dom loves.

But if he's just going to walk out through the elevator again, past me in a skimpy outfit and all my delicious food, who am I doing it for?

I thought I had him yesterday. The way his stomach growled said he wanted the food I'd prepared, even if he didn't want *me*. But he'd resisted, and he left. I couldn't call him after, even if I'd been brave enough to try, because no one thought to give me his number.

What would Serafina do?

I close my eyes as a tear slides down my cheek, the warmth surprising me. I thought I'd cried out all my tears over the past month, but they still sneak up on me.

I don't like to imagine what she would do, in this hypothetical situation she's never been in. I don't like puppeteering the memory of her for my own comfort. While Rafa and Dad work and Mom and Carlo drink, I'm the one who has to hold her memory perfectly preserved inside me. No one knew her better than I, and no one deserves suffering more than I do.

It's up to me to hold vigil for her—a fishwife waiting at the docks for a ship that'll never come.

At least I don't have to pretend to *be* her all the time. Mom already canceled her classes and sent emails to the school, claiming grief on my behalf—not that I'd be able to perform to Serafina's level. Everyone thought she was just some dumb, pretty girl, but she always got As in her science classes, and she pushed herself hard in ballet. I'm pretty sure Mom canceled everything as much in fear of me getting outed as of me embarrassing her by not doing as well as Serafina.

Church is out of the question, too. Serafina was a good, pious girl who went every Sunday. They'd recognize me in a heartbeat. The safest thing while we're uncertain if there's still a hit out for me is to stay in Dom's penthouse unless there's an emergency. Mom, especially, was serious about it, like I'd want to sneak out to go socializing around Chicago while pretending to be my sister.

I lie in bed for hours, watching the hue of light change from cool to warm on the ceiling and rubbing the smooth cotton of Dom's bedsheets between my fingers. He must've changed out his sheets before he went on his camping trip, because his bed smells like fresh laundry and only faintly of him.

When my stomach starts gnawing on itself, I wait another hour and finally push myself out of bed. I pull my hair back into a ratty bun on the top of my head—I can't remember the last time I haven't spent at least half an hour styling it—and head downstairs. I pull the cold leftover focaccia out of the fridge, pick off the anchovies—I have no idea how Dom can tolerate extras of the salty little fish— and eat half. I drag the single, grey blanket off the couch and sit on the rug in the living room to watch doll-sized cars and people drifting through the streets far below.

DOM CAME HOME LAST NIGHT.

After crawling back into bed, overcome with exhaustion even though I did nothing all day—a lovely side-effect of grief, or so I've learned—I still couldn't sleep. I lay under the blankets with my fingers interlaced across my belly and listened to the whispering sounds of his arrival in the guest room next to mine.

By the time the morning came around, I had a plan.

I dragged myself out of bed just as the sun was beginning to rise. In the en suite bathroom, I showered, and like I have every day this week, set a timer for thirty minutes and cried my heart out—big, ugly sobs with tears and snot running down my face as I let all my grief, my guilt, and my longing for my sister pour out and spiral down the drain.

When the thirty-minute timer went off, and I felt like the human equivalent of an open, pulsating wound, I washed myself and stepped out. I braided my hair into two boxer braids, applied the perfect amount of makeup that a man would never notice, and sat down on the rower Dom has in a pocket corner, perfectly placed in front of the guest room's door.

I can't tell if he's up, but I haven't heard anything from his room yet, so I'm sure he's still in bed. Thankfully, the rower isn't electronic, so I grab the handles and start rowing. After a few minutes, my heart's pounding and my legs are fatigued, but I keep at it. I'm at my lowest weight since high school. I've slept like shit over the past few weeks, and I haven't exercised in as long. These are basically the worst possible conditions to start an intense cardio workout, but I grit my teeth and keep going.

I want to make Dom see me.

After fifteen minutes of heaving over the rowing machine, his shadow finally floats under the door. I tap into an unknown energy reserve. With each stroke, my thoughts get louder and louder.

What does he expect me to do all day?

He can't just leave me by myself like this.

I am his wife.

Dom swings the door open and steps through. His gaze snaps to mine, and my world freezes for a split second. I track the sight of his muscular thighs filling out his jeans and a black button-up that exposes a shiny gold chain buried in his dark chest hair. The fur-trim coat he wore on our wedding day adds another thick layer of bulk to his already considerable frame. His dark hair, laced with silvery greys, hangs loose and damp around his face. I'm thankful I'm already on the rower, or I wouldn't know what to do with my hands.

"Dom," I say breathlessly. I don't know if it's because of the sight of him or the exercise.

Instead of answering, he gives me a look of mild disgust

that spears an arrow into my heart before he starts toward the stairs next to me.

"I need to ask you something," I blurt out.

Dom doesn't turn toward me, doesn't acknowledge me in any way except to stop in his tracks.

"What do you want for Thanksgiving dinner? It's next week." I'm grasping for straws. I already know exactly what he likes—he loads his plate with the same heaping servings of calorie-dense foods every year.

Just his profile is visible, and he looks annoyed.

"I don't need you to make anything," he rumbles, his voice thick with sleep.

"Well. I *want* to make something. For us." I hesitate. "And I'll need money. To buy groceries."

He places his left hand on the banister, and if I weren't paying so close attention to his movements, I would've missed it. The flash of a gold wedding ring on his left hand, with a band thicker than Dad's wedding ring. He bought a new one.

The rower's handle slips from my sweaty palms, cracking against the machine. Dom snaps his head toward the sound, and his gaze lands on me.

His eyes flick *down*. He takes in the sight of me, sweaty, in my black leggings and sports bra, my chest rising and falling with each deep breath.

For a moment, a hopeful balloon swells in my chest. I'm able to fake confidence as I pick up my hand towel off the ground, and with Dom's eyes glued to my every movement, I run it over my face, to the back of my neck, and down to the space between my breasts. I leave it over the top of the machine, and his gaze flicks to the folded fabric.

The tendons in his hand flex as he squeezes the banister, his wedding ring winking at me again.

I lift from the machine fluidly, silently thanking Mom for always keeping us in ballet, and take a step toward him.

Without taking his eyes off me, he reaches into his back pocket and pulls out his leather wallet. He passes me a black credit card.

"Spend whatever you want," he says.

I take the card and look up at him, my lips parting.

"What do you want?" I ask in a low voice. "Is there anything I can do for you before you leave for work?"

His expression is stoic, but his voice is crushed gravel when he asks, "Like what?"

I swallow. A man like Dom would appreciate the direct approach.

"I would love to suck your cock."

Dom's eyes blaze and, for a second, I think he wants that too, but then he grins and *laughs* in my face.

"I don't want a fucking blowjob from you, *Serafina*," he says.

He knows.

My eyelashes flutter. He grins, shakes his head, and walks down the stairs.

When he disappears around the corner, I fly back to my room, slamming the door behind me. I lay a flat palm against my racing heart as I suck in a steadying breath. Then another.

Fuck.

I undress quickly, goose bumps rising across my skin from the drying sweat in his freezing cold bedroom.

Fuck!

Dom knows I'm not Serafina. What else could his tone have meant? And if he knows, he's going to tell Turi, and if he tells Turi... well, I don't know what'll happen exactly, I just know it'll be *bad*. I don't know Turi all that well, but even I know he doesn't like liars. And if he finds out Dad, who's supposed to be his trusted advisor, has been lying to him?

I walk quickly to the bathroom, set a timer on my phone, turn on the shower, and step inside. The water's so cold, I suck in a shuddering breath, my stomach caving in, but I don't leave the icy spray. I scrub my face with my palms, tears already leaking from my eyes. I've trained my body—showers are for crying, although the embarrassment of being rejected so completely is plenty of fuel on its own.

New plan. I stay as far away from Dom as possible. I don't give him any reason to suspect anything different about me, and I cook delicious meals every night to build up some goodwill in the meantime.

And if he changes his mind and comes into my bedroom?

Hot and cold spiral inside me. I wouldn't deny him, if that's what he wanted. But for now, I'm nothing. I'm a mouse, living in the walls of his home. I won't give him any reason to dislike me.

A sob wracks my chest. I can't hold the tears in anymore. Hot and ashamed, I cry my humiliation under the water until my timer goes off.

Then, I pull myself together and get dressed.

A FEW HOURS LATER, the elevator door dings, and I stand at attention.

I'm wearing my best black skirt and a cashmere sweater, and my makeup is tastefully done just like Serafina used to do. After my second crying session, I took a long nap, only stirring when Mom called to say she was headed over.

Mom sweeps into the penthouse in a pair of cream wide-leg trousers, a mauve sweater, and a trench coat that couldn't possibly be warm enough in this weather. Behind her, a tall woman about my age with a bob of black hair struggles forward with several grocery bags. I vaguely recognize her face from family events, although I can't place her name. I remember her brother, though—Stefano, an ambitious asshole who hangs around my brother Carlo sometimes.

"Serafina," Mom says. "You know Valeria? She's going to be helping with your grocery deliveries."

I smile blandly at her.

Valeria eases the groceries onto the kitchen counter and takes a step back. She's dressed stylishly in a black Nirvana T-shirt, jeans, boots, and a big black coat. She's pretty, but she always looks at people like she just heard their favorite food is stale bread, so I've never tried to get to know her—I get enough judgment at home.

She measures me for a moment before cracking her cold, uninterested expression with a tiny, surprisingly warm smile.

"Let me know if you need help figuring out where anything goes," Mom calls over her shoulder.

Valeria's smile disappears, and she sets herself to putting up the groceries.

Mom wraps me in a hug, then pulls me back for a good look. Her eyes, hidden by sunglasses, catalog my appearance. She touches my hair briefly.

"You've lost weight," she says approvingly. Over her shoulder, I see Valeria freeze for a split second before she continues pushing a bag of sugar into the pantry.

Just a few hours, and I can crawl back into the warm bed.

"Thank you," I say, trying my best to inject some

sincerity into the words. But by the way Mom's mouth twists in frustration, my best isn't very good.

With a sigh, she pats my shoulder and turns to the kitchen. She sheds her coat and folds it over one of the stools before she walks to the refrigerator and opens the door. "Did you feed Dom last night? There's a lot of leftovers in the fridge."

She points to the single square of leftover focaccia that I picked anchovies off of. "Oh, sweetheart, he likes extra anchovies."

I suck down a retort and join them in the kitchen to help Valeria unpack the groceries.

"Valeria," Mom says in a too-casual tone. "Your mom was telling me you're going to be the event planner for your dad's celebration."

"That's right, Mrs. Barbara," Valeria says in a flat tone.

"While you're going to school and working as a bartender? Your parents raised a hard worker!"

"Thank you."

"You know," Mom says, "Serafina's *very* passionate about floral arrangements, and she'll need something to keep busy while Dom's at work."

My stomach sinks.

Mom turns away from us to rummage in the cabinets. Valeria and I glance at each other behind her back.

"Your mom said you could use another set of hands with the preparations. Serafina would love to be able to help out anyway she could." Mom smiles at Valeria. "What do you think? She's great with people. I think she'd be a wonderful helper."

Valeria pours a bag of apples into the fruit bowl on the kitchen island. She tucks one hand into her coat pocket and leans back, her impassive face trained on Mom. "It's okay, Mrs. Barbara. I have it handled."

"Trust me." Mom reaches for a corkscrew in one of the drawers and a bottle of white wine Valeria brought over. "It sounds easy now, but planning out an event for the whole family is a big task. Serafina would be happy to help. You just let her know what days work for you to come over, and she can do whatever you need."

Behind Mom's back, Valeria raises one eyebrow at me, as if to say, *really?*

I shrug. *I guess.*

"Okay, Mrs. Barbara," she says. It's hard to tell, but she does look a little relieved at the offer of help. "That'd be great. Thank you."

Mom flaps a hand in her direction. "Don't mention it. That's what family is for."

Valeria nods toward me. "I'm free tomorrow. I'll text you."

Just as she's pulling out her phone, the elevator, tucked in the short foyer around the kitchen wall, dings. I snap my head toward the sound.

Dom? Back so early? Or... *no, it's not... it can't be...*

I can't move, my feet glued to the tile, my heartbeat sputtering like the flame of a flickering candle.

"Sera?" Valeria asks, staring at the side of my face.

Three women I've never seen before round the corner, each of them with a suitcase or backpack, and the panic inside me withers.

"Jan!" Mom exclaims, spreading her arms wide and approaching the oldest woman of the group.

They wrap each other in a hug, then turn to me.

"Serafina, this is Aunt Jan," Mom says, like that name means something to me.

I'm still trying to catch my breath from the insane thought that those women were hitmen sent by my late husband's family, and now I'm fixing my mouth into a frozen grin as I dig through my memory for this woman's name or face. Did Serafina know her?

"Bah! You don't remember me," Jan says with a raspy smoker's voice. "I used to change your diapers when you were a kid. Your mom and I go way back."

She gives me a firm hug, dousing me in floral perfume, her soft body pressing against mine. When she pulls away, she sifts her fingers through my hair, and I actively repress a full-body shiver at being handled by a stranger.

"So, what're you thinking?" she calls over her shoulder to Mom while she examines my hair. "Highlights?"

BY THE TIME the women are finished with me, I feel as sexy as a plucked chicken. I've been waxed from the neck down and had my eyelash extensions filled in. My acrylics are replaced with glossy, champagne-colored nails, and I've been given a pedicure and a facial. My hair now has the same subtle lowlights Serafina used to wear.

Except for the waxing session, which I thankfully got to do upstairs, Mom hovered over us the entire time like a bee at a picnic, voicing her opinion often. Valeria escaped hours ago.

After all the beauty treatments, I stand to the side in the kitchen, an abandoned doll, while Mom and Jan catch up on family gossip.

Serafina and I always had a rigorous beauty routine, but Mom's added a few extra steps since I've been gone. I don't know how Serafina kept up with all of this—all I want to do is go lie back down and take a nap.

I consider sidling out of the kitchen to head back to my room. Would Mom follow?

Just as I'm on the cusp of sneaking away, Jan finally says her goodbyes and leaves the penthouse.

Mom picks at a few grains of rice on her plate, leftover from the sushi she ordered us all for dinner and licks the sticky grains off her fingers like she's not counting every calorie.

I glance at her coat, just within arm's reach.

"So," Mom says, as she carries the takeout containers to the trash. "A visitor came by the house the other day."

I couldn't care less, but maybe she'll leave faster if I play along. "A visitor?"

"Giulia Chiarelli."

My mouth goes dry, and Mom gives me a knowing look.

"She spoke with Dad. Said the family's heartbroken about her son's death. They want to have dinner with *you*," Mom says in a meaningful voice that makes me break out in a cold sweat.

"I can't," I whisper in a choked voice.

When Giulia sees me, she'll know. If anyone from Frederico's family sees me, they'll know.

"You'll have to, but we have time." Mom circles the kitchen counter to lay her hand over mine. Our nails match. "We'll make sure everything's perfect, okay?"

I thought I wasn't going to see anyone from that life ever again. That was the whole point in marrying Dom. He's supposed to protect me and my family.

I swallow. "Mom—"

"Sweetheart, you need to do this for yourself as much as for your dad."

"What have you done?" Mom asked me when I stood, exhausted and weak, at my parents' front door. Shock and horror painted her face. "She's dead. What did you do?"

"Don't be difficult," she adds before kissing my cheek and leaving.

I LIE SPRAWLED over the living room couch later that evening, wearing only Dom's shirt again, and raise the bottle of Chardonnay to my lips, lifting my head just enough to keep the wine from spilling out of the sides of my mouth.

I've never done this. I've never been alone with my thoughts, and definitely never long enough to relax. After Dom's rejection and Mom's attention, I was exhausted and jittery until I spotted Mom's open wine bottle in the fridge. I haven't yet forgotten her motherly advice the day before my wedding.

Get him drunk so he doesn't realize there's no blood, and get pregnant as soon as you can.

It was a great plan with only one flaw—my husband doesn't want to fuck me.

I take a big swig, ignoring a prickle of anxiety. I won't be like Mom and Carlo, who escape way too often into a bottle —I'm just getting drunk tonight, and then tomorrow, I'll use the rest in a sauce.

I squint at the digital clock on the microwave in the kitchen. Well, technically, I'll make the sauce today, seeing as how it became "tomorrow" about an hour ago. I should be in bed, but with my fucked-up circadian rhythm, I'm wide awake.

At least the sparkling lights of the city below and Dom's fish tank make me feel like I'm not the only one up so late.

It'd be almost comfortable if it weren't for the creaking sounds the high-rise building makes in the far recesses of the penthouse.

Creeeeeak.

I glance upstairs. I know the sounds happen because the building is flexing with the wind—it doesn't make it any less creepy.

I bet Dom doesn't get scared of the sounds. He probably never gets scared of anything.

I take another swig of wine.

People are supposed to drink because it makes them happy and loose, so why does each sip sink me deeper into a bad mood? I scowl at the microwave clock. How is Dom not home yet?

Completely alone, I scoff loudly.

I still can't believe he said no to a fucking *blowjob.*

He doesn't want me?

Good.

Great.

I don't even *like* giving blowjobs, and I hate gagging. I've already had to grin and bear it for one husband. I'm glad Dom doesn't want that, too.

My chest rises and falls, and I sip a little more from the bottle.

What I want is a man to please me for once. I want to be the selfish one who gets to come, roll over, and fall asleep, exhausted and sated. I want a man to tend to my needs. To see me storm into the house and anxiously wonder how he'll guide me to the bed to eat me out, to dissipate my anger.

I only realize I'm smiling when it slips off my face. I take another gulp of wine, crisp and bitter.

Okay, I don't want that, necessarily. I'm not an asshole.

I just want a man to care.

I huff bitterly into the mouth of the bottle. Fat chance.

First, I found a husband who wanted too much, then I found one who doesn't want anything. Maybe I'm just not cut out for marriage.

I swing my head back and blink slowly at the ceiling. So, then what?

The elevator dings.

I sit up immediately, the world blurring a second too slow around me.

Is he home early?

Part of me panics at the thought of being caught unawares, tipsy, and wearing only his shirt like a lover. The other part of me, the old programming that's determined to please him, thrills.

Try to deny me now.

I lurch off the couch toward the foyer to catch a glimpse of the elevator just as the doors split open.

And there's no one inside.

The sweet anticipation curdles in my gut. My mouth goes dry, and my heart thuds in my chest. The short foyer tunnels to the completely empty elevator, opened wide like a dying man's last desperate breath.

It shouldn't do this. It only opens if someone has a key code or they call up first. This is impossible.

The doors stay open for a long time, as if tempting me to enter, to let myself be eaten, but drunken bravery—or fear —keeps me rooted to the spot.

The moment the doors whisper closed, I bolt.

8

DOM

Serafina never would have been as bold as Annetta was this morning.

Turi still hasn't gotten back to me, but by now, I know I'm right. Serafina didn't cook, and she never cried. Annetta thinks I can't hear her sobbing for exactly thirty minutes through the walls, but it's become my new, fucked-up morning alarm.

I'm not scared of a woman crying. It's easy, actually, to manage an upset woman. You sit next to her, silently offer her tissues and sugar, and tell her she was right. But I'm not going anywhere near Annetta until she fesses up to why she's been lying to me.

Or until Turi rips the truth out for her.

The night is young when I finally get to Plunder, the shitty little bar just south of Humboldt Park. I pass by a man on the street corner openly snorting cocaine, and a couple of women wearing glittery dresses underneath their oversized coats, who all take one look at me and don't even try to get my attention. I wouldn't be surprised if they know who I'm with. The whole neighborhood knows us—that's why

I'm not worried about my car. No one is enough of an idiot to touch a car that nice in a neighborhood like this.

Everyone inside the bar turns to look at me as the bell on the front door jingles.

"The usual?" the bartender calls out to me from behind the bar as he reaches for a whiskey glass.

The rest of the barflies turn back to their conversations.

"I'll take the IPA tonight, thanks," I say.

He hesitates for only a second, but he's smart enough not to ask questions as he fills up my beer in a smudged glass that I bet clean-freak Turi would refuse to drink from. "They're all here."

I nod my thanks and head upstairs. I have to crouch to get through the tiny, spiral stairs that lead upstairs, and the wood groans its annoyance at my weight the whole way up.

Upstairs, in a dim glow cast by one overhead light, half a dozen familiar faces turn toward me, first with hostility, then with welcome—fake or otherwise. I grin widely and hold my beer aloft.

As I reach the top step, I purposely bump into the bathroom sign hanging from the ceiling.

"Ah, shit," I say, gripping my head. "I really gotta watch where I'm going."

A few men around the table chuckle, easing the tension a little.

I spot Carlo, Serafina's oldest brother, and his friend Russell at the far end of the table. Judging by his red-rimmed eyes, Carlo's already high as a kite. Next to him, Russell looks like a pissed-off babysitter.

I'm glad Russell's here to keep Carlo out of the worst of trouble—and even better, he keeps his mouth shut and brings back the money he's supposed to. It's obvious he's using Carlo to step up in the organization, but Russell keeps an eye on the Barbara heir, so no one gives him any shit. He keeps his nose clean, and he'll be a made man in no time.

Carlo, on the other hand, is a fuck-up. He likes our life-style because it means he can get a bunch of badass tattoos and sexy women, but he'll jump through a lot of fucking hoops to avoid doing a single job, and more often than not, I'm the asshole who's gotta drag him back through said hoop. Barbara always took care of my family back when I was a lanky, angry nineteen-year-old with five siblings and shitty parents. So now, I take care of his.

Carlo isn't so bad, though. He's got a good sense of humor that reminds me of Turi's younger brother Matteo, when he was still alive.

"Where you been, Dom?" A dopey smile on his face, Carlo slides his empty glass of whiskey onto the table. "They said you went camping while the rest of us were working like dogs out here."

These men are all soldiers or wannabes, yet they're drinking on a Thursday night. I doubt there's much hard work going on.

I drop into the empty seat next to Russell. "You know me. Had to leave the whole city just to get enough space to air out my balls."

The men burst into laughter. There's not a full glass of whiskey at the table, and this is their regular meeting spot. Turi would have a field day if he saw this. When was the last time these idiots swept the room for bugs instead of getting shitfaced and gossiping?

"You know what they say, the bigger the balls, the smaller the dick," Russell calls out.

I laugh good-naturedly with the rest of the men. It takes guts for him to talk shit to me, I'll give him that.

A couple of hours later, I've gotten to my eighth watered-down beer, and everyone else is on who-knows-what round of whiskey by the time the conversation turns to business.

"All I'm saying is that," Riccardo says, "I'm hemorrhaging money over here dealing with these *pulotti*, and I shouldn't be. It wasn't our damn fault things blew up at the warehouses. I don't see why I gotta pay off every pig that sticks his lard ass where it doesn't belong. The Irish fucked this up, so Gavin should be paying off the cops. They're his, anyway!"

His buddy Ettore emphasizes this with a clank of his empty glass on the table. A few of the men around him nod and mumble in agreement.

"It's bad enough the cops are riding our asses all the time, but now I hear the boys in New York are coming for us too." Riccardo stares down at his glass angrily. He flicks his gaze up to me. For some men, Riccardo is intimidating. He's thin and severe-looking—but he also has a full head of straw-like hair that makes him look like a scarecrow with stuffing leaking out, so I'm not too threatened. "We've been handling our own business for years, and now some fuckers are gonna waltz in and tell us what to do?"

I know for a fact he wouldn't challenge Turi's orders to my face if he weren't drunk, and if he didn't think I was too. Not so lucky for him, I had the bartender cut my drinks with seltzer water six beers ago.

I meet his gaze and shrug lazily, letting my beer slosh out. "What're you gonna do? Them's the breaks."

Riccardo scowls.

Before he can think of more complaints, Ettore chimes in with drunken cheer, "Mario said we're going to start marrying their daughters."

Russell wrinkles his nose. "You know how those girls are," he grumbles.

Everyone grunts in agreement, even though I'd bet my left nut not a single one of them other than Carlo has visited New York.

Russell continues. "I'd want proof I'm getting a cherry with the sundae, you know what I mean? I'm not trying to catch something."

I take a big swig of my watered-down piss drink, regretting my sobriety. I've been hanging out with straight-edge Turi too much. I should have been drunk to deal with this lot.

"Man's got a point." Riccardo points his beer at Ettore. "Remember when you got chlamydia?"

"*It burns!*" someone shouts.

Ettore yells over the burst of laughter, "It was *one* time!"

"Getting more drinks," Carlo calls out among the noise and dips down the stairwell.

When he's turned the corner, Russell shoots me a defiant glare.

Interesting.

"Dom, you lucked out, huh?" he says, his voice barely audible over the men cracking jokes at Ettore's expense.

Looking into his glossy eyes, I realize Russell's had a lot more to drink in the past hour than the rest of the night.

"There's no one sweeter than Serafina," he says. "I can't believe her dad signed her off to you. She must have the sweetest, tightest—*gak!*"

I don't think. Just act, swinging a fist into his windpipe.

Russell dry heaves over his lap, clutching his throat, while the men sit up straight.

The room falls into dead silence except for the radio playing downstairs and Russell wheezing and coughing.

I take a sip of my beer as I lean back.

Ettore leans over to Russell, who's turning a mottled

shade of red. Russell knocks over his glass, which drops to the ground with a thud and rolls away. Ettore looks up at me in mild panic.

I wrap a hand over Russell's shoulder, and he tries to jerk away, but I clamp down harder.

"You're a kid, so I'm going easy on you," I say. "This is a good lesson to learn. Next time you speak disrespectfully about my wife, I'm not holding back." I look out across the men.

A mix of fear and resentment looks back at me.

"That means in *private*, too. *Il diavolo ascolta sempre.*"

The Devil's always listening.

I don't drop Turi's nickname often, but when I do, I make sure it's for good effect.

"Yes, boss," a few of the men mumble.

Riccardo scowls into his glass, but he says it along with the rest. I know that look. Every man here has fought and scraped to the top of his tiny world, and it can be a jarring realization to be reminded they're little more than shit on the bottom of my boot.

"Ettore," I drawl, "take Russell to the doctor."

Ettore's already on his feet and dragging Russell toward the stairs before I finish my sentence.

My work here is done. I'm exhausted, pissed off, and way too fucking sober.

But I'm not going home.

I sift through the conversation tonight.

"Riccardo," I say, and he lifts his head toward me like a beaten dog. He might hate me, but he's got enough self-preservation to keep that thought off his face. "That fuck that keeps shirking his debts? What was his name?"

"Hoffman, boss." Riccardo's thin shoulders are bunched up around his neck, and he consciously lowers them.

"Get the fuck up. We're going hunting."

CARLO WAS PISSED when he found out I crushed his friend's windpipe, but when I told him it was in his sister's honor, he sucked from his vape and slunk off. I'm going to have to talk to his dad about him soon. Carlo's thirty-two, and unlike his younger brother, he's showing no sign he's cut out for our lifestyle.

Unlike me, too.

My knuckles are throbbing from beating the absolute piss out of that slimy, rich fuck. A deep satisfaction, like the kind after a solid workout, loosens my muscles. I was a little disappointed he ended up coughing up the dough when I finally held my knife to his pinky finger.

Riccardo was annoyed. He and his men had been trying for weeks to do what I'd done in a single night, but he was begrudgingly grateful. I set up another night of drinking with him. Men like Riccardo think they want to be top dog, but what they really want is to submit to a bigger, badder man.

They crave the hierarchy.

Tonight, as I step into the penthouse, I catch the scent of meat and spices. I approach a copper slow cooker sitting in the kitchen, one I've never seen before in my life.

Annetta cooked dinner last night, too, leaving me a plate of food in the fridge with carefully written reheating instructions on top. I took it and ate the whole thing cold, like a starved animal.

Something in my chest twists.

I've been a complete dick to her, yet she's made sure I have a delicious meal waiting for me when I get home.

There's a clean bowl and spoon on the counter next to a dish of butter and what I suspect is a loaf of homemade bread.

I prepare myself a bowl, filling it to the absolute brim, and scarf it down, standing over the counter. By the third bowl, I'm completely sated, my belly an overstuffed sausage.

Fuck.

I've always appreciated a woman who can cook, and Annetta can *fucking* cook. I wouldn't admit this under the scope of a firing squad, but she might even be a better cook than Conchetta.

I clean up the food and drag my feet upstairs. I need to get the truth out of her. A younger me would have happily taken her up on her offer of a blowjob, but I have the unfortunate benefit of experience. If your gut is telling you not to sleep with a woman before you get all your ducks in a row, then you'd better listen. Turi will get back to me any day now, and I want all the information in my back pocket in case she tries lying to me.

But she's beautiful and she cooks well, and a man's only got so much willpower. I'll give it a few more days, and then I'll sit her down and get out the truth my own way.

My guess is that it has something to do with that husband of hers dying, which would be a damn shame. I'd definitely have to tell Turi, and he won't be happy about it.

Who knows? Maybe she had a good reason.

I scrub a hand over my jaw and stand in front of my old bedroom door. I keep forgetting—she's behind this door.

I would love to suck your cock.

That, I won't be forgetting anytime soon. I barely managed to stave off an erection until I got in the elevator, laughing at her because otherwise I was gonna say something stupid.

Just thinking about her now, though, with her face flushed pink and her chest heaving from the rower, wakes my dick up—although thinking about the fact that she's my *wife* now has it deflating again.

I didn't ask for a kept woman. The idea of a half-dozen angry little Doms running around and a miserable domestic servant for a wife has my balls shriveling up inside me. I got enough of that growing up.

I turn from my bedroom door and head to my guest room, but when I twist the door handle, it stops halfway.

Locked.

"What the fuck?"

Did Annetta do this? The only other person who visits the apartment is the house cleaner but she doesn't come for a couple of days.

"Dom?" a soft, timid voice calls from inside the room. She sounds terrified.

I rap on the door, my blood pressure spiking. "What's going on? Are you okay?"

The door handle jiggles, and then the door swings open.

"Fuck," I say aloud before my brain can make me shut up.

She's wearing nothing but one of my shirts. Heat zips to my groin at the sight of my young wife's nipples poking against the white cotton and her smooth, slender legs stretching out from under the hem.

The room reeks of wine. She gazes at me hazily from under her long eyelashes, wavering on her feet, and her hair is messed up. I've never seen her like this.

"Why was the door locked?" I demand, although I should just be walking away. Nothing good comes from a drunk girl with no pants.

She leans against the doorjamb and exhales a soft breath. "The elevator door opened."

I raise an eyebrow and cross my arms. "And?"

Her gaze dips over my forearms—I resist the urge to flex—then it slides back up to me. Her mouth is flushed a deep pink. She darts out a tongue to wet her lower lip. "And there was no one inside."

"So you locked yourself into my room and got drunk because the elevator's on the fritz?"

Even though I'm almost sure this is a half-baked scheme to get in my pants again, on the off-chance she's telling the truth, I make a note to talk to Turi about it tomorrow.

"It makes me feel safe."

She must be plastered. I'll be surprised if I get into my room and there's not vomit on the bed. Yet another reminder that a relationship with this woman would lead to disaster—less than a month in and she's already getting blackout drunk. I'm not trying to play babysitter for a twenty-year-old who is discovering alcohol.

She blinks, and it looks like it costs her serious effort. I'm half-impressed she's still standing.

"It makes me feel safe to touch your things," she says. "You smell really good."

"That'd be the wine talking," I say, although I'm already turning to hide my growing erection and give her space to walk past me. I place a light touch against her lower back to guide her out of my room. "Come on, you'd better sleep this off."

Instead of moving pliantly like I expect, she digs her heels in and juts her chin up at me. "It's not the wine. I've been in your bed for the past week. When are you going to fuck me?"

I grit my teeth and push her forward, even as she presses her slender back into my palm. "Don't say shit like that."

"Shit like what?" She laughs a little breathlessly as I lift her a few inches in the air. My fingertips bite into her tiny ribs. She's so fucking light. "That I like when you touch me? Like how I used to make excuses to bring food to everyone when you'd visit because it meant I could see you?"

I force myself to ignore what she said, throw open her bedroom door, and sling her inside. Except I misjudge my strength and have to lunge forward to catch her by the upper arm when she stumbles forward, so she doesn't crack her head against the nightstand. She wheels herself into me with a graceful turn—*she's a dancer*, I remember belatedly—and presses her hands against my chest.

Her feet are between mine. We fit well together.

She clutches my shirt like she did at that fucking church, and I pray to every known and unknown god that she doesn't see the raging fucking erection in my jeans as I force her to her bed.

"You make me so mad," she murmurs.

That, along with a jerk of her little wrists, knocks me off balance. I throw out an arm to catch us at the last moment, my hand sinking into the mattress, and hold her against me to ease her onto the bed. Her legs swing up to lock around my hips at the same moment, her hair fanning out on the bed. Her small, pouty mouth flushes, and a delighted look crosses her face.

My brain grinds to a fucking halt as all the blood rushes to my groin.

I don't give a fuck what my dick is telling me—she's too goddamn drunk.

"I'm not gonna fuck you." *Not tonight, anyway.* And if I were as wise as I think I am, not ever—not after this display.

But as her heels dig into my lower back and she wrenches at my shirt, my body screams at me to give in.

Wrong. Wrong. Wrong.

She snaps her hips up, and I jerk back as her hot little pussy grazes my aching cock. She gives a soft laugh. "Are you going to let me fuck someone else then? Should I take him home? Fuck him in your bed?"

I squeeze her upper arm, but instead of backing down, she grinds herself against me again. All thought flies out of my head.

"You take another man home," I murmur in a low, deadly voice, "and I'll kill him."

The last sound I hear before I slam her door shut is her quiet, satisfied laughter.

9

ANNETTA

It's only when I drag myself downstairs and take my first sip of coffee that I remember last night through the dull pounding of a hangover.

I told Dom I like it when he touches me.

That if he doesn't have me, I'd take another man to my bed—a bald-faced lie.

I set my mug on the counter, press the heels of my hands against my eyes, and groan. Who did I become last night? My face is burning so hot that it feels like my hair will ignite. And all for what, an elevator door opening?

Against the starburst of light and dark behind my eyelids, the memory of his response sends a shudder through me.

I dig through my hazy memories for the sensation of Dom's hard cock against me. He felt so *big*, like I knew he'd be. Big, and barely holding back.

I moan at the memory, secure in the knowledge that I'm alone in the house.

So much for fading into the background.

I drink deeply from my coffee, letting the almost-too-hot liquid scald my throat and warm my insides. Outside, thick grey clouds sleepily weave through the high-rises.

At least I know now he wants me. I can work with that.

A COUPLE OF HOURS LATER, I add the finishing touches to my snack trays. Unlike whatever's going on with Dom and me, *this* makes sense.

I have one tray of cut veggies for Valeria if she's on a diet, and another stuffed with crackers, meats, and cheeses, in case she's not. After I found the thermostat and cranked the heat up from Dom's original arctic settings to a toasty seventy degrees, I'm dressed in a casual, but not-too-casual, off-the-shoulder sweater, and leggings. No wine tonight—the thought makes me nauseous—but I have coffee brewing and tea ready.

Dom doesn't have a TV, which was probably the most unexpected thing about him, but I did find some Bluetooth speakers embedded in the ceilings to connect my phone to, and piped in classical study music.

My skin crawls when the elevator door pings—I'm learning to hate that sound—but I relax when Valeria steps inside, wearing a thick jacket with the sleeves rolled up, black baggy jeans, and sneakers. She hefts a thick binder and a stack of books to one arm when I step forward to hug her, but as I lean forward, she shifts and pokes me in the eye with the edge of her binder.

"Sorry!" she blurts out.

"No, it's okay." I rub my eye and wince.

It wouldn't be so bad if I weren't already hungover, but I don't mention that part.

She grimaces. "I'm not great at hugs."

"Maybe we can go for a high-five next time," I say, laughing.

She gives me a tiny, grateful smile as I lead her into the kitchen.

"What do you have so far?" I pull out a couple of plates, and when I turn, her expression has turned businesslike.

She nods and spreads her binder and books across the counter. "Let's start with the theme."

Several cups of tea later, I have the distinct impression that her dad's set her up to fail. After he fired his event planner for high prices, he threw everything at his daughter and told her to *figure it out* and do it cheap. The only expense he's budgeted for is renting out a huge yacht on the pier and a catering company he already picked out—a favor to a friend, I guess. From what I can tell, Valeria's never planned a party and has no contacts outside of the family. Because she's going to school and working as a bartender— and now as my delivery person—it's almost impossible for her to find the time for this.

"At least we have the florist settled." She thumbs through one of the floral arrangement books, stopping for an extravagant, avant-garde display.

I roll a lock of my hair between my fingers as I look over the glossy photos of high-society dinners and sticky notes with scrawling handwriting.

My tongue is thick in my mouth. I've helped Serafina with her arrangements before, but I was never good at deciding what to pick or figuring out the structure of the arrangement. She always made it look so easy.

"Here." Valeria points to a few arrangements with stone vases and structural designs. "What do you think about these? On the second deck of the yacht, there will be dozens of small, circular tables, so we'll need something low and circular to mimic those shapes. My mom took a look at the arrangements I picked out, but she said the men wouldn't like sitting next to something so *girly*. We'll need 'manlier' flower arrangements." She rolls her eyes. "Any thoughts?"

Apparently not, as I look through these. The flowers all remind me of my sister. Calla lilies, tulips, roses. I can almost smell them and see her touching them.

"I—" My throat closes up.

Valeria glances toward me with a touch of panic. "This is too much, isn't it? I told Mom…"

With a supreme force of will, I drag myself out of the river of grief threatening to tow me under. "It's not too much. I can handle it." I sip from my tea. "What about moss? You could do something more forest-y?"

She stares at me a little longer before she finally nods. "I'll find some reference photos."

I sit up straight. "I can do that." Finally, something to do that isn't waiting around all day for Dom to come home and tell me he won't fuck me. "We have the theme figured out. I can mock up some invitations and send them over to you."

"No, I wouldn't impose—"

"You have exams coming up, right?

She drums her fingers against the counter, then meets my eye like accepting my offer of help is a bomb she's about to snip the red wire on. "Yeah. Alright, that would be great. Thank you."

I stand and busy myself with our glasses and cups to hide my smile. "So, same time next week?"

We tidy up in a comfortable silence. When she's done, she hovers at the kitchen island, tapping the marble again.

I eye her across the sink. "What?"

"Do you…" She firms her mouth and stands tall. "Do you want help? Getting out of here?"

I blink a few times.

She wants to rescue me?

She doesn't miss a beat. "I have a little money saved up. Eight thousand."

I look into her dispassionate face and think that I might've misjudged this woman.

"You can have it. I can get it to you tonight, and you can take my car."

Is she offering *me*—a near stranger—everything she owns?

Staring blankly at her, I lower my soapy hands into the sink. "Where would I go?"

"Get a plane ticket. Go to Europe."

The thought is at once infinite and crushing. Europe? I could see the world. I'd be free to reinvent myself. I could ask Rafa, too. He drove me in complete secrecy to get my IUD weeks before my marriage to Frederico. He would give me cash if I asked for it, too, and he wouldn't tell a soul.

My family would be safe, wouldn't they? If I left. Dom would be happier for it. He never asked for a wife.

My chest squeezes.

I don't *want* to leave.

Valeria watches me with something like compassion. "If he's hurting you…"

My eyes widen. "You mean Dom?"

I know he's not a good man, I'm not lying to myself about that, but I've seen him on the couch, groaning from a belly full of my mom's *arancini*. I've seen him play princess tea time with my baby cousin and dig his thick fingers into the muddy coat of Cousin Tito's dog. He's not the kind of man who'd hurt me just because he could.

"Do we know another Dom?"

"He's not hurting me." I dry my hands on a kitchen towel before meeting her eye. "But, thank you for asking."

She shrugs. "So, you like him then?"

I wipe my hot palms on the sides of my leggings as I walk around the island.

God, this feels ridiculous. "Yes, I like Dom."

The corners of her mouth twitch. "I mean, like, *like*?"

We both grin, and I stand on my toes to nudge her shoulder with mine. She relaxes and waves a hand around to gesture at the penthouse, lit up by warm lights that cast a glow on all of Dom's belongings. The city outside sparkles from an uncharacteristically bright sunlight. "What's it like? Being married?"

It's a bit odd to think we're the same age. Valeria doesn't convey a look of *innocence*, necessarily, but she seems like a normal, if a little serious, twenty-something-year-old, as she waits for an answer.

"So far, he mostly stays out of the penthouse," I say.

She clears her throat, looking away from me. Something flickers in her expression. "What about kids?"

The thought makes my skin crawl. Does *she* want kids? It's hard to imagine Valeria in her all-black outfit, cooing over a baby.

"Not for a long time." *Not ever, if I'm lucky.* I glance at the wall clock in the living room. "Didn't you say you had to make it to work around six?"

She blows out a long stream of air, her shoulders slumping down. "Yeah, I did, didn't I?"

As I walk her to the elevator and we wait for it to arrive, she gives me a long look, the kind Mom usually gives me when she's about to say something I won't like. I want to peel the doors open and shove her inside before she can let the words out.

"You know," she says while I fix a frozen smile on my face, "at Annetta's wedding, I thought she was the most beautiful bride I'd ever seen. She was like a real-life princess, and she looked so happy. I'm glad she had that. She got to be happy."

The elevator doors open. She squeezes my shoulder and steps inside, and the moment the doors close, I let grief pull me under, and I sob.

Waves crash over me, each stronger than the next. I suck in a mouthful of dirty water and flail my arms to stay afloat. The water is syrupy and dense, and I can barely keep my head far enough above the waterline to take a breath before the next wave crashes over me.

I'm going to die here.

My mind cleaves in two.

Let go.

Fight.

I don't know which to listen to, but I don't have to wait long to decide. A pair of hands grips my shoulders. I go limp. They'll rescue me.

The hands move to my neck, and instead of lifting me, they constrict and push me further under the waves. My lungs burn as I hold my breath and claw at the hands, kicking at the water and doing everything I can to stay alive a few moments longer.

I wake up in the dark. I can't breathe. I scrabble at my throat and kick at the bedsheets, trying to get a lungful of air. The only thing I can do is choke and gasp like a dying fish.

BOOM.

My bedroom door swings open, and a massive man storms inside.

A scream lodges in my throat. I clamber back, my legs catching in the sheets, still clutching my throat.

The man grabs my ankle and hauls me toward him.

"No." I scream and sob, kicking with my free leg as hard as I can and driving my nails into the bed sheets to claw for purchase. "No. No!"

The man grabs both my legs and pulls me against him, presses me against his chest, and—

It's Dom.

He's saying something. His hands move across my back, searching. I choke out a sob, curling myself into him.

"Do I need to call the doctor?" he asks. "What's going on? Talk to me."

I suck in a deep breath, and his scent coats my insides like a warm vapor, calming me. I press my face against his furred chest. I'm sitting in his lap, my legs on the top of his thighs, and his belly against my body. His arms band against my back, making me feel, for a moment, safer than I've ever felt.

I shudder out a sigh. "I'm okay."

I nestle deeper into his chest and wrap my arms as far as I can around his waist. He's so strong and *warm.*

His cock, not entirely soft, presses into the bottom of my thigh through the fabric of his boxers, his only piece of clothing. I shift my leg to grind into it, but at the same time, Dom clears his throat and slides me onto the bed. He kneels on the floor like he's going to say his prayers, hiding his lower half behind the bed.

"What was that?" he asks. Since when does he wear

glasses? The unfamiliar black frames lend an air of sharp sophistication to his features.

"A bad dream."

I like the way he's watching me, like I'm taking up all his awareness. Already, the terror of the dream is being chased to the dark recesses of my mind.

"About what?" Dom leans in slightly.

For all my fears and hesitancies, the big man before me doesn't scare me. I wish I were on his lap again, wrapped in pine and smoke as I press my face against his chest.

"Bad things," I murmur.

Dom huffs an angry laugh, shaking his head. "That wasn't your run-of-the-mill bad dream. You were shouting 'stop.' Did someone hurt you? Who did that to you?"

I skate my gaze down Dom's form. When will I get another chance like this? His broad chest and arms are on full display. I lean forward. Would he let me touch him if I didn't say a word? We could pretend it was a secret.

"You have something to tell me?" His voice strokes against my body, still thrumming from the emotion of the dream.

I suck in a breath and lean back on the bed. "No one hurt me, husband."

Dom's mouth twitches at *husband*, and I wait for him to storm off, but he stays.

"Tell me," he says in a quiet, deadly voice.

I'm not sure if we're still talking about my dream.

"Since when do you wear glasses?" It's half-distraction, half-burning curiosity. I thought I knew everything about Dom, but he keeps surprising me.

"I need them to read."

"What were you reading?"

He exhales. "Wouldn't you like to know?"

"Yeah, I would." I reach toward his waist, but he rises in one fluid motion, treating me to an eyeful of the bulge in his boxers and his thick, muscular thighs.

"You let me know if you remember anything relevant."

He strides out of the room, his muscular ass filling his boxers.

My mouth is dry as I call out to him. "Goodnight."

He doesn't answer.

10

ANNETTA

Squealing erupts from the stove. I curse and flick off the burner, blowing into the frying pan as curls of blackened pork drift smoke back into my face.

Usually, I like cooking. If I follow the rules, I get a specific result. Every time, without fail.

Except today.

I already burnt two pork shoulders, my roux was too watery and then too dry, and I skinned my finger chopping the carrots.

I blow out a long stream of air, throw my apron onto the kitchen counter, and sit cross-legged in front of the massive living room windows, leaning my forehead against the cool glass with a soft *plonk*.

I'm learning to sort my days into good and bad.

That first month at my parents' house after I came back to Chicago? Bad. I barely remember those days, but I recall how dark it was, like I was one of those jagged-tooth, eyeless fish floating at the bottom of the Mariana Trench. Except, even that sounds kind of cool. I was more like a sea cucumber, barely existing in the gloom of my grief.

I laugh a little, my exhale forming a mini cloud on the window pane. Serafina would lecture me about calling myself a sea cucumber. She didn't like to hear me insult myself.

"Don't listen to Mom," she had told me as I brushed her hair into a tight, high bun for her ballet lesson.

Mom made no attempt to lower her voice as she bragged to her sister over the phone that Serafina was going to be the lead for her next dance recital and that I "was such a good helper." I'd called myself Serafina's stage mom.

"If you practiced with me, you could be just as good," Serafina said.

I remember smiling through all the bobby pins in my teeth as I shook my head. That was something Mom and Serafina didn't get, although at least Serafina tried to understand. I didn't care about being the best in ballet or the strongest in Pilates or having the highest grades in high school. It mattered if I was helping the people I loved. I *liked* being a helper. I was the first person anyone in the family called when they needed babysitting. Serafina came into *my* room when she needed someone to quiz her or to listen to her presentation.

Those things used to give me purpose, but I now know that they shielded me from reality—nothing I do matters. Serafina was the best at everything she did, and a hit-and-run killed her. I was a good wife to Frederico. He still cheated on me.

There's supposed to be this benevolent God who's marking off good deeds and bad ones, but in the end, being good or bad doesn't change a thing.

The pre-heated oven beeps at me.

I take a deep breath. It's just the bad day talking. Sometimes I wake up, and I know it's going to be one of those days where the grief stains everything in dark, muddy colors, and all I can do is move as little as possible. The emotions are supposed to exist only in my head, but they feel as real as a brain tumor. Sometimes I can fight them off, sometimes I just want to laze in them and cry, and sometimes they're a low hum in the background, but they don't ever go away, no matter how much I wish they would.

In a few minutes, I'll stand again, turn off the oven, take a thirty-minute shower, and go back to bed. Valeria can bring takeout for Dom. I won't want to eat today.

Tomorrow, I'll pull out Serafina's laptop and make another design for the party invitations. I'll slow cook the pork—delicious, and hard to mess up. I'll get on the rower again after Dom leaves the house.

I don't want to face his rejection. It's too humiliating, and I already have plenty of negative thoughts to deal with.

Maybe if I go through all the motions of what I used to enjoy, I can trigger some forward momentum.

Maybe tomorrow will be a good day.

As I move to stand, one of the cars in the street below the apartment building catches my eye. It's a shitty silver car, out of place compared to the others in this neighborhood, mostly luxury vehicles. It sticks out like a sore thumb. I've noticed it a few times before, but I thought nothing of it.

Today, though, the driver is standing outside the car.

He has dark hair. And a white shirt.

I throw myself back, crawling on my hands and knees until I can't see him anymore. My heart pounds in my chest.

It's an overreaction. Just a random man on the street. Not... not my late husband looking up at me through the window.

My hands shake as I run them over my hair, and a laugh

strangles out of me. Paranoia, that's all this is. The depressed woman with major trauma finally has a mental break.

My phone in the kitchen catches my attention.

I could call Dom, but he already thinks I'm a fool for making such a big deal about the elevator. What about my brothers? Dad?

I clench my hands into fists.

I could talk to him—the person in the car. Or at least, I'll get close enough to see his face. I can leave the penthouse. Dom has guns all over the place.

I'll do it myself.

I march toward the kitchen, aiming for the gun I know is tucked away in one of the drawers. But as I step forward, the elevator dings.

All the courage drains out of me. Icy fear roots me to the spot.

It's just another empty elevator. It's on the fritz.

The doors peel apart, and a flash of dark fabric moves behind the sliver of an opening.

I run.

I quietly hurl myself up the stairs and race to the master bedroom. My fingers crash against the lock, clicking it shut, and I dive for the nightstand table to yank out Dom's gun. With its cold weight in my hand, I hide behind the bed and point it right at the door.

For several minutes, I can barely breathe, listening for any sound.

When nothing happens, I pull my phone out of my back pocket.

"Please," I whisper to myself as I call Dom. "Please."

He doesn't pick up.

I call him three more times, my heart pounding as I strain my ears to listen for movement in the hallway.

He doesn't *fucking* pick up.

My vision blurs with tears as I call Carlo next. He always has men with him and drives fast.

When he picks up on the first ring with a, "What's up?" I nearly sob with relief.

"Carlo, there's someone in the house," I hiss into the receiver. "Please hurry. Dom's penthouse. Hurry."

Tires squeal, and a man yells at Carlo.

"Shut the fuck up!" he shouts at them. Then, to me he says, "I'm coming. Where are you hiding?"

"I'm in Dom's room. Upstairs."

"I'm not far away. Just hang tight. I'm on my way—"

The call drops.

My phone rings again, but something in the hallway rustles. I quickly turn off my phone with trembling hands.

Skritch, skritch.

There.

I think?

I can't tell if my mind's playing tricks on me, but just as I'm about to turn my phone back on, there's a dull thud outside the bedroom.

It's a Glock, so there's no safety to switch on. I've shot one once before with Rafa at the range. My hands sweat, but I hold it as steadily as I can.

I can do this.

I can do this.

Footsteps slowly grow louder until they're in front of the bedroom door. The door handle jiggles. My finger twitches on the trigger.

And they walk away.

I wait for a long time, what feels like hours, expecting them to return, but they don't.

With my left hand, I pull my phone back out and turn it

back on. There are a dozen missed calls from Carlo and one from the apartment complex.

I call Carlo first.

"Tell this fucker to let me up," he screams into the phone.

"Sir, if you don't calm down, I will be calling the police," says a voice I recognize as the doorman's.

"It's my brother," I whisper. "Please let him up."

The doorman sighs, but several minutes later, there's a knock on the door. "Hey, it's me. Carlo."

I throw my gun on the bed and race to the door, scrambling to unlock it. Carlo wraps me in a quick hug, then looks me up and down.

"There's no one here," a man calls from downstairs.

"You okay?" Carlo asks.

"I—yes. They didn't come into the room."

"Did you see who it was?"

I shake my head, and he looks a little doubtful, but he doesn't say anything about it. "Why don't we get some food downstairs?"

I don't want to make food for my brother's friends, but my hands are trembling, and I want to be alone even less, so I nod.

Downstairs, three of Carlo's friends are splayed out on Dom's couch. Russell has a bandage around his neck and is the only one not openly staring at me.

"Heard a ghost, Serafina?" Mark asks. He's my least favorite of the bunch, with his dead eyes and stupid jokes. He sprawls his thin limbs over the couch like a creepy puppet.

I ignore him and turn to the kitchen to pull out cut meats for a snacking tray. This is what's expected of me. I stay silent. I make food.

As I slice paper-thin cuts of the meat with shaky hands, Carlo's friend Checkers speaks up, "I can't believe we're missing the Velvet Kitty for this."

"Yeah, Carlo, when are we getting out of here?" Mark asks. "Your sister ain't gonna strip for us."

"Shut up," Carlo says without any heat.

Same old, same old. All the men in my life do is talk about honor and loyalty, unless it's their friends stepping on their wives or sisters.

"You doing okay?" Carlo murmurs.

I press down on the knife with the heel of my hand, carving away a nearly transparent slice of meat. My hands are moving steadier now that some of the adrenaline has drained away and a fog of apathy is settling back into place. "Yeah."

Carlo scrubs the back of his neck. "Do you want to come with us? We're going to get a few drinks."

There's no such thing as a few drinks with Carlo, but when I glance up and see the dark skyscrapers stretching out beyond the windows of the living room like a handful of jagged teeth, I feel lost.

Dom still hasn't called me back.

What's the point of all this?

Without looking at Carlo, I shrug. "Sure."

I GRIP my seatbelt with white knuckles as Checkers drives us down a dark neighborhood street. Music blasts through the car, and the guys are all laughing and joking at Checkers striking out with some girl at the last bar.

"I told you she was a fucking bitch," Checkers says.

Carlo punches his shoulder with a raucous laugh, making the car swerve.

I squeeze my eyes shut. My heart is a ticking bomb.

"Watch it!" Russell barks out from the middle seat, next to me.

I'm crammed against the door with my forehead leaning against the window, but Russell's thigh is still pressed against mine.

I offered to drive because they've *all* been drinking, but they laughed at me. When I asked Carlo if he could take me home, he promised me he would after one more stop.

"You okay?" Russell murmurs. He captures my knee in his hand.

"We gotta turn back," I say to the others.

"It'll be quick!" Carlo says.

I cram myself against my car door. Russell slides his hand up an inch higher.

I can barely breathe. The car stinks of men and alcohol, and my chest is tight. I want to go home, but I don't know how to find it from here.

Checkers swerves into a parking spot in front of the Velvet Kitty.

"We'll be right back," Carlo shouts and stumbles out of the car.

Checkers follows suit.

Panic seizes my lungs. I'm going to be stuck in here with dead-eyed Mark or handsy Russell.

I fumble for the door handle and throw myself out of the car into the freezing night air. I don't want to go to a strip club, but it's better than being stuck in the car.

"I'm gonna get a smoke," Russell calls out in a raspy voice. He nods to Mark. "I heard Tatiana's gonna be here tonight."

That seems to capture Mark's attention, because he stumbles to the club entrance after Checkers and my brother.

Of the four, Russell's had the least to drink, but it hardly puts me at ease with the hungry way he looks at me.

"Want some?" he asks, offering me a freshly lit joint.

I shake my head, tightening my coat around me. I glance at the bandages wrapped around his throat and quickly look away.

He laughs and holds his joint away from his clothes, leaning against the car door next to me. On this side of the building, it's just us in an empty parking lot. A lone car drives past on a faraway street. "You couldn't get enough last time."

For a moment, I have no idea what he's talking about. Then I remember.

He still thinks I'm Serafina.

"Last time?"

He flicks off the bright red cherry and hides away the joint in a tin in his pocket.

He got it out just for Serafina.

"I'd never seen you so high." His voice drops low. "Or so horny."

Liar. He's lying. "*What?*"

"Is your new husband mad you're not a virgin?"

No.

No fucking way Serafina had sex with this fucking wispy-mustached *loser.*

He rakes his bug-eyed gaze over me with an unearned familiarity, and even though it makes my skin crawl, I don't back down.

"Don't lie," I say.

He laughs. "One of us is a liar here, and it's not me. I

know you haven't told your husband about us, or else I'd be a dead man. You still got a soft spot for me, Serafina?"

I find my voice after a moment. "No. I don't even know what you're talking about."

He shoves his hands into his pockets. "Always fucking lying."

Serafina never lied.

"I'm not a liar."

Russell scoffs. "You lied to your sister, didn't you? Made her get married instead of you, because you were so fucking scared they'd find out you didn't have a cherry—"

"Stop."

"—and you've made up this whole scenario to Carlo just so I'd come over. And now you want to be a little tease about all this? I wonder what sort of lie you'd tell your husband if he drug tested you. Bet he'd be pretty disappointed to find out his sweet wife's sucked dick more than once for a little bit of weed."

Russell leans in, bathing me in the sour scent of beer and weed. "Can that old man even get it up, or are you already missing what I can give you?"

Something like anger licks through my veins. How dare he? Russell picks up on my quick breathing and misinterprets it.

He chuckles. "That's what I thought."

Just when my hand twitches with the urge to slap him— hurt him, *somehow*—he takes a step back.

"I have to go make sure your brother's not being a fuck up. Sit your pretty ass in that car and think about who knows the real you." He leans in and touches my hair. His breath reeks. "We both know it's not that husband of yours. Ask yourself who loves the real you."

He inhales and tilts back to give me a long, searching

look before brushing past and disappearing into the strip club.

I turn in the other direction. For a silent moment, I stand out in the cold, staring at the dark, empty storefront windows across the street, willing my breath to slow, for my hands to stop trembling.

Was he telling the truth?

Did my pure, sweet sister let me sacrifice myself to my bastard ex-husband so she could get her rocks off with this loser?

Angry tears spring to my eyes. I exhale through gritted teeth.

How dare she?

I shake my head. No. Russell was lying.

I'm going to tell someone, Dad maybe, about all this, and then he's going to break Russell's legs for what he said. First, I need Carlo to take me home.

Quick footsteps striding across the asphalt warn me of Russell's return. I don't turn, forcing myself to calm the rage vibrating through my veins.

He crashes into me, throwing me into the car and pressing his body against mine. My head bounces off the hood, and a flash of pain blinds me.

"Got you, bitch," a strange man says.

Fear plunges me into cold shock, freezing me to the spot. The man has my whole body pinned to the car like a bug. I can't move. I cry out in a weak voice.

"This is for Frederico."

My heart stops. The stranger's hot breath ghosts over my cheek, and he slides me across the car door. I scrabble at the metal, barely able to gain purchase in a seam of the door with my acrylic nails.

His hands jerk away from me, and the weight of his body disappears. He spits out a curse.

I don't do anything brave. I don't even beg. I tuck into myself against the car door and cower, anticipating more pain.

A familiar, booming laugh sounds behind me. "Of all the stupid motherfuckers they could've sent. Are you fucking kidding me, Mikey?"

Dom?

I hold my breath and turn.

Dom, looking like an angry grizzly bear in his brown fur-trimmed coat, pins a smaller man I don't recognize onto the road. The other man—Mikey—struggles, and Dom laughs cruelly as Mikey's cheek grinds into the asphalt.

A huge, ugly gash rides up Dom's swollen left eye to his hairline. His face is covered in blood, but that doesn't stop him from grinning at the man underneath him.

Red flushes Mikey's face, and dark blood streams from his nose as he fights against Dom. The parking lot's empty. Carlo and his friends are nowhere to be found.

A few feet away, a knife glistens in the streetlights.

"This has nothing to do with you," Mikey spits.

He cries out as Dom scrapes the side of his face into the road. I glimpse Mikey's scarlet cheek—raw like ground beef. Dom's palm is cut and smears more blood onto Mikey's face.

My stomach churns, but I can't look away from Dom's brutality.

He's doing this for me.

"Is that what they told you?" Dom laughs like Mikey told him a great joke. "You wanna know why they picked you? Because you're the only man fucking stupid enough to go after the Butcher's wife."

Dom glances up at me, his one open eye dark and hard like flint, and his grin falters a little. My breath catches.

"Let me go," Mikey says. "I didn't know!"

Dom's grin grows wider as he looks back down at him. "Of course you didn't. Now, Mikey, where am I starting? Your fingers? Nose? How about a foot? Maybe I cut off your dick and call it a day, huh?"

Mikey's eyes go wide, and he flounders against Dom with renewed effort. "No, no! Come on, Dom! Please, I'm sorry! I didn't know!"

With some effort, Mikey scrapes his face against the road to look up at me. The look he gives me freezes me in place—the Hail Mary of an evil man.

But I don't want to save him. He was going to kill me.

Dom pulls out a wicked-looking knife from a holster on his leg.

"You're dying tonight, Mikey, make no bones about it. But you can do one useful fucking thing in your life and tell me who gave you this job. You know who I work for. I'll find out either way, but I sure will be grateful to get a faster answer from you. Maybe you can make it to hell with all your parts intact."

Mikey groans through gritted teeth, his facial features squeezing together in agony.

"Time's up, Mikey."

"Wait! Wait," Mikey screams. "The Chiarellis. The Chiarellis have a hit out on her."

Dom's gaze cuts up to me, and we lock eyes. Even with a man wriggling underneath him, his muscles straining to trap him down, and half his face covered in blood, Dom's expression is relaxed—amused, even.

"And why would the Chiarellis have a hit out on *Serafina*?" he asks me.

"I-I don't know." Mikey starts to blubber. "But it's not Serafina—I-I mean, she's not that they—who they w-wanted—"

"Dom," I say. It's almost a whisper, and Mikey stops struggling to look up at me, hope shining in his eyes. "Hurry up."

A wail bursts from Mikey's mouth as he thrashes against Dom.

"You see my car?" Dom calls over Mikey's cries.

I look up sharply. It's not far away, only a few parking spots from us.

"Go sit inside," Dom says while Mikey wriggles under his hand like a worm on a hook. "Lock the door until I get there."

Mikey looks up at me with pleading eyes for the briefest of moments, until I turn away and do as I'm told.

His muffled cries follow me as I take thirty-four steps to Dom's car, counting each one. I open the passenger door and lock myself inside.

I stare straight forward through the windshield out onto the dark scene.

Dom rises from the shadow that is Mikey's body, where it lies there, unmoving.

I expect Dom to come to me, but he goes to the strip club instead. For a long, breathless moment, my vision locks onto the club's door as my imagination runs wild at the thought of beautiful women rubbing themselves against him.

But it's not beautiful women he comes back outside with. Russell has his hands hooked onto Dom's wrists as Dom drags him outside by his throat. Carlo and the rest of his friends follow behind. Checkers is stumbling so much that it looks like he might fall over. Dom tosses Russell toward Mikey's dead body, points at it, and walks toward me.

His wild grin fills my body with sunshine. He's got one of those perfect smiles—a wide mouth, brilliant white teeth, and a hint of dimples hidden beneath his salt-and-pepper beard—that make it impossible not to smile back. The corners of my lips raise.

Then he seems to remember himself, and his mouth plunges into a deep scowl.

He throws himself into the driver's seat of the car, turns the radio on, and drives. "Start talking."

11

ANNETTA

He's hurt.

But it's hard to tell by the way he's carrying himself. The radio's tuned to a pop song, and after he wiped his face with his shirt and—thank God—opened his other eye, he's driving steadily through the dark streets like he doesn't have a care in the world, like he's not covered in his own blood.

"You're supposed to be talking," he says.

Annoyance flares inside me.

"You were supposed to answer my calls," I bite back.

"I was busy—"

"Doing what? What do you even do all day? All you do is avoid me and leave me *alone* all the time."

"You want some fucking company? Get a dog or go move back in with your parents. I didn't ask to be your babysitter."

He's got a point, and that pisses me off more than anything else.

"It's too late. We're married now. How many women marry men they hate and still have to smile and pop out babies for them and cook and clean for them? Why do *you* get to pick your fate when I can't?"

"Is that your fucking problem? Daddy stuck you with me, and now you're crying because you're not fucking Russell?"

I blink a few times, my anger blown out like a candle's flame. "...Russell?"

He couldn't possibly be jealous.

"Don't even say his name," he grits out and bursts into a dark chuckle. "If I hear his name on your lips, I swear to God, I'm driving back there, and I'm going to make you watch me finish strangling him."

Finish...?

The bandage around Russell's throat. That'd been Dom?

It's difficult to think through the pleasurable haze that is the understanding of my husband's jealousy.

I lean into him, wanting to sip from it like from the juices of a ripe fruit. "He's nothing to me."

"Maybe you're too sheltered to know what a man thinks when he sees a woman like you, but it was pretty fucking clear he wants you." Dom pauses. "I forbid you from seeing him again."

I burst into laughter, and judging by the white skin on Dom's knuckles on the steering wheel, he doesn't like that. I couldn't care less about seeing Russell again, but I'll be damned if I let my absent husband boss me around.

"What gives you the right to tell me who I can talk to?"

He snatches my wrist and shakes me, a groan of pain escaping his lips. The idiot—he's grabbing me with his own injured palm.

"This ring gives me the right," he says. "You say I'm stuck in this—you are too. So, you're going to be my wife, I expect obedience."

Fuck no.

I twist my hand and dig my finger into the cut in his palm.

He nearly swerves off the road. "Fuck!"

He jerks his hand out of my grasp and swings the car to the side road, hitting a strip of sidewalk before he slams to a stop, inches from hitting a brick fence.

I brace myself against the side door of the car, heart racing, eyes wide.

"Dom," I say in a weak voice. "You're scaring me."

He laughs. "You're scaring *me*. Here I thought you were my sweet, innocent wife, and now I learn the Chiarellis have a hit out on you?"

My tongue goes dry. "You need to go to the hospital. Get stitches."

He sucks in a breath through his teeth. "Alright," he says. He turns off the car and tosses his phone on the dashboard. "Get out. Leave your phone."

Is it trust or fear that has me scrambling to unbuckle myself after him? The way his massive form stalks around the hood of the car makes my breath catch, even now, but I still wait for him to open the door as an act of tiny rebellion —he can do it, since he wants me outside so badly.

The door swings, and he stands outside the car for me like my personal bodyguard.

I slip out lightly onto the street, my boots clicking onto the asphalt.

"Where's your phone?"

"I left it in the penthouse."

He eyes my coat. "You gonna be warm enough in that?"

My coat's plenty warm, but I still cross my arms and glare at him. "No."

He chuckles as he shrugs his massive coat off and slides it onto my shoulders. The smell is intoxicating, and I have to resist shoving my face in the fur lining. Maybe this crush is just self-destruction dressed in lingerie.

Mom picked Dad even though Aunt Karen said he would cheat on her constantly until she got pregnant with Carlo. I've seen the ways she molded herself to be a woman Dad would never think to leave, until there was nothing of her old self left.

And if Serafina and Russell really were together, that's another woman in my family who chose a man who couldn't be worse for her.

If I could turn off my attraction to Dom like a switch, wouldn't I? Or is it written in my DNA to pick men who're bad for me?

"Come on," Dom says. "Let's walk."

Blades of grass poke through a frost-crusted hill behind the brick fence we almost drove into. Nearly invisible in the darkness, tombstones jut out of the ice like shards of broken pottery.

My breath catches in my throat. It's a cemetery. I spot a placard on the iron fence above the bricks. *Oak Woods.*

Serafina's body isn't here.

Dom lays a hand on my shoulder before I can spiral down that line of thinking. I'm tempted to shrug his hand off, but I'm equally as tempted to lean into it, to kiss the blood off his knuckles.

He might be a fucking asshole, but he killed that guy for me. Mikey.

"You really need to get looked at," I say after several long moments of silence as we stroll down the sidewalk like two midnight lovers. This is the first time we've ever been together, just the two of us in public like this, though there's no one to see.

"I will soon."

We pass a few other parked cars and a homeless man sleeping—at least I hope he's just sleeping—on the sidewalk, before Dom finally says what's on his mind.

"Why are you pretending to be your sister?"

I trip, stumbling forward at the same time that he shoots a hand out and snags the back of my coat. I turn to stare at him, open-mouthed, and he gently guides me forward.

"Keep walking," he says. "And start talking."

"What did Mikey say?"

Dom scoffs. "Cut the shit. I might be dumb, but I'm not that dumb. You and I both know I had my suspicions. I didn't need Mikey to figure it out. This your idea?"

My mind flashes to my parents, hard-eyed in the soft glow of their living room while I stood out in the cold.

What have you done? Mom asked.

"Promise me," I say. "Before we talk about this, promise you'll keep my family safe."

"I promise." He doesn't hesitate, and I don't know if it's the easy confidence of a practiced liar or of a person who knows an absolute truth about themselves.

I remember the way he held Carlo outside my bedroom door. He loves my parents and brothers. He's always been a part of our family—I have to believe that.

"Mom," I whisper, my mind spinning. My grasp on his coat loosens.

I wish he'd say something, but he's completely silent as he waits for the rest of my confession—and of course he is. I've heard about what he does when he's burnt out from work. He goes to the woods and hunts. The image of him, fierce and deadly, aiming an arrow at my heart in his kitchen, sends a frisson of heat through me, throwing my emotions off-balance. I can't control it.

"She wanted to protect me," I say in a low, slow voice. "She said I had to be Serafina."

We're walking next to a cemetery in the dead of night. Could someone be listening in, even now? My mind flashes with images—a boat, beer bottles, a flailing hand, an open mouth filling with water. Fear and pleasure stir deep inside me.

I continue. "Before I left Florida, my husband and I fought. I ran, and his family is after me now. They think I killed him."

"Did you?" Dom asks.

I want to tell him the truth. I have to.

But the moment I do, I'm throwing myself at the feet of a man not known for mercy, who's done little more than ignore me since I've moved to live with him. I want to laugh. What I'm thinking about doing is almost suicidal. Where else would I go? What other options do I have? He won't accept a non-answer from me, and if he sends his boss to look into this, I'll be especially screwed. Not even Valeria's offer of cash could save me.

He wanted to know who hurt me when I had that nightmare. What feels like a lifetime ago, he promised me Aldo wouldn't hurt me.

I take Dom's hand, more for my own comfort than anything—like I might have another way to probe his emotions if his face doesn't expose his thoughts, or like the softness of my hand will remind him to treat me gently. We stop dead in the center of the sidewalk, and I lock eyes with him, nodding once.

I catch a look of amusement, of all things, which shouldn't be a surprise coming from Dom, but it is.

He turns to continue our walk.

"Dad thinks they mixed us up—"

"They did."

I glance sharply at him.

Dom squeezes my hand. "It was Mikey. He mixed you up with Serafina, and the Chiarellis know. They wouldn't pay him until he finished the job."

I stop in the middle of the sidewalk. "How much?"

"I didn't ask."

Whatever it was, it couldn't have been enough, not to take away my perfect sister. I wish...

"You should've let me watch."

One of his eyebrows ticks up, all the amusement wiped clean from his face. "That's not the kind of thing you need to see."

I imagine it anyway—Mikey's blood, dark and thick as it pools underneath his body. His eyes turning dull as consciousness slips away, a small comfort for my loss.

"That's not the kind of thing you get to decide," I say, even as my stomach churns at the mental image I've created.

Dom takes my shoulder in his good hand and peers at me, his gaze so kind and gentle it cuts into my chest. His palm is molten hot even through the layers of our coats. "You're young. Burning away what's left of your innocence isn't going to bring your sister back."

It's a miracle I'm able to hold back my tears when I finally look him in the eyes. "There's nothing left to burn."

He looks sad as he scrapes his thumb along my jaw. "I'm not going to let them touch you, okay? I'll take care of this."

My mouth quivers. "Let them have me. I'm nothing. I'm not Serafina—I'll never be her. Not as good as her. I'm her rotten fucking shadow. Giulia and Marco Chiarelli are going to take me, and it's just a matter of time."

"Don't say that shit, *reginetta*. You have me. I told you I'd protect you, and I will."

Reginetta. Little queen.

The nickname pisses me off.

"*You*," I spit, slamming my hands against his chest. "You call me a queen, but you can't even stand to be in the same room as me. You didn't pick up my call tonight. You said you would protect me, but you *lied*."

Everyone lies—especially husbands.

Instead of backing down, he grins, capturing my hand with his bloody one. "What a pair we make then, eh? You promised me an innocent wife, and what I got was a killer."

"You're one to talk, *Butcher*."

That gets the reaction I want. He inhales sharply at the nickname, a wide, dangerous grin spreading across his face. The rough calluses of his hand scratch against mine, his fingers so thick that it fries my brain for a moment.

"What reason have you given me to trust you?" I ask harshly. "When you were throwing a tantrum at our wedding? Or when you've been avoiding me and rejecting me in our home? I'm not the only liar here. The difference is, you lie to yourself. I'm willing to be your wife, and you're too much of a coward to look at me."

Dom lets out a cruel laugh. I hope his injuries are killing him.

"You don't fucking want me," he says. "You just think if you flash me a pair of tits, I'll let you lead me around by my balls. That if you feed me and suck my cock, I'll be your little lapdog." He leans down until we're eye-to-eye. "That shit's not gonna work with me."

I grab his shirt, and although we both know I couldn't keep him anywhere he didn't want to be, he lets me hold him in place, and, for a moment, I think I could.

"Of course, it would," I say, and his grin widens. "That's why you won't let me."

A single, charged moment passes between us. I lean forward. Maybe he'll step up to the challenge and finally let me have a taste of him.

Instead, he pulls my hand off his collar like it's nothing more than a spider and stands tall.

"You want me to protect you, after you lied and manipulated me?" He shrugs. "Fine. I've watched over you your whole life—I'm not just gonna stop now. You don't have to fuck me to make me do it."

I should be relieved. An offer of help with nothing asked for in return? For once, I can exist without the crushing weight of expectations I didn't ask for.

But I'm furious.

"Why not? You know I'm not a virgin. We already live together, and we're married, for God's sake! Give me one good reason we shouldn't."

Dom flicks three fingers into the air. "I'll give you three. One, I got my balls snipped years ago. I'm not giving you kids. Two, I don't trust you. You and your dad schemed to trick me into this, and you killed your last husband. Why the fuck would I want you in my bed? And three, I'm too fucking *old* for you, Annetta. I'm twenty fucking years older than you."

He waves his bloody hand at me. "Look, I get it. I've been in your life for a long time, you've got a little crush and a ton of daddy issues, and I'm a convenient older man to play out that fantasy for you, but you're not seeing the future here. Maybe I don't want to be a burden to you."

He sighs, tugging at his short beard. "I've been alone for a long time. You can live with me, and I'll take care of you, but I don't need a wife."

A storm of conflicting emotions rages through me. "I don't want kids—"

He scoffs. "You're twenty. You'll change your mind in two years, five tops."

I cross my arms. "You're thirty-eight. You think you don't want a wife? This is when men like you settle down. You'll change your mind in two years, three tops."

He chuffs a laugh.

I press my advantage. "You said it yourself—you've known me my entire life. You know I wouldn't lie without good reason, and I wouldn't hurt someone without one either. We know each other. You know we could work together. We already like a lot of the same things. You listen to more girly pop than I do—"

"I listen to what's on the radio—"

I throw him a doubtful look, and he laughs.

I continue. "I like to cook, and you like to eat. You say you don't want a wife, but look me in the eye and tell me you haven't liked coming home to fresh-cooked meals."

He meets my gaze, but he doesn't say a thing as he folds his big arms across his broad chest. He's shutting down, which means I'm getting to him.

"I like working out, you like working out. You like hunting? I like camping. You're too old for me? I love ancient history."

He cracks a smile, and I match it. I take one daring step toward him and rest my hands on his arms. I can see it in his eyes. He's softening.

"What if you let me in?" I ask.

Dom rests one heavy hand on my shoulder, threading his fingers into my hair. "You're already in my house, *reginetta.*"

I tap him on the chest. "That's not what I meant."

"What do you think being married to me looks like? I can't stay inside the house with you all day. I can't be a good husband to a young, grieving woman, especially not now—not when Turi needs me."

Even if his words are bitter, his face is gentle. I think of him hugging Carlo in my parents' house.

"Lucky for you, my standards for husbands are very low."

He frowns and presses his palm against my neck.

I lean into his fingers. "I know you're a good man, Dom. That's why I asked Dad to marry us."

His breath puffs over me in a little cloud as he laughs. "Of course you did. Barbara could never say no to his girls."

"He could if he had to, but he trusts you, too. Do you remember who broke Tommy Halle's arm when I was a freshman?"

"What the hell are you talking about?"

I spread one hand over his forearm, greedily soaking up the sensation of his firm muscles beneath my fingers. He's covered in his own blood, but for a fighter like him, it suits him.

"He was a senior," I say. "He kept making jokes about a threesome with Serafina and me, and he followed us home one day, harassing us the entire time. The next day, he came to school with a broken arm and wouldn't look either of us in the eye."

Dom's mouth presses into a firm line. "Your dad asked me..."

"When I turned eighteen and Cousin Red was making jokes about me being legal? What did you do?"

Pine and smoke surround me, mouthwateringly tempting.

"I don't remember."

"You took him to the back of the house, emptied a bottle of whiskey on him, and told him if he cracked another joke, you'd light him on fire." I rise, just an inch, onto my toes. "I saw you do it. Can you blame me if all I see when I look at you is a good man?"

Dom releases a short exhale, his pupils swallowing all the light. "Those aren't things good men do."

Heat blooms in my body. I can barely feel the cold in this moment. "To me, they are."

And I can see it on his face. I thought he'd forgotten the night of my eighteenth birthday that I've carried with me all these years like a little secret jewel of happiness. He remembers, too—he must.

"Dom, please."

Last time, he looked kind and a little patronizing. This time, he's watchful. But he plays along anyway. "Please what, *reginetta?*"

"Please kiss me."

I rise on my toes, nearly *en pointe*, to close the space between our faces, planting my hands on his sturdy chest, which rises and falls with more speed than I would've expected. I affect him more than I thought.

He reluctantly drops his head down, his heat enveloping me.

"*Fuck,*" Dom whispers.

He drops his mouth to mine.

At first, it's a hard press of his mouth to mine and the feel of his lips against me. I wrap my arms around the back of his thick neck and thread my fingers into his hair, pulling us together at the same time that I lick along the seam of his mouth like I did at that church.

Let me in.

This time, instead of pulling away, he falls forward over me with a deep moan, like a skyscraper toppling. His wide hands splay over most of my back, and his mouth finally opens. Excitement fizzles through my chest.

I suck at his tongue, tasting mint again, and when I nibble at his bottom lip, he chuckles against my mouth. Maybe I would feel self-conscious about it with someone else, but with Dom, it's a compliment. He may be a big, scary guy, but he likes to laugh, and he loves to *play*—and I realize, I do too. I want to be with someone fun and relaxed. He's not just a faceless protector for me, even if that's what I've been telling myself. I don't want him for what he can do for me—I want *him*. I want to be around someone whose smiles are like sunshine and whose laugh you can hear through the entire house. I want to be around someone who chases the nightmares away.

His arm bands around my back, lifting me into the air. I'm weightless and breathless. I wrap my legs around him, and he shifts so he's supporting my weight with one strong hand under my ass.

Warmth floods my panties. It's been too long since I've felt anything like this. I luxuriate in the taste and feel of his breath, his heady scent, his tongue playfully rubbing against mine.

I draw back, my mouth raw from our efforts, and lock eyes with him. My heart slams against my chest. More than anything, I want him to believe in us like I'm starting to.

I take his broad face in my hands and slowly kiss his cheek, his temple, his eye, the places he was cut defending me, until I return to his lips and lean back to look into his eyes.

The wicked smile he usually wears has been wiped away, leaving behind a wary expression. If I kiss that look off his face next, what'll be left?

I thread my fingers into his hair, pulling the base of his

ponytail down, and he willingly exposes his neck to me. *Mine.* He's all mine. I squeeze my thighs around his waist and tug down his shirt collar to kiss and suck on the spot where I bit him, mostly healed over, but still lightly bruised.

His low voice rumbles against my mouth. "You gonna bite me again?"

"You want me to?" I nip at his neck.

He flinches, and we both laugh.

He doesn't lower his head again until I've finished kissing and sucking along his neck, lavishing extra attention to my bite. I don't feel bad for it, though I should. I like knowing he's strong enough to take anything I could do to him, and I like knowing I'm there, right under his shirt collar, invisible to the world but still *real*, a secret we share.

When I pull back, I find what I'm searching for—hungry curiosity, like he's waiting to see what I'll do next. Excitement thrums through me.

A car honks, breaking the spell, and Dom jerks me off of him, whipping us around and pinning me to the brick wall behind him so he's shielding me from the road with his body.

The car drives off into the night, leaving us heaving against each other. Dom's exhale rustles the top of my hair while I bury my face into his chest and smile.

"We can't stay here," he says.

He's right, of course, although I almost want to make him promise that he'll be the same when we return to the penthouse. I don't need a long drive to sober his thoughts and return his conscience. I need him just like this—pliable and willing to let us have what we both want.

I nod against his chest, and we walk back to the car.

In the passenger seat, my body's loose and relaxed, but

my mind's on a knife's edge. He's given me a taste of him, and I've discovered I'm starving.

He keeps looking over at me as he drives, stealing long glances. I want to make him wait. I want to stretch his resistance into a thin strand, and then I want to make it snap.

When he misses the turn back to our penthouse, I speak up. "Heading to the hospital?"

"No. We're going to Turi's."

12

DOM

"He's going to kill me."

"Annetta." I stop. Her name coats my tongue in sweetness.

She's scared and pissed, but the sound of her name affects her, too, judging by the little inhale she makes.

"Annetta," I say again. I'm fucked and I know it, but I can't bring myself to regret kissing her in that cemetery. "I trust Turi with my life. He's not gonna hurt you. He wanted us to get married. He'll help us."

He won't be happy about it, but he'll do it regardless, which pretty much sums up our working relationship.

"That's because he thinks I'm Ser—that I'm my sister. You said you were going to protect me, but he's going to hurt me. He could hurt Dad."

"Trust me. You'll see."

She sits back and crosses her arms, glaring out her window. I drive on, secure in the knowledge that I'm right.

Annetta.

Most nights I sleep like a fucking baby. I'm going to hell

anyway, so why should I keep myself up at night about the decisions I've made? Guilt's not a word in my vocabulary.

But *something* like it poisons my delight at the knowledge that Annetta's in the car with me and not her sister, and I know how fucked up that is. I'm not happy her sister's dead. Serafina was a nice girl. She covered her mouth when she laughed, had delicate, ladylike hobbies everyone approved of, and she went to church every Sunday. The world's worse off without her in it.

But *Annetta*.

Almost three years ago, I caught Annetta sneaking out on her eighteenth birthday to Rizo's Bar. They didn't card then—still don't. I was relaxing after a long day and trying to get into the pants of some woman I'd met there, and then Annetta Barbara had waltzed inside without a single escort.

I had excused myself from the woman and slipped into a dark corner to watch.

For a long time, Annetta just stood there with her arms crossed over her chest as she took in what I'd assumed to be her first bar. She wore makeup I'd never seen her in, a deep red lipstick and dark eyeshadow that didn't suit her at all— something she probably thought made her look older—and a black blouse and pencil skirt she must've found in the very back of her closet.

Then she caught the eye of some random, sleazy old man. As he walked up to her, she lifted her chin and said in a voice I couldn't hear, but could guess at from that distance. "Buy me a drink."

And that fucking scumbag did.

I figured I'd let her have her fun but keep an eye on her for her family's sake. She was getting married and shipped off to Florida in less than a month, and her bachelorette would probably be boring as fuck. As the night went on, she looked less and less like she was having fun. The guy's hands started drifting under her clothes, and every time she'd shove him off, he'd laugh and try again.

When I stepped in, the look of shock on her face still makes me smile to this day. She thought she'd been so clever sneaking out of the house.

"Can I dance with you?" I asked after I sent her partner away with a single look.

She whispered her answer. "Yes."

I remember how tiny she was in my grip, like a little bird. We danced one dance together, and I took her hand to leave.

That little bird stood her ground, jerked me back, and made a drunken demand. "One more dance."

I was so tickled that I let her have her way—my first mistake.

She took my hands and placed them on the curve of her waist, and she danced against me like she wanted to weave herself into me in a dozen little ways.

When the song was over, she straightened and took clipped steps out of the bar like she was headed to the guillotine, and I was her executioner.

I paid for a taxi to take us to her home. At her house, I followed her, expecting her to walk begrudgingly to the front door. Instead, she led me past the rose bushes planted against the side of the house until we stopped underneath her bedroom window. She'd left a ladder to get in and out of the second floor.

"Alright, I'll hold the ladder." I was ready to get home and shake off this weird night. "Get inside."

She put her hand on the first rung and looked up at me. "I don't want to get married."

Which went against the rumors that she'd seduced Frederico Chiarelli to steal him from her more popular sister. I had it on good account of what she'd done to wrap that man around her finger. Looking at her then, a plea in her eyes, I realized I should've given her more credit.

She wasn't a malicious person by nature. She was self-sacrificial.

"And Serafina?" I asked.

"She was scared."

So, she'd thrown herself at Frederico to save her sister from getting married. "Someone else will come along to marry her."

"I know, but she just wanted more time."

I thought of myself as another member of the Barbara household, but I'd never thought twice to look into those rumors about Annetta being a husband-stealing slut. She didn't deserve that.

"Don't fight this," I warned, because what else was I supposed to tell her? Frederico would make her a good-enough husband.

"Dom, please."

"Please, what, *reginetta*?"

It was too late to get out of that marriage of hers, though I knew she'd try. Maybe she'd beg me to use my connections and help her get out of it.

She fixed her gaze on me. "Please kiss me. I've never been kissed before."

It had shocked me. If she's a girl now, she was even more so back then.

But a single kiss?

It was so *innocent*.

And it burned me to know she'd sucked Frederico's dick, but he'd never even kissed her. Selfish bastard.

I understood what she wanted—a taste of freedom before she moved from one gilded cage to the other.

I leaned forward, intent on kissing her cheek and wishing her a good night. At the last second, she'd swiveled her head and kissed my mouth, snatching my shirt into her little fists.

I froze. She was clumsy and eager, licking at my lips and trying to kiss me like she wanted to eat me alive.

When I pulled away, I saw a look on her face I'd never seen before. A look that seared permanently into my brain, no matter how often I tried to forget.

She was serene. Taking control suited her.

She accepted her fate with grace as she looked me in the eye and told me, "Good night, Dom."

I helped her into the house and didn't wash her kiss off my mouth until the next morning.

WHEN I PULL up to Turi's house, most of his SUVs are parked in the gravel lot. Annetta stares forward with wide eyes, wringing the seatbelt across her lap.

I lean over to rest my cut hand on her thigh, and I swear to God, it feels a little less painful from the touch. "I promise, no one's going to hurt you."

She looks fucking terrified, but she still whispers, "Or my family."

"Or your family."

Her shoulders ease a fraction. "I trust you."

I know it's a plea, an emotional jab to make sure I do what she wants, but she doesn't have to do that. I already want to help her. And for as long as her dad and I have been watching out for each other, this is a loyalty that runs deep.

We walk the short path across the dark, cold driveway to the burst of warmth and light in Turi's house. This late at night, only two guards are circling the grounds. The rest of the house staff have left for the day.

I know without checking that Turi and Marisol will be awake. If the moon's out, they're up.

Before I head upstairs to Turi's watchtower, my phone buzzes with a text.

TURI

Meet us in the basement.

Nothing ominous about meeting in Turi's designated torture room.

She couldn't have read the text, but Annetta takes my hand in hers. Her fingers are slender and cool, and it makes me feel good that she's still wearing my coat, like it's my small way of protecting her.

I bring her to the basement door. "Wait here."

Before I can knock, Turi opens the door. His icy gaze ticks over me and Annetta, landing on our joined hands. "Inside. Both of you, now."

Annetta stifles a scream as we enter the room.

A man's strapped to a metal chair, blood gushing out of his mouth.

Next to him, Barbara's in a white undershirt and chewing a cigar, his breathing almost as loud as the man next to him. His bloodied hand rests on the man's shoulder as he watches his daughter enter the room. The man in the chair is vaguely familiar with his wispy brown hair and shitty tattoos on his arms, but with most of his face bashed in, I can't place him.

Turi is spotless as he walks over to the medical tray near the stranger and plucks a set of pliers from the top. He looks at the stranger as he swings his pliers toward Annetta and me.

The room seems to hold its breath as we wait for Don Salvatore to speak.

"Tell them what you told us."

The man lifts his head eagerly.

Annetta sucks in a breath. This is probably the first time she's seen something like this. I grip her hand firmly and shift her so that her body's shielded by my arm. She presses in close to me like I can protect her from what the man's about to say.

"I saw you," the man says to Annetta.

She stiffens, and I squeeze her hand, cutting a glance to her dad. Only the muscles in Barbara's jaw, grinding his cigar into tobacco pulp, give away his nerves. He's worked hard to make sure his girls never see shit like this.

"You were at the Blue Rooster and your friends were talking about going to a titty bar and you went with them, and I knew—"

The man's burst of words is interrupted by loud, gunshot hacking, blood spraying over his knees as he coughs.

"Sorry, I, uh, I remembered your face, 'cause Mikey—he doesn't do girls much, so when I heard he was looking for you, I figured I'd look you up and…"

He swallows and glances up at Turi. Even though he's covered in blood, I recognize him. Rodney, but he likes people to call him Rod because he thinks it sounds cooler, even though no one gives a damn. He's a piece of shit who beats up his own mom.

He continues when Turi doesn't react. "Yeah, so I remembered your face. I called Mikey and told him where you were headed."

"Annetta," Turi says as he approaches Rodney.

Rodney's chest rises in quick succession, his focus split between Turi and the pliers in his hand.

Turi snatches Rodney by his hair and exposes his face to us. "Do you recognize him?"

"N-no." Even as it trembles, Annetta's voice carries across the small room.

"No," Turi echoes. "Neither did your brother. Or Checkers. Or Mark. Or Russell. None of you noticed a man making a call to a hitman with your name at the top of his list. And none of you noticed you were being followed."

Annetta trembles against my arm.

Turi smacks the pliers against his palm once.

"It took quite a bit of effort to get this out of you. I'm glad you finally told me the truth, but I already told you what would happen if you lied to me."

On cue, Barbara steps behind Rodney and squeezes his face to hold him still.

I wrap my arm around Annetta and shove her behind me so she won't see, but I can't protect her from the screams. They echo off the basement walls as Turi tears the man's tongue from his mouth with a set of slip-joint pliers. He drops it into a bucket with a *splat,* and the pliers clatter in afterward.

He takes a knife and stabs Rodney through the base of the skull.

When the screams silence, the only sound left is the *click, click* of Barbara's lighter as he lights up his cigar.

"Annetta," Turi says in a perfectly calm, quiet voice. He picks up a shop rag and wipes his hands clean before dropping that into the bucket too. "I want to hear from you, and no one else. Why do the Chiarellis want you dead?"

She shifts around me slowly. Her eyes are trained to the

ground, and she's shivering, even in my coat. In the softest voice imaginable, she answers, "I killed Frederico."

Barbara's cigar burns a bright red on his inhale.

"Why did you kill your ex-husband?" Turi asks.

"I saw him in bed with someone else." Annetta swallows. "An underage girl."

I jerk my head toward her. The fuck? A fucking *girl*?

"Could you have been mistaken?" Turi asks.

"No," she says, and her voice cracks on the word. "They'd been bringing girls to the house for years. I just believed the lies they told me. I didn't want to know the truth."

"How did you kill him?"

"We were on his boat on the lake. I let him get drunk, and I pushed him overboard."

"You saw the dead body?"

"Yes."

"Are you sure?"

Annetta's voice is a thin whisper. "He can't swim. I watched him drown."

"Then you drove home, the Chiarellis called a hit on you, and Mikey killed the wrong sister. Is that right?"

"Yes, sir."

Turi broods on this for a moment. His weird amber eyes are flat in the basement's dim light. "That's good you told me. Honesty is an essential trait to have in our family, don't you think?"

"Yes, sir."

"It's good we understand each other." Turi exhales and glances at his watch. "You're my advisor's valued daughter and my right-hand man's wife. Your enemies are my enemies. Is that right, Annetta?"

Sweat trickles down her temple, despite her shivering, and her nails dig into my wrist. She doesn't look at the man in the chair.

"Yes, Don Salvatore."

Turi's gaze ticks to me. "It goes without saying that we don't need anyone else finding out who she is before I can nail down the Chiarellis."

I nod.

"Get your wife home."

~

AFTER A LONG, shitty day, the tentative light outside my living room windows tells me another is about to start.

We had to stop by Dr. Macaluso's house to get stitches. Annetta sat in his living room with her arms crossed, staring forward and not moving a muscle the entire time. She didn't speak, even while I explained to her that the person in the elevator had been my house cleaner and the man on the street was one of our own men.

She doesn't speak now either, turning on her heel after she removes her shoes and going upstairs.

Exhausted, I follow her.

I head to my guest room, take a half-assed shower with my stitches sticking out of the water, and try to pass out in bed.

But as much as I toss and turn, I eventually find myself staring up at the ceiling with Annetta's terrified face playing in a loop as that unfamiliar feeling of guilt wriggles around in my chest. It weaves through my internal organs like a fucking parasite I can't get rid of.

Annetta deserves better.

She's been forced into so many roles in her young life—

a wife, a killer, a widow, a liar—and she didn't ask for any of this.

I remember coming to her parents' for dinner and hearing how she'd be late because she was volunteering or helping with cleanup after Serafina's ballet recital or babysitting Joey's kids. At the time, it made me feel good to be near someone who wasn't a fucking blister on society's foot like all the other soulless fucks I work with.

Annetta didn't deserve Turi scaring her like that. She didn't deserve to be married to her piece-of-shit ex-husband or to have to make such difficult decisions while she was with him. She never deserved what happened to her sister.

And she sure as hell deserves better than me, some old criminal bastard who's never home.

She's fought hard in her short, shitty life. She should get to live a real life now, not be stuck in hiding. What she needs is a therapist, maybe a dog, and a nice vanilla boyfriend who takes her on vacation to Niagara Falls.

My jaw's already clenching at the mental image.

I shouldn't have let her kiss me at the cemetery.

I shouldn't have let her kiss me before that.

But we just kept circling each other, didn't we? Like celestial bodies, or carrion birds.

A knock at the door startles me from my thoughts. I reach for my jeans on the nightstand, but the door swings open and Annetta slips in.

In the darkness, I can just make out that she's wearing an old, black T-shirt of mine.

Neither of us says a word as she takes one step, then another, and another until she's on the other side of my bed. She burrows under the covers and huddles along one side of the mattress.

I don't think, and I sure as hell don't say a damn thing as

I roll closer and wrap an arm around her shoulders. She flips toward me, buries her head against my chest, and we fall asleep, holding each other as the day breaks.

13

ANNETTA

I would have thought it was a dream, except that I only have nightmares these days, and I woke up in the wrong room.

I reach in the darkness for Dom's cold pillow and drag it to me to inhale his rich, masculine scent like it's a bump of coke to start off my day. It sweeps through my bloodstream how I imagine a drug would—pricking my nipples into attention, flooding my clit with an achy pressure that doesn't go away even when I grind against my palm. My hips jerk forward of their own accord when I remember his lips against mine.

The rest of the night catches up to me, and I still, the lust bleeding away. Last night was messed up. Seeing Dad there in his undershirt while he held another man's face still for a set of pliers has my stomach twisting in knots. I've always known what Dad did or, at least, suspected it, but it was another thing entirely to witness his cold obedience to his don.

I hug the pillow to me and stare up at the ceiling.

Dom protected me last night, even though I'd been lying

to him about who I was and what I'd done. Maybe obligation forced him to save me from Mikey, but what other explanation could there be to shield me from the vision of Don Salvatore and his pliers? He stood in front of me the entire time, between me and his don.

All of that pales in comparison to the fact that he wrapped his arms around me last night after I crawled into his bed. After everything that happened, he offered me simple comfort, without any strings attached. Affection swells in my chest.

I want him so badly it hurts.

And after that kiss last night, I think he might want me too.

I roll onto my belly to rub my face into his pillow and blame the sharp aphrodisiac of his scent when I thrust my pillow between my thighs. My libido feels like it's waking from an ancient slumber as I settle into my favorite position. I could use a release right now, but more than anything, I want to be close to Dom, even if I have to imagine it.

I sandwich my hand between myself and the pillow and rub against my palm, imagining it's Dom's hand. A moan bursts out of my mouth.

I've *never* made any sort of noise while I masturbated. I've always had to do it stealthily, biting down on a pillow and straining my ears for someone else in the house.

Why can't I be loud this one time? I bet Dom is loud. I bet he roars as he comes. I bet he makes a huge mess, coating his entire hand with his salty cum.

"Dom," I moan. The pressure builds inside me, and I get even more excited. "Dom!"

The door slams open.

I scream, jerking Dom's T-shirt over my lower half and flipping onto my back.

Dom storms in, looking like he tumbled out of my fantasies in his boots and thick coat, with his hair pulled back from his face. He looks *furious.*

He slams the door shut—and locks it.

"What the fuck are you doing?" he asks in a low, demanding voice.

I could not have been caught more red-handed than if I'd had a sign that said "DIRTY PERVERT" in neon letters over my head.

His gaze touches my face, skates down to my hard nipples, and lingers for a half beat longer at the pillow between my legs, before he grits his teeth and focuses on my face.

"Dom…"

"Why the fuck were you calling for me?"

"Because—you know why." I sound like a huge idiot right now, but I was masturbating in the privacy of my own home, and he can't burst in here to yell at me about it.

He takes two long steps closer, and the room constricts around him.

I inhale sharply. He's not coming to help, is he? I sit up, pushing my hips against the pillow a little further.

Dom notices the movement and stops.

"Eduardo's here," he grits out.

"Okay, so?" I have no idea which Eduardo he's talking about—we have at least three in the family.

Dom takes one more step until he's at the edge of the mattress. "So, he could hear you."

Oh.

My cheeks burn.

"I didn't know that," I say in a weak voice.

He exhales, glancing over me again. "I have to go meet with your dad and a few other people today. I just wanted to stay long enough to introduce you to Eduardo. He's going to stay in the penthouse as your bodyguard." He pauses. "You gonna be able to control yourself?"

For a moment, I can't meet Dom's eye as my face burns with embarrassment. Of course, I don't want Eduardo to hear me.

But this is *my* house too. And I'm sick of being stuck again around a bunch of men and a husband who won't satisfy me. My core aches with the discomfort of my ruined orgasm.

"What if I can't?" I whisper. I look directly into Dom's eye, and when the corners of his mouth twitch, certainty spreads through my chest. "Make him wait outside until I'm done."

Dom takes a step forward and hooks one boot on the edge of the bed frame, amusement spreading across his face. "That's a security risk. He can't wait outside if he's supposed to be protecting you."

"A security risk?" I burst into laughter, despite the flush of heat at his proximity. "If it's such a security risk, then you should be taking care of me, shouldn't you?"

"What do you need then?" he asks so suddenly that it takes me a moment to process what he said. He nods toward my hips. "To come. What do you need?"

Oh fuck, oh fuck, oh fuck.

I don't waste a second.

"Finger me." I scramble to kick the pillow out from underneath me with all the grace of a newborn deer. "I need you to finger me."

I spread my legs, exposing myself to him, trying my hardest to look sexy and unaffected and not awkward and thrilled.

Please. Please, please, pleeease.

He stares down between my legs, his body shifting forward, like he's being drawn in. The tendons in his forearms stand out deliciously as his hands clench into tight fists. I watch, fascinated, as his cock grows heavy in his jeans.

"And your"—he swallows—"your panties?"

Rip them off with your teeth and incinerate them in a campfire.

"Take them off," I whisper. I clench the bedspread into tight fists to keep from trembling like an overeager chihuahua.

I think he might back out at the last moment, but he shifts forward, and like a dance, I shift back. My elbows press into the mattress as he creeps his hands up my thighs.

I always imagined he'd be hard and rough in bed, like he is with everything else, but he moves against my skin like I'm made of spun glass.

Every brush of his fingertips against my thighs sends sparks up my body and coats me in goose bumps while my pussy throbs so angrily, I think I might combust from lust.

His gaze is fixed firmly between my thighs until his fingers gently hook on the waistband of my underwear, and I gasp. He freezes, glancing at me with wide eyes like he's done something wrong.

"Please," I say. "Please, keep going."

He inhales sharply, and this time, as he pulls my panties down my legs, he watches my face carefully. When he finally glances down, he rumbles a low, strained laugh like he can't believe what he's seeing. His hands rise to my midthigh and squeeze me lightly. "What do you need from me?"

A giddy excitement swells inside me. "Shove your finger in me and rub my clit with your thumb."

He glances at me like he wants to make sure he heard

me right, and then back down at my spread legs. "Eager, huh?"

"A little."

His hand slides forward, and he skims two knuckles against my wet slit. I hold my breath as he pushes his thumb between my lips until it grazes against my clit.

"That's good," he says.

The anticipation, the build-up, his soft praise—I nearly come.

"Just your fingers inside me for now," I blurt out. I mentally list all the purse brands I can think of and the ingredients for dinner tonight. I don't know when he'll give me this again. I don't want it to end too soon.

Dom's free hand trails down to adjust himself, drawing attention to the long, hard outline in his jeans. I whimper and squeeze my eyes shut.

"Are you sure you want this?" he asks in a low rumble.

I'm not looking to see if he's teasing me or earnest, but it spikes a messy panic in me.

I almost cry. "Please don't stop. Two fingers, please."

He presses a single finger against the wet mess I'm making. And then he slips it inside.

I groan with unabashed relief and slump down onto my back. Oh, thank *God*. The pressure against my inner walls feels amazing, better than I could've hoped, and he was right just to start with one. I would've come straight away if he'd given me more.

The slow rhythm he's set is perfect, stoking the fires enough that I can enjoy what he's doing, but not finish immediately. I rock my hips along with the motion of his hand. That feeling again, of *affection*—though I'd give it a different name if I were brave enough—swells inside me. He's doing this for *me*. He's taking care of *me*.

He sinks his second finger inside me and curls both, and in a few strokes, it builds up enough pressure that I can't fight it anymore. I clench down as hard as I can against the impending orgasm, but it only brings the rush on stronger, and then Dom rubs against a spot inside me.

If I'm gonna come, it'll be with my eyes open.

A beautiful flush covers his face, and when we lock eyes, I gasp out his name as waves of starburst pleasure rock through me.

He slows his pace until, gradually, he pulls his fingers out of me. Once we're separated, he stands fully, and we stare at each other for several seconds. I've never seen the expression on his face before—like he wants to whisper a secret he's never told anyone before.

I glance down at his hard cock. "Can I help you with that?"

He palms himself, grinning, before dropping his boot back down from the bed to the floor with a *thud*. "You just helped me plenty."

I lie there, bewildered as he throws me a wink and leaves, shutting the door behind him.

It's only after an hour of lying in bed in the most relaxed bliss I've ever experienced in my life that I search for my panties on the floor, in the sheets, and finally realize he took them with him.

I'm making a mess.

The flowers Valeria delivered this morning litter the dining room table, scraps of petals and stems. The few that made it into the stone vase are all quietly rebelling. Stems that should be rigid are drooping nearly to the table, and a few of the rose heads are so overplucked that they look like half-bald Barbie dolls. I pause the video that promises a "Simple, Beautiful Winter Floral Arrangement" and groan, dropping my face into my hands.

Once I'd gotten out of bed, the easy bliss from this morning burned away as quickly as a fog in the morning sun.

Mom and Carlo had sent me texts saying Carlo would be stopping by to "check up on me", and I'd come downstairs to find that my least-favorite Eduardo was my new bodyguard—the one whose sense of humor is firmly stuck in the third grade. Thankfully, he seems mostly content to raid the fridge every hour and splay out on the couch as he watches videos of women in bikinis bouncing around in front of cars.

The elevator door dings, and I look up through my fingers to see Carlo slinking in, wearing a ridiculous orange beanie. He waves at me, tossing his coat and a brown lunch sack on the kitchen counter—leaving his sunglasses on—as he walks to the fridge.

A moment later, with a new bottle of lager hissing open in his hands, he joins me at the dining room table. "Nice flowers."

"Nice beanie."

"I paid Cousin Steffie twenty bucks for this." He flicks the bright yellow pom-pom on top of his orange beanie. "You don't support women-owned businesses?"

My mouth twitches. I lean back in my dining room chair, stretching long until my back pops. I didn't realize how much I've been hunching over these flowers all afternoon. Mom would kill me if she saw me in that posture.

You'll get a hump if you keep doing that.

I glance over at Carlo, slumping into the chair next to me, posture-be-damned as he drags the bottle to his mouth.

"You really think they look that bad?" I ask.

"They look drunk." Grinning, he takes a swig of beer to punctuate his point. He glances at Eduardo in the living room and leans toward me. "Don't sweat it. Mom said she can hire someone to make the design if you can't hack it."

I fume. "Well, you can tell Mom—"

"Whoa, whoa." Carlo throws his hands up in a "don't shoot" pose. "I'm just the messenger. Take it up with Mom. You bringing this attitude to Dom? Because that would explain a lot."

I try not to look too interested as I focus on tidying up the flower petals on the table. Even hearing his name sends a pulse through me. "What's that supposed to mean?"

"It means he was in a weird mood today. Barely gave me any shit about last night and could hardly pay attention to Dad."

I bite back a smile. "Oh."

Carlo leans forward, squinting at me like I have something on my face.

"What?" I ask innocently.

He jerks back in his chair. "Oh! *Ew!* Fucking *gross!*"

"What?"

"You *know* what, you sicko. That's nasty. I don't need to know about my sister like that."

"*Oh!*" I throw my hands up. "Like I didn't have to sit in the same *fucking* living room while Alexis Harris gave you a handy under the blankets. Newsflash—you guys were *not* subtle about it. I had to burn that blanket after!"

Carlo slams a fist on the table. "That was Alexis. Fucking. Harris. She could've offered me a handy while I lay bare-assed on the front driveway, and I would've accepted!"

I snatch a rose off the table and whack him with it, and we both burst into laughter. When we finally catch our breaths, Carlo stands, tosses his bottle, and picks up his coat.

"Just stopping by to traumatize me, then?" I tease, following him into the kitchen.

"Yeah." His smile drops a little. "About that... about last night. I just wanted to say, I didn't think things were gonna go off the rails like that."

Listening to Carlo dance around an apology is about as fun as pulling teeth.

"Don't sweat it." I wave him off and glance toward Eduardo to make sure he's not listening. I lean in, muttering to Carlo, "Speaking of last night, were Russell and Serafina ever, you know, a *thing*?"

Carlo bursts out laughing. "Fuck no. He wishes, but she never gave him the time of day."

I want you to think about who loves the real you.

I smile despite the lingering doubt in the back of my mind.

Carlo pulls me in for a side hug. "Thanks, sis." He shuffles his coat from hand to hand. "The, uh, other reason I'm here is because I'm going to see *her* later today. I wanted to know if there's anything you wanted me to bring."

We don't need to say her name. We already had this conversation several times in the past month while I stayed at Mom and Dad's house. Carlo thinks he'll find closure by visiting Serafina's grave, but there's nothing there besides a bunch of rotting bones. She's gone—in every sense of the word—completely smudged out of existence like she was never here in the first place, all at the hands of a careless man. Maybe Carlo will find closure there, but there's nothing there for me to visit.

"I'm good."

"I think it'll be good for you—"

"No." I smile. "Thank you, though. Seriously."

"Alright." He nods toward the lunch sack he left on the kitchen counter. "Mom told me to bring that to you. She said it was real important." At my expression, he laughs. "Just think, it probably can't be worse than anything you dealt with last night. Take care, sis."

He says his goodbyes to Eduardo and leaves through the elevator.

Frowning, I pull the brown lunch sack toward me and unfurl it to peek inside. There are several boxes with the words "ovulation" and "pregnancy" printed over the top next to pictures of smiling babies.

I crumple the bag like I found a nest of black widows inside and drop it into the trash, my heart beating loudly in my chest—from fear or anger, I'm not sure. I shove it to the bottom of the trash can under dirty towels and old food. My breathing is deep and intentional as I lean over the kitchen counter.

I always thought it'd be Frederico who would grow disappointed with my mysterious inability to have kids.

But it was his mom.

Frederico was perfectly content to let me offer any of my holes before he'd disappear for the night with his brother or his colleagues. So, it was his mom who sat me down at the dinner table one morning while he slept in.

"How long have you been with my son now?" Giulia Chiarelli asked in Italian.

She was a short, round woman with a kind face and soft hands. After her husband went to jail, Frederico had become the de facto don for the Tampa mob, but Giulia raised two good boys who listened to their mama, so she always had her say.

"Two years, Mamma," I answered in the same language.

We all called her that.

"Two years and six months, sweetheart." She took my hands in hers. "And I couldn't be happier. You are the daughter I never had."

She tucked a strand of hair behind my ear, the only part of me she never criticized. "Just between you and me, are you trying your absolute *hardest* to get pregnant?"

I held her gaze without blinking. "Yes, Mamma."

Giulia smiled warmly, the edges of her eyes crinkling. She patted my cheek. "That's good to hear, sweet girl. We're going to the doctor's tomorrow to see if there's anything we can do to help you and my son. If you're not able to have a baby... well. Let's go to the doctor first."

That night, I tore out my IUD myself and buried it in the garden.

14

DOM

I miss her cooking.

The thought comes to me, unbidden, as the waiter from Salt & Stone brings me a still-sizzling ribeye steak.

"What'd the cow do to you?" Aceto teases from across our four-top table. "That's a grade-A cut of meat, and you're giving it a look like it talked shit about your sister."

I pick up my knife and fork, grinning. "Guess I got my mind elsewhere these days."

"Hey, I understand. You've got a lot on your plate. Congratulations, by the way, on the marriage. Serafina's a lovely girl. She's helping my daughter Valeria get the flowers and decorations set up for my promotion dinner."

Riccardo weighs in from Aceto's side. "She's a good girl. Damn shame about her sister."

"Yeah," I say unconvincingly.

Riccardo would have zero fucking knowledge of any of my wife's qualities, so I'm not sure why he's opening his mouth.

Aceto cuts in. "Did she tell you I'm renting out a yacht for the party? I know what you're thinking. 'In the winter, are you fucking crazy?' But have you ever seen the Navy Pier in January? Me and the Missus…"

As Aceto drones on, I nod and chew through the rest of my steak, slower than usual. It tastes like shit—it's overcooked, and practically swimming in butter. Annetta keeps a little jar of bacon grease next to the stove and cooks with that, but hell if I know what her secret ingredient is. All I know is, for the first time in my life, I'm pushing aside the meal in front of me in favor of the one I know I have waiting at home.

"This place is known for their steaks," Aceto stops his own monologue to say. He glances nervously at my half-eaten plate. "You get a bad one or something?"

I shrug. "Something like that."

Aceto goes on about the caterers he's going to hire—some company he scammed to work at half price, and my thoughts drift back to Annetta and what she's cooking back at the house. Maybe I can get her to bake up more of that cheese bread she made the other night.

I'm painfully aware of her hooks in me when my next thought is a jealous stab toward Eduardo for *smelling* her food. He already heard her moans drifting downstairs—the only reason he's not a dead man is that she was saying *my* name.

I've never had to wrestle with jealousy like this before. When my ex-girlfriend Marla cheated on me after two years together, I was over it in a day. The trash took itself out. So what if she complained that I picked the Family over her? She knew what she was signing up for when we got together. I treated that woman to extravagant vacations and fancy jewelry, and made her come every night. If a woman can't be loyal after all that, then that's on her.

But Annetta? She already knows the Family comes first,

and she's been loyal, even when all she's seen is the worst of me. The grumpy, asshole me when I'm sick and begging her mom for hot soup. The way-too-fucking-loud me when I'm drunk with her brothers. And now, she has a clear idea of the fucked-up shit I do with her dad. I haven't treated her like a wife for a single moment since she's been in my penthouse, and all she's done in turn is treat me with kindness and home-cooked meals.

That's not a woman you give up easily.

Mom was like that. No matter how much Dad yelled or how badly he beat us, she stayed. She was loyal to a fault, and all it got her was misery. But I'm not interested in carrying on Dad's legacy. And I don't want a woman to be with me because she thinks she doesn't have other options.

I'm not fooling myself about Annetta. She already told me why she wants me—I can protect her, and her standards for husbands are in hell. She deserves more than the bare minimum of a man who doesn't hit her and shows up to eat her food.

This morning was different. Her soft, peaceful contentment when I walked out of the bedroom? While she's with me, the least I can do is make that happen for her every chance I get.

"So, tell me, Aceto," I say once he's done blabbering about his stupid yacht. "How're the *houses* doing? Still got a bunch of *buzz flies*?"

Riccardo had been complaining about all the police at their warehouses, but I haven't heard anything about it since. It's rare for a situation like that to go away on its own, though wouldn't that be peachy?

Aceto strokes his mustache and smiles, but the expression doesn't quite reach his eyes, the first interesting thing to happen tonight. "They're doing real good. Got all the *buzz flies* taken care of."

I make note to swing by for a little surprise inspection of Aceto's warehouses in the next couple of weeks. Just long enough that he forgets about this conversation, and just short enough that he doesn't change anything up. I know a lie when I see one. There's no way he *took care* of all the police buzzing around his warehouse without Turi hearing anything about it.

Goddamn, I hope it's something good. I've been needing a little stress relief lately.

As Aceto brags about how great his drug distribution is going, I get a text. After that shit with Annetta getting freaked out by the house cleaner, I've been pulling out my phone for the slightest phantom vibrations.

I barely read the entire message before leaping up from the table.

"Dom?" Some of the politeness melts off of Aceto's face, probably because he's worried I won't pay for my food. Fucking cheap fuck.

I pull out my wallet, throw a thousand dollars in cash on the table, and I'm gone.

ON THE DRIVE HOME, I squeeze the steering wheel until it feels like it might fold under my grip, but I don't speed, even now. I call up Turi.

"Dom."

"How the fuck did a hitman get into the building?" I know I'm shouting, but I'm spiraling, stuck in this vehicle like a caged animal.

"He only got as far as the lobby." Turi's reaction to me

yelling has always been to get quieter, and right now, it's pissing me off more than usual.

"What if he had a bomb? Aren't you and Marisol supposed to have alerts for killers entering the building? And what about Mauro? He was on street duty. I'm going to *fucking* kill him."

"Mauro called it in. He thought the guy looked funny."

I don't have anything to say to that.

"Why don't you check up on your wife? The guy's getting delivered to my house within the hour. If he's got something to say, we'll know soon."

I grit my teeth. "Fine."

He doesn't say a word, but I swear to God, I can hear the stupid smile on his face before he hangs up.

I jab at the penthouse elevator button and pace around the small metal box in tight circles as it creeps to the top floor.

When the doors open, the scent of warm, sweet bread curls around me like a housecat's tail. Her bodyguard Eduardo is lounging on my living room couch.

"Go home," I bark.

He jumps up and vanishes into the elevator as I turn the corner to the kitchen.

Annetta, wearing a light blue apron with handfuls of flour dusted across the front, and her honey blonde hair swinging in a ponytail, turns to greet me. Unfiltered delight at seeing me—*me*—spreads across her face and violently cracks into my heart. The future lines up before me like a stack of dominoes. This—what if *this* could be what I come home to every night? A beautiful woman, home-cooked meals, and smiles? For the first time in my life, I realize I've been missing out on something big.

"Annetta," I say, stopping only a few footsteps from her.

She sucks in a breath, looking up at me with longing. "Yes?"

There's a thin line of green through her brown eyes that I've never noticed before, though it's swallowed by her pupils the longer I stare.

"Dom." She reaches forward with her mom's engagement ring still faithfully worn on her left hand and touches my arm.

"There was a hitman." My voice is lower, softer than normal. Her eyes widen, and I can't tell if it's in reaction to what I said or the clear desire in my voice. Holding back my hunger for her feels like trying to contain a river behind a leaky dam, and after almost losing her *again*, I don't want to. "I came to make sure you're okay."

"I'm okay," she says, cupping her hand along my forearm. "Thank you."

"I didn't do shit." I can't believe I wasn't here to stop her would-be attacker. That's supposed to be *my* job. "Turi took care of him."

"Yeah, but you came to check on me." She stares at my mouth for a beat too long, and the kitchen seems to fold around her, squeezing us together. "I want to kiss you again."

I'm falling forward before she's even finished saying those magic words, wrapping myself around her body and lifting her into the air with a tight hug. Her breasts press against my chest. This, at least, is something I can do for her.

"Tell me what you need," I murmur against her neck.

Her legs straddle wide over my hips, and her delicate hands thread into my hair like we're long-lost lovers finally reuniting after months apart. "I want to taste you."

"No," I growl, and she stiffens against me. I knead my

hands across her back, all sharp bones and surprisingly firm muscles. "I don't want…"

Fuck, I can't articulate this right now. There's nothing more that I want than to feel her warm, wet mouth on my cock, but I don't want to just take from her—not yet, not when I haven't done a damn thing to earn my keep.

She laughs into my hair. "Then I want you to eat me out."

For a moment, the only audible sound is the whisper of air pumped through the ventilation.

She's holding her breath.

I can do that for her.

I ease her onto the kitchen counter, and she shivers.

"Cold?" I ask, running my palm up her arm. She's got goose bumps.

She shakes her head with a smile. "I'm excited."

Considering the fact that my dick is about to bust through the seams of my pants, she's not the only one. Knowing my knees are going to hate me for it, I kneel, putting my face at the perfect countertop height.

"Oh," she exhales. She combs a hand through my hair in a possessive gesture that coils heat down my spine.

"You like that, *reginetta*?"

She bites her lip and nods.

I cup her calf next to my head and press a kiss there, covered in a thin layer of spandex I can't wait to peel off. I trail my hands up her legs until I find her waistband and tug the fabric down. She steps onto my shoulders to lift her hips into the air.

"Why don't you tell me what else you like?" I ask as I reveal her panties—a see-through lavender set with embroidered flowers on it and a huge wet stain in the center that makes me salivate.

"I like the way you look at me," she says, and I tear my gaze away to glance at her, surprised.

"How's that?"

She laughs nervously

I sit on my heels, rolling down her leggings and patiently waiting for her answer.

She swallows and says, "Like you're scared of me."

"I am." When I glance up at her and see her staring at me so earnestly that it makes my chest squeeze, I add, "You're known to bite."

She knocks her foot against my head, and I grin. I tug her leggings off each heel and press a kiss to her bare calves.

"I'm sorry about that, by the way." She sighs contentedly as I kiss my way up her legs.

I laugh against her skin. "No, you're not. But that's okay. I might even ask you to do it again."

She shifts her ankles so they're locked behind my head, trapping me between her legs and shooting a roll of arousal through me. I love her quiet rebellion—she's been trained all her life to be someone's obedient housewife, but in our private moments, she can't help the hunger and desire bleeding through her every touch.

I rub my face against her thighs, into her lavender panties, like a dog coating himself in his favorite scent. I want to wear her as my new cologne.

"I think you're scared of being soft around me." Her voice reaches me distantly, muffled by her thighs.

"Maybe I'm scared you won't find anything soft." I nip at her inner thigh and rumble a laugh when she squeezes her legs around my head. "I'm the same man all the way through—funny, charming, incredibly handsome, and always *hard*."

She gives a breathy sigh as a serene smile melts across her face.

"You want me to eat you, *reginetta*?"

She nods.

"Use your words."

She grins, delighted. "Fucking eat me, Dom."

I press my mouth to her pussy, opening my mouth on instinct, tongue lolling out long and flat like a serving platter. I can *just* taste her through the underwear, and it's fucking infuriating, like sucking on a lollipop through the wrapper. The frustration drives me to eat her harder, like I can dissolve the barrier between us if I want it badly enough.

Her hands sift through my hair in long strokes while her hips rock against my mouth in a steady rhythm. I flick open my belt buckle with a snap.

I pull out my dick with one hand and snatch the waistband of her panties with my other. She shifts forward, balancing on my shoulders with her pussy shoved in my face. She tastes so *fucking* good—raw and carnal and *woman*. *My* woman. I finally get her underwear off and lunge forward, catching her ass in my hand to feed her to me and thrusting my tongue between her lips.

She screams, her soft thighs cinching around my head.

I jerk my hand away from my cock so I don't come too early. My entire body feels like a rubber band about to snap, but if I can do this for her, it feels like I can do one good thing in the world. I need this—more than her, maybe. The underside of my tongue twinges, and the muscles in my mouth ache, but my thoughts slip by. There's only desire and want.

I cant her hips to and from me in a rocking motion, feeding her pussy to my mouth in a steady rhythm until her legs tremble. She pushes herself off the counter, crushing her pussy against my mouth and grinding hard.

The knowledge that she's riding me like this, *using* me for her pleasure—I can't hold back anymore.

I groan into her as I clutch her wadded-up panties and come into them, so much that it soaks the fabric and burns a path down the side of my hand.

"Are you—are you coming?" Annetta jerks her hips up, gasps, and clenches my face in her hands as she comes on my tongue.

I'm yours. Use me.

The thoughts pound through my head, but I only groan in the affirmative for her, and she squeezes harder and uses me to ride out the aftershocks of her orgasm, her pleasure filling me with a deep, honest satisfaction.

When she's finished, she floats backward, and I lunge forward to catch her in my arms. I feel like a dirty old satyr that's caught himself a nymph. She looks down at me and smiles like she did this morning, as if I've solved all of her problems just by making her come.

Her mouth parts, and my fingertips press into her back. I *need* to hear what she's about to say, even if I won't be able to make myself believe it.

The oven beeps, snapping us back into reality.

She laughs weakly, slipping down the counter to collapse against me.

"My cinnamon rolls."

15

ANNETTA

TODAY'S A GOOD DAY.

But tears track down my face.

I woke up in bed with Dom by my side for the second night in a row, and for the second night in a row, I slept without any nightmares. I lay there for a long time, tucked against his warm body, and watched the snow drift outside onto the sleeping city. His steady breathing next to me was the only sound in the room until my need for the bathroom grew too pressing.

Fragile as a newly-hatched butterfly, I crawled out from under his arm and floated to the bathroom. So much tension had unwound from my body at Dom's hands and talented mouth that I hadn't even set a timer when I stepped into the shower.

The second the water pelted my face, a switch flipped, and I sobbed into my open palm so I wouldn't wake him up.

The same old emotions coil around me. Fear for myself and shame that I could ever be worried about my life when I should be grateful that I have one at all. Everything is drowned out by the deep longing I have to talk to Serafina one more time.

She never cried. She didn't like doing it in front of anyone, even me, even though I would've been there for her if she did.

If she'd been thrust into my life, to need to make the decisions I did, would that have broken through her emotional shell? If she'd been haunted by the attempts on her life and the cold terror of Don Salvatore's implied threat in his basement, would that have made her as unrecognizable as I'm becoming?

I can't think about it.

My phone buzzes harshly against the bathroom counter, shocking me into the present. I rub the warm water out of my eyes and draw the shower curtains to one side. Valeria's name flashes on the phone screen.

I hiss a curse and fumble with my towel before swiping several times against the glass screen with damp fingers.

"I'm heading up with your groceries in a few minutes," she says.

I wince. She can't wait for me all morning to finish crying. She's got classes today.

"Okay," I say, trying to cover the raw tone in my voice with a high-pitched enthusiasm. "I'm in the shower, but I'll get dressed now."

We hang up, and I rush to finish washing my hair and wrap myself in a fluffy towel. I nearly run out until I catch a glimpse of myself in the bathroom mirror. Puffy eyelids, blotchy skin, and a red nose. I consider going into the bedroom anyway—what would Dom say?—but I don't want to ruin what we had last night. I pat on a thin mask of concealer until I appear mostly normal.

When I swing open the bathroom door, the sight of

him stops me in my tracks. He's awake now, sitting up against the pillows with the crisp, white bedsheets pooled along his waist—and he's shirtless. His hair hangs loose and a little messy over his shoulders. A gold cross sits nestled in his chest hair, and I have to clamp my jaw shut to keep it from falling completely open at the sight of his broad chest and arm muscles eating up the width of the bed.

"Who was that?" He glances up from his phone in his palm, looking at me over the top of his sexy glasses.

"Sorry?" I fiddle with the edges of my towel, calculating how much time I have before Valeria gets here. Definitely not enough time to have sex, but maybe he'd finger me again and help me release all that stress from the shower...

"On the phone. Who called?"

"Valeria," I exhale. I'm nearly on the verge of asking him to touch me again until I realize he's been staring at my face for a little too long, and I break out in a quick smile instead.

I'm doing fine with my thirty-minute crying sessions. I don't need to bother him with them, and I definitely don't want to go back to him treating me with kid gloves. I'm moving forward with my life, no matter how much the past tries to drag me back.

I drop my towel to the ground, and interest lights up Dom's face. He slings one arm over the top of the headboard as the outline of his dick grows long under the bedsheets.

"I have to meet with her to talk about the party stuff before she goes to her classes today. Will you be here when I get back?" I force myself to turn away from the beautiful man in my bed to rustle through the closet naked, pushing my ass out a little more than usual.

His voice drifts in through the shirts I'm filing through. "I'm yours for the rest of the day."

"Really?" My heart lifts. "I should have hitmen come to the apartment more often."

"Very funny. That reminds me. I want you to learn how to shoot a gun."

"I can shoot a gun." I tug on underwear and a pair of leggings before turning back to Dom and taking my sweet time to drag on a thick, chunky sweater while he watches. I should probably blow-dry my hair, but Valeria will be here any second now, and I'd rather spend the time flirting with this brand new Dom.

"You get anywhere near the target?" He looks too relaxed in the bed, instead of tense and seconds away from ripping my clothes off like I'd prefer.

I lean back against the doorjamb of the closet, crossing my arms. "A few times."

He scoffs, tapping lightly on his phone. "Eduardo will bring a few things I ordered later today. You train with me, and I'll have you hitting the target every time."

A strange thrill passes through me. "You want to train me? Like, to shoot?" I think back to the cold terror of Mikey pinning me against the car door. Of Don Salvatore looking at me in his basement. "Can you teach me to fight, too?"

He glances over at me. "Fight what, a flea? You weigh a hundred pounds soaking wet."

I frown. "Yeah... I guess you're right." The elevator door faintly dings downstairs, and Valeria calls out a distant greeting as she steps inside the penthouse. "Valeria's here."

I'm strangely disappointed as I leave the room with Dom's gaze burning my back. Why would he go through the effort of teaching me to shoot and not to fight? Is it really that big of a joke to teach me how to defend myself?

Valeria is digging through one of the two giant paper

sacks of groceries and flowers when I enter the kitchen. Her eyes linger on my face just like Dom's did.

"You doing okay?" she asks too casually as she pulls out a bag of leeks.

I pat under my eyes self-consciously. "I didn't think it was that obvious."

"It's not." Valeria turns to the fridge. "Would a hug help?"

For a few moments, I'm not sure if she's joking or not, until she cracks a tiny smile.

Is she *teasing* me?

"Only if you promise not to blind me again," I tease back.

Valeria measures me for a few seconds. I think I might've offended her, until she takes a bracing breath like she's about to plunge into an ice bath and steps forward to hug me. Her long limbs wrap around me with all the comfort of a stick bug, but I appreciate the sentiment as she awkwardly pats my back.

"You've been practicing," I say.

"Shut up."

When we finally release, a light blush lingers on her cheeks as we work together to get the rest of the groceries put away.

"I got the party invitations printed out." She pulls a thick, book-sized package from her bag. "They look even better in person. Are you sure you can mail them all out? I can still do it."

I snatch them from her. "I've seen your handwriting— trust me, everyone will thank you for delegating." I cast my gaze over the flowers we've laid out on the kitchen island, a few ideas already forming in the back of my mind. "I'll send you some pictures of the flowers later. The chicken wire you brought over the other day should help. Did you ever hear back from that pianist?"

The pieces are starting to fall together for us. If I can get my flower arrangements to look less "drunk", and Valeria can get the pianist she paid last week to sign her event contract, we'll be in a good place for the party. I should be happy we're figuring this all out, but mostly I wonder what I'll do once this event's over. I like cooking, and I don't mind cleaning, but being a housewife for Dom feels like falling into the same old song and dance.

Valeria's gloomy face falls. "No. I keep meaning to stop by his house, but I haven't had the time. If I don't get him to agree to go, I'll have to fight for the deposit. I might use some of my cash to hire someone else until we can get it back."

"Deposit for what?"

Valeria and I turn as Dom comes down the stairs, dressed in a pair of soft dark brown pants rolled at his ankles and a black T-shirt that stretches across the heavy muscles of his chest. My stomach somersaults at the sight of him, and he flashes me a grin that makes my knees weak. Despite his size, he's completely silent as he walks barefoot from the stairs to the kitchen and kisses the top of my head.

Blushing furiously, I turn to Valeria—who's completely stone-faced. Little by little, her expressions had been opening up, I realize, only to shut down again at Dom's arrival. Dom, on the other hand, is completely unbothered as he opens the fridge and rustles through the interior.

"It's no concern," she says woodenly. "Just a few snags for the party. I'll get it handled."

"I can call him," I say. "Cousin Joey's kids used to be Girl Scouts, and I've helped run their cookie stands sometimes. I'm good with people."

"Someone's not coughing up their deposit?" Dom's voice rumbles ominously behind me.

"Dom," I say warningly and turn to Valeria. "I'll call him today, okay? And maybe I'll have Cousin Carmen draft up some legalese to scare him if that doesn't work. We'll have it back by the end of the week, promise."

Valeria's eyes flick up to Dom, before she meets my eye and nods. "Okay. Thank you."

"THEN UNSPEND THE MONEY," I snap at the meek nerd on the other side of the phone. I rub my temples.

Getting angry isn't going to help, but we've been talking in circles for ages now. Dom glances at me from the living room as he measures the water levels of his aquarium and writes them into a little black notebook.

Pages of Valeria's contract spread out over the kitchen table, ready to serve as a quick reference when I called Neil the pianist, expecting to dive into an argument with a grown man, not a guy who sounds like he's barely out of high school.

"I told you, Mrs. Lombardi," he says. "I asked my landlord, and she won't give me an extension. I really need this gig, but I need a little time to borrow an electric piano from someone."

My chest squeezes at the desperation in Neil's voice. I'm too soft.

"If I find you one, can you promise you'll do the event?"

"Really? Yes, wow, thank you!"

He could be scamming me. It's not like I haven't dealt with liars and con artists in the family before, but the pure gratitude in his voice sounds sincere, and I'm pretty sure he's not orchestrating the organic sounds of a couple screaming at each other in the distance. I'll buy the kid a nice piano with Dom's credit card—he has plenty of money to spare—Valeria and her dad never have to know, and everyone's happy.

"We'll chat soon."

He thanks me about a hundred more times until I'm finally able to hang up.

"He give you back the deposit?" Dom asks, glancing at me from over the top of his glasses. He's kneeling before his massive aquarium with a strip of wet paper in his hand, his huge forearms perched on the ledge of its wooden stand.

"I'm working on it."

The last thing I want to do is send the *Butcher* to scare some poor kid. I grab my coffee cup, leaving behind the half-finished flower arrangement on the kitchen table, to sit on the couch facing Dom.

He looks doubtful but says nothing about it as he prints out a few surprisingly tidy notes into his notebook. Several glittery fish dart toward the edge of the tank, watching him.

We exist in an envelope of comfortable silence as I sip at my coffee and luxuriate in the warmth of my husband working near me. Normally, being around someone like this stresses me out—I can't fight the compulsion to play hostess or cook—but with Dom focused on his fish, I can exist as myself, at least for the moment. The sun slowly melts the snow off the skyscrapers outside as I ease into the soft leather underneath me.

At Christmas, Mom would take out the snow globe collection she had since she was a girl, and I would stand at the mantle, fascinated by watching the snowflakes fall in their safe little bubbles. Does she still do that?

I celebrated the past few Christmases with Frederico's

family, which were tense affairs while I watched Giulia make backhanded compliments about my gifts and sat next to her son, who did nothing about it.

Dom still hasn't told me who sent the hitman yesterday, but I already know. She's the same person in my nightmares, standing at the edge of a boat with a vicious light in her soft face, watching me drown. The same person who called me at my parents' house to say she knew what I'd done.

Frederico and Marco never knew to what extent their mother pulled the strings, smoothing their failures and elevating their successes, but Giulia always made sure I saw as she played the part of family matriarch. I know there's no depth she won't sink to.

I exhale a long, steadying breath. She can't touch me here. Maybe Don Salvatore's willing to wait to act, but Dom and my dad have their influence too. Dad loves me and will protect me, and Dom, well, I'm working on that.

"What's that little sigh for?" Dom asks, waving his black ballpoint pen in my direction.

My first instinct is to clam up. I don't have anything to say.

It's stupid. It's nothing.

Dom grins knowingly and leans against the wooden aquarium stand. "I got all day, *reginetta*. You take all the time you need."

I remember the way he looked at me when I told him what I did to Frederico. If anyone deserves open honesty, it's Dom.

I take a sip of my lukewarm coffee to stall for a few seconds longer. "I've been wondering... what kind of wife you want me to be?"

Dom raises his eyebrows. "What the hell kind of question is that?"

I rub my thumb against the smooth surface of the mug. "I mean, I'll cook, obviously. You could let the housekeeper go, and I could clean. We're on the same page about kids. Do you want me to get a job?"

He shifts so he's facing me on one knee, all the relaxed fluidity from earlier stiffening with what looks like irritation. "You and I, we didn't get married for love."

The reminder shouldn't feel like a glass shard to the heart, but it does. I resist the urge to rub my chest.

He continues. "So, you and I, we're gonna take it day-by-day. I like your cooking, but if you hate it, we can order take-out. I'm not firing the house cleaner—she's been loyal for years—but you can clean if you want to. You can get a job too, if you want to." He taps his pen against the aquarium stand. "It goes without saying that you shouldn't leave the house unless you're with me or we get all this mess sorted out. In the meantime, you have my card. Buy or do whatever you want."

The longer he talks, the more I burn with wild panic, like a massive, swelteringly hot spotlight has just swiveled in my direction, and I never learned the show's routine.

What I want to do?

When has that ever been an option?

The panic refracts, focuses like a beam of light, to *anger*. "Whatever I want?"

Dom grins. He knows a trap when he sees one.

"Will you teach me how to fight?"

"I never said I wouldn't."

I scoff. "You said I'd only fight a *flea*."

He barks out a laugh, and despite myself—even if I'm still holding onto my anger—I smile too, a little bit.

"I'll teach you to fight, *reginetta*. Is that what you want?"

And just like that, the anger dissolves, leaving behind

electric anticipation in its place. Every time I expect him to go left, he goes right. I think he'll be cruel in bed, but he's tender and generous. I'm scared he'll throw me to the wolves after I lie to him, but he comforts and holds me through the night.

I take my time to answer him, inching forward as his gaze touches all over me, to set my mug on the coffee table with a clink.

I brace my elbows on my knees. "Are you going to treat it seriously?"

A hungry look passes over his features. He leans toward me, on one knee, like he could lunge at me at any moment. My stomach flips.

"Dead serious."

"Alright." I rise from the sofa. I can almost feel the current of tension between us, dragging us toward each other. "Then teach me how to escape."

He laughs, but his fingers give him away, tightening over the ledge of the aquarium stand. His thigh muscles flex. "Right now?"

I shrug, although I'm anything but casual. I roll back and forth on the balls of my feet. "Why not? I should always be ready to run, right? You can... critique my evasion techniques."

"That what you want?" he asks in delighted disbelief. He pulls off his glasses and folds them.

My heart beats a hundred times over. "Count to five and find out."

I turn and vault over the sofa, racing to the stairs.

His voice rumbles behind me like a distant roll of thunder.

"One..."

16

ANNETTA

I'M HALFWAY up the stairs by the time he gets to three. When I leap onto the top step, my chest heaving and calves burning, he's reached five.

I peek down the stairs, and he rises from the floor with a smug grin, taking measured steps toward me.

He thinks he can do this without working up a sweat? I turn tail and race across the hallway, catching a glimpse of him at the end of the hallway before I fly down the second set of stairs. I'm going to hide in the kitchen—the island will give me space in case I need to dodge him.

Behind me, his steps thunder down the stairs, giving me enough time to dash into the kitchen. I tuck myself behind the island, peering into the reflection of the oven door for his head.

I hold a breath in as he passes by, his footsteps heavy.

I know with every single fiber of my being that Dom would never hurt me.

It doesn't make sense for me to trust him, and I know that too. He's bigger, older, and more vicious. He's hurt *other* people—I've seen him kill a man with his bare hands. It's not like I have a good track record of understanding deep truths about people, so it's almost impossible to know if it's a lie I tell myself, but I believe it all the same.

My name is Annetta.

The Earth is round.

Domenico Lombardi will never hurt me.

That's what has my heart slamming against my chest in a sort of trusting, blind panic. The rollercoaster's about to tip over, the blonde girl on the TV is about to walk into the basement, and my big, scary husband's just turned the corner.

I'm terrified, but I'm safe. I'm not calm, but I am in control. Once I hear a loud footfall out of sight of the kitchen, I crawl on my hands and knees away from him. Maybe I can spy on him from the opposite set of stairs.

I lift to a crouch, balancing myself carefully on the balls of my feet to set out in a silent sprint.

The moment I lunge forward, a hand circles my ankle.

I shriek giddily and kick at him, but he's already wrenching me toward him, final and certain as a ship to a dock.

"Well, well, well." Dom flips me so I'm on my back underneath him. His thick thighs trap me against the cool tile, and his hand splays next to my head, the edge of his thumb brushing against my cheek. "What do we have here?"

The sight of him knocks the air out of my lungs.

"You caught me," I whisper breathlessly. My chest heaves like I've just won a sprint.

The same wolfish grin as always grows arrogantly across his face, but his eyes are tender. "I'll always catch you, *reginetta*."

I suck in a breath. My heart swells against the underside of my chest, and three little words press against my throat, even when I swallow. I don't know if this is love, but I'm certain I want him, in all the ways he'll give himself to me.

I press my palm flat against his chest and dig my fingertips into the muscle there.

If I could just take his heart without asking, I would.

"It's time," I say.

He brushes his thumb against my jaw in a slow caress. I want to pull out his ponytail so badly, feel his hair tumble over my face. I want to live inside his skin.

"Yeah. It's time." He leans down and kisses me like he's starved for every one of my exhales. Like he wants to guard every piece of me inside him.

My hands move up to his ponytail, tug, and a curtain of hair falls over us.

He chuckles against my lips. "You like that?"

"I *love* your hair."

He groans deeply, pressing me back against the tile floor with his mouth until the back of my head sings in pain.

I drag my legs from between his to circle around his waist, pressing against his sides with all the strength in my thighs, free in the knowledge that I can't hurt him, even if I tried. I collect his hair into my fist and tug, leading his head up in a slow arc to bare his throat to me, and he lets me do it. I curl forward to shove my face into the crook of his neck, wanting to smother myself with him, to shake apart from the vibrations of his moans. I kiss the scar I left on his neck.

Energy thunders through me. He said I could have *whatever* I want.

"Take your shirt off," I urge into his ear like the devil on his shoulder.

Dom rises onto his knees and tugs his shirt off with one hand. I don't know where to look first—it's all delicious, all of the tattoos, scars, hair, and muscles. I like that he keeps his hair long. I like that he doesn't suck in his belly. I like his patience, his confidence, and his appetite. I like that I can see a future with him.

He leans down as I push my hips up, and then he scoops me into his arms, easily lifting both of us off the floor with his intense strength.

"Where are you taking me?" I ask, wrapping my arms around his neck and kissing behind his ear.

"Upstairs. My knees can't take this tile floor shit."

My laugh follows us all the way to the master bedroom —our bedroom.

Dom tosses me lightly on the bed. He's breathing a little heavier after our trip.

I rub my thighs together. "Tired?"

"Not even a little."

I wet my lips. "Alright." Time to test how serious he was about giving me what I want. "Get undressed then."

If he thinks today is a repeat of our last encounters, that I'll use his mouth or hand and let him come into my panties without touching him in return, he doesn't show any sign of disappointment as he drops his pants and boxers to the floor and his cock springs forward. It's uncut—and every bit as thick and heavy as I imagined it would be.

He's confident, as he should be, as he stands there in the center of our bedroom, waiting for me to finish my inspection of his body. I know some of the stories of the tattoos covering his body, but not all of them. One day, I plan to fix that.

Since I've been here, I haven't noticed him working out in his personal gym upstairs, but his body is stacked with thick, well-defined muscles like he's been sneaking off to chop firewood in the forest while I sleep.

I slip a hand between my legs and rub against the achy

pressure there while he watches. I think if I asked him to stand there and watch me get myself off and told him he wasn't supposed to touch me, he would listen. I don't know if it's a form of love or kink or patience or something else entirely, but for me, it feels like power. For once, I get to sink my teeth into it.

"Everything to your liking, *reginetta*?" His cock bobs gently in the air with a pearl of pre-cum gleaming in the bright daylight.

The idea that this could all be for me and not the idealized woman I mold myself to be is a little terrifying, but it's a different kind of scary, where there could be something good at the end of it if I can just be willing to open myself to him.

I swallow.

"You are the most beautiful man I've ever seen," I murmur in open awe. "And I want to taste you now."

His physical reaction is immediate. His cock jerks upward, fists clench, nostrils flare.

"Yeah," he says in a voice like gravel.

His reaction—his clear arousal for *me* fills me with confidence.

He's so damn tall that if I kneel at his feet, I won't be able to reach his cock. I slip onto the ottoman at the foot of his bed. "Come here."

He takes one long step forward, spilling a drop of pre-cum onto the carpet.

"Aren't you going to undress?" He sounds hopeful, but I don't think it's to see me naked. I think he wants to spoil me with his generosity again, to get me off.

This time, I want to give him the same gift.

"No." I grip his cock in my hand.

He groans.

His hands rise to touch my hair—but he said I could have *whatever* I want.

Before my brain can tell me to stop, I glance up at him. "Hands behind your back."

We lock eyes—I've gone too far, no man likes being spoken to like *this*—and just as I open my mouth to apologize, to take it back, he complies. His arm muscles flex as his hands disappear behind his back.

"You like telling me what to do?" He sounds dangerous.

Anticipation needles at my skin. "Is that okay?"

He tilts his head back with a grin, only a sliver of his dark eyes visible. "Angel, you can tell me what to do any day of the week."

Warmth floods my panties at his masculine, borderline arrogant, confidence.

I turn to his cock and give it an experimental tug, his hips chasing my hand's path, and my clit pulses at his eagerness. I slip one hand between my legs, over my leggings, and dip my head forward to lick the slit of his cock.

Ocean saltiness explodes across my tongue. We moan in unison, and then I go back for seconds and thirds. I suckle at the head, tugging lazily at his shaft, drawing out the sensations for him with long, slow movements.

My nipples prickle painfully against the knitted fabric of my sweater, and I soothe myself with an echoing circling against my clit, dulled by the layers of clothes on top.

"*Reginetta*," he groans after several minutes of me teasing him. "Let me touch you."

I glance up at him. Pain and desire are etched into every line of his face.

I release his cock and lean back—he sighs, reaching for me.

How far will he let me go?

"Did I tell you to move your hands?" I murmur, searching for the hem of my sweater with my fingertips.

His arms snap back behind him, and he chuckles darkly. "No, you didn't, *reginetta*."

"That's right. I didn't." I feel more myself than I *ever* have. I'm the version of myself that's been passed through a hundred filters, leaving behind the heartbreak, pain, and insecurity to distill into the purest essence of me.

I pull my sweater over my head and toss it to the floor.

Dom releases a gruff sigh, looking like a barely restrained wild animal, muscles flexed with a light sheen of sweat across his face and chest. I rub myself at the sight of him, that he wants me as badly as I want him, and in the same way.

"Tell me when you're about to come." It's the only warning I give before I suck his cock into my mouth.

He fills my mouth up entirely with only a fraction of himself, and instead of trying to force myself to deep throat him like I know he'd enjoy, I do the things I feel like doing, things that please *me*. I run my tongue up and down his shaft like I'm licking a popsicle, I suckle the head, and I stroke him with both hands threaded together. All the while, I slowly soak into my panties until I'm slipping back and forth on the ottoman. It doesn't help that Dom groans broken utterances above me the entire time.

He begs. He pleads. He persuades. But he doesn't move his hands.

"*Reginetta*, give me a turn. You know I can make you feel good. Let me taste you, angel. I'll take care of you. You can use my hands again, do whatever the hell you want. God, you look so fucking sexy. You're making me so hard, you're making me fucking *crazy*. *Reginetta*, I'm going to—"

I pull off of him with a pop.

He's panting. His belly flexes as he curls inward, his head bowed. He looks like he's hanging on by a thread. I had felt him thicken, tasted the pre-cum on my tongue.

I blow a stream of cool air onto his cock, and he winces, his thigh muscles spasming.

"You're doing so good," I say.

When he groans, more wetness gushes into my poor underwear. He is so good, though. I just want him to see that I know that.

I wrap my hands around his cock and push the foreskin further back, that wonderful contradiction of hard and soft weighing in my palm.

He rocks forward. "I'm going to…"

I release him.

We play this game several more times—or I play, and he suffers.

Until he warns me too late, and white-hot cum splatters over the corner of my mouth, my chest, my belly. His breath is ragged.

"*Reginetta*…"

I run my finger along his mess, collecting it on my finger. "You made a mess."

"Yeah. I'm sorry." He doesn't sound very repentant, although that's hardly something new. He's not a man who experiences guilt like the rest of us.

But now? In this topsy-turvy world, where I can be a queen and he, my servant? We can play pretend.

I pull myself onto the bed until my head rests against a pillow and hook my thumbs under my waistband, pulling my leggings and underwear down and tossing them to the ground.

"So clean it up." I lift a brow, daring.

His cum's still warm across my belly and chest.

A fierce grin breaks across his face as he drops onto the bed, the mattress pitching toward his substantial weight. With his hair hanging loose and the ominous look in his eyes, he looks like a feral beast that's crawled into my bed from the forest.

What big teeth you have.

He dips his head low to nuzzle his face between my legs and inhales deeply. Heat blankets my face, but I force myself to spread my legs for him, pushing past the embarrassment. For once in my life, I have everything I want, and I'm not going to ruin it.

"You drive me fucking insane," he murmurs from between my legs, rolling out his tongue to press into my pussy. The wet heat of his tongue slips between to spread over my clit and dips to dig inside me.

I squirm, bucking up into his mouth. Just a moment longer and—

With a wicked gleam in his eye, he trails his tongue up to my belly to finish licking up the splatter of his release.

I watch him, breathing faster and faster, my body shuddering under his touch, under the threatening promise of his massive weight hovering over me as his tongue traces a line of hellfire over my body. I left my demand open-ended to see what he'd do, how far I could push him. That he's willing to use his own tongue to clean me up is unthinkably arousing.

His chest and belly and cock drag over my body as he works his way up me. I rub my legs together to catch a sliver of relief, but I'm far past the point where it might help. My clit burns for his touch. When his beard scrapes against one of my nipples, I nearly scream.

He rises all the way to my neck, and I snap.

"Kiss me." It's more broken plea than demand.

His eyes widen, and his lips curl in a grin as he drops his face over mine. I open my mouth eagerly, and the moment his tongue slips against mine, I suck every trace of cum from it. Judging by Dom's deep groans, the slow bucking of his hips, and the dig of his stiffening cock into my thigh, he likes this as much as I do.

"Can you go again now?" I ask, although it's almost pointless to worry about his refractory period when his cock jerks, half-hard, against my thigh.

"Yes, *reginetta.*"

He guides himself toward my entrance. I'm so wet that the head of his cock notches perfectly into place. He inhales deeply, looking up at me with a flash of unrestrained lust.

"Dom?"

Arousal flits across his face.

"I want you to fuck me now."

He lets out a broken moan. The first push of his hips comes with a delicious, burning stretch that has me crying out. He starts to pull out immediately, but I hook my legs around his ass and keep him locked in, even as I slip down the bed with his movement.

"Don't you dare," I grit out.

He looks conflicted. "I don't want to hurt you."

My heart squeezes.

I cup his cheeks with my palms, and he melts into the touch. My gentle giant.

"Go slow, okay? We're going to make it fit."

He nods into my hands and does as I ask. Slowly, inch by inch, he feeds his thick cock into me while the pain and the burn slowly ascend into something pleasurable. His hazy gaze ticks over my face like he's trying to read my thoughts until he drops his head down to let our foreheads touch. It's as if we're sharing one breath.

This thing between us is so tender and dangerous. I can feel it swelling inside my chest, expanding against my ribs like a balloon. I know he understands, too, that whatever we have, it's rare. It's precious.

I urge him forward with my heels, and he acquiesces, filling me slowly until his groin kisses my ass and he's fully seated. I wrap my legs tightly around him and weave my fingers into his salt-and-pepper beard and his wild mane of hair, and he sneaks light kisses against my fingertips.

This is what it means to make love.

He curls inward to kiss me and unfurls his body into his full length and drives into me with long, slow strokes that build pleasure inside me until I don't want to hold it back anymore.

"That's it. Dom, I'm—" Electricity seizes my body, pinning me to the bed while Dom feeds me his cock over and over again, drawing out a life-shattering orgasm that has me seeing the birth and fall of constellations.

When I'm finally spent, he lets me float to the bed, light as a down feather. He starts to pull out, but I catch him with my legs again. He raises an eyebrow.

After all we did, I'm bashful. My cheeks heat.

"Roll over," I urge in a whisper. "I want you to stay inside me. Just for a little bit."

Understanding dawns on his face. He scoops me up and rolls us so he's on his back and I'm on his chest, with his heavy cock perfectly seated inside me.

"Thank you," I whisper as a deep sense of drowsiness washes over me.

He huffs a laugh and tightens his arms around me.

17

DOM

"WHAT DO YOU MEAN, he's got *nothing*?"

I pace the entirety of my downstairs floor while Turi speaks through the phone. Eduardo's here too, setting up the finishing touches for Annetta's surprise, and she's upstairs crying in the shower. If I thought a little bit of dick magic would cure her grief, I was quickly enlightened when she snuck off to shower and quietly sob like she has every other morning.

I'd hope a call to Turi about the hitman would deliver some good news, but I should have known better.

Eduardo gathers up his tools, waves, looks longingly at the *cornetti* Annetta made yesterday, and leaves.

"If he had something to tell us, he would have," Turi says dryly. "He got an order and a payment, and he didn't ask any questions."

"So what now?"

"I'm negotiating with *Ottavio* now." Turi says his father's name like it's a curse. "He is adamant that we can't have more instability in the Family. We have to do this right. Barbara's going to Florida this week to identify a loyal replacement for the Chiarelli Don, and Marisol and Worm are working on digging up some dirt."

"*Dirt?* How much more do we need? How many times have they tried killing my wife now?"

I wish I had something heavy and don-shaped to punch as Turi pauses on the other end of the line.

"Your *wife*?" he says with an annoying note of amusement.

I pinch the bridge of my nose. "I'm going to drive down there and strangle you with my bare hands."

"I have everything in motion now. The Chiarellis won't be a threat to *your wife* for long."

Annetta's light footsteps sound at the top of the stairs.

"Goodbye, Turi."

He exhales a laugh as I hang up.

Annetta's eyes grow wide as she comes around the bend and sees what I have laid out for her. She stops at the edge of the kitchen, taking in the sight of our kitchen turned arsenal. I figured if I couldn't bring her to the gun range, I'd bring the gun range to her. After my call with Turi, I couldn't be more glad.

Airsoft, BB guns, gel pistols, and plastic aiming attachments are scattered all over the kitchen island. It's not a perfect solution, but if she can't practice with real bullets, then a variety of weapons should give her a comfortable understanding of how to shoot if the time comes.

She approaches the guns like they're a nest of live snakes. "This is all for me?"

I come up behind her, circling my arm around her waist, and she leans her head back against my chest like we've done this a hundred times before. My heart lurches against my ribs.

"You're still going to teach me to fight, too?" she asks.

"Eduardo's bringing over smaller weights and a tread-mill today." I kiss the top of her head. "We'll start tomorrow. Those fleas won't know what hit 'em."

She slaps my arm, and I laugh.

"Pick one out and let's see what you can do, Miss I Can Shoot a Gun."

Her mom's old engagement band glints off her fingers as she lifts a lightweight airsoft off the table and faces the end of the hallway where Eduardo and I set up a hazardous, homemade gun range made of plywood, nets, and paper targets shaped like men.

I hadn't realized that I expected she'd be timid about this, or that she might back out when faced with the reality of this training, until I'm surprised by the effortless way she raises her gun and aims it down the hallway. Something stirs inside me at the sight of her looking so sure of herself.

She pulls the trigger, and the airsoft pellet tears through the paper target and hits the plywood behind with a *plonk*.

Her shot went wide, and her stance and grip could use a little work, but she did better than most people do on their first time. Déjà vu passes over me as I think to myself what a good hunting partner she'd be.

She squints down the hallway and frowns. "That was bad."

"It was your first try."

I step behind her and nudge her right foot a little wider. It's not strictly necessary, but I press my chest against her back to fix her grip.

"Remember," I murmur, my mouth brushing against her hair, sweet from her almond shampoo. "Trigger hand grips loose, and your support hand grips tight."

She pushes her back against me, and I rest my hands on her hips as she shoots again.

"Good. While I'm gone, you'll do just that, but about a thousand more times. Start up close and then try again with more distance as you hit the target consistently."

"Are you leaving now?" She shoots again, truer this time.

Blood rushes to my dick. Is this the Annetta that's been hiding underneath her obedient princess mask all this time? A coolly competent sharp shooter? And—I think back to last night—a hellcat in the bedroom?

"Yeah. As soon as Eduardo gets back, I'm heading out." I pull her tighter against me, and she shoots again, missing the hallway entirely and embedding in the drywall. I laugh.

"You're distracting me." She doesn't sound that upset.

I lower my head to the crook of her neck and kiss the delicate skin there. "Maybe you need a few distractions."

She gasps as I suck at her neck. "You're a lot more than a distraction, Dom."

I chuckle against her neck. My hands drift lower, playing with the sliver of exposed skin just above her leggings.

"That's exactly what I am."

She lowers her gun, and I brush my fingertips along the underside of her arm in a light suggestion to keep her arms raised.

"That's what you *want* to be?" she asks.

"It's what I'm good at."

She gives a frustrated exhale. "Alright." She spreads her legs a little wider and shoots off another pellet. It hits the dead center of the paper man's heart, and my hips jut forward. "Then distract me."

The failure of the hitman, of the Chiarellis, of her mom's engagement ring on her hand as she fires off another round —it all slips out of my mind as I reach into her leggings— she's not wearing panties—and slide my fingers against her already wet clit. Desire slams into me, urging me to pump my fingers inside her, skip to the good stuff. Instead, I circle her clit and soak in the feeling of her body melting against mine.

"Arms straight," I murmur into her ear.

She makes a valiant effort to straighten her arms and shoots.

"Put a finger in me," she urges in a delicious demand.

I might be more tempted to push back and make her wait, but Eduardo should be back soon, and we're in open sight of the elevator, so I do what she says. I slide two fingers down her slick pussy, but when I push them inside her, I take my time. The breathy little moans she makes and the way she's fighting to keep control of her own arousal are driving me wild, but I force myself to be patient. This is what I'm good for—it's what she's asked for. There'll be time for more tonight. And tomorrow, and the day after that, even though I said we'd take this day by day.

Her inner walls contract around my fingers as I pump in and out of her. She's so *tight*, even just for my fingers, and it stirs the memory of that same tightness squeezing my cock. She rocks against my hand, her arms trembling from a mixture of arousal or fatigue, and rolls her head against my chest, her eyes shuttering closed.

"Keep shooting," I tell her.

Her head jerks up, and she unloads the rest of the magazine in several rapid-fire shots before she tosses the gun to the kitchen island.

"I want you inside me, Dom. All of you. Now."

I don't think—I lift her into the air by her waist as I keep up the pace of my thrusting with my free hand. I'm too big to fuck her standing, so I bring her to the couch. She understands my intent and holds onto the couch arm to anchor herself, her belly across the couch arm, and her legs dangling in the open air.

I drop her leggings to her ankles.

We're looking directly down the foyer to the elevators now, and I'll be damned if Eduardo gets an eyeful of her like this.

I snap my belt open and pull out my cock.

Underneath my palm, her back tenses.

"Start slow," she says, a touch of worry edging her voice and twisting my heart.

"Whatever you say." I bend down to kiss the small of her back, and then—*fuck it*—I drop all the way to my knees and spread her thighs apart to lick up her pussy. She's already soaking wet, but after a few more licks, she's *dripping*. I lap up to her asshole and stand, fisting my cock at the base.

I could come right now, and judging by the way she was clenching around my fingers earlier, she's not far off.

Grinning like a madman, I feed the head of my cock into her.

We groan in unison.

"You're so big, Dom," she says, her voice muffled by the couch cushions. "God, you feel so good."

I'm hypnotized by the sight of her pussy taking every slow inch I give her, and the feel of her strangling my cock in her warm, wet heat in my own little slice of heaven.

"Yeah?" I tease, just because I can't help myself. "What do you like about it so much?"

I seat myself fully inside her and pull back out to set a slow rhythm.

"I like feeling how safe I am with you," she says. "I like feeling this close to you."

She comes into focus—her golden hair splayed over her face, and the smooth arc of her back.

I'm old enough to know better, but the marriage, her cooking, and the warmth in her laughter have me spilling my guts.

"You'll always be safe with me," I say, winding a hand around her hips to strum against her clit.

She jerks into my hands and clenches so hard around me, I nearly finish inside her.

"I know, Dom, I know," she whines against the cushion. "You're a good husband."

Fuck. I grit my teeth and fight the surge of electricity riding down my spine.

Then she says, "You're so good to me."

I'm spent.

I thrust into her as a wave of pleasure folds me on top of her, a single thread of consciousness the only thing keeping me from entirely crushing her. I don't stop circling her clit, and in seconds, she's crying out underneath me as we come together. Satisfaction fills every atom of my being at the total pleasure of coming into a woman I've made finish with my hands and my body.

She sighs. "That was perfect."

Her body is completely boneless against the couch.

I hesitate. But I've never been a man of half measures, so I tell her, "You're perfect."

A LITTLE VELVET box rests against my thigh as I drive to my last stop for the night.

You're so good to me.

I called her perfect. And it's the way she was *glowing* after the praise that has me adjusting myself now as I wait at a stoplight.

When she moved in, I thought she'd be a little broken birdie I'd have to take care of. She'd stay scared and timid, and I'd protect her, but our relationship would end there.

The confident Annetta who fills up the penthouse with her flowers and bread and demands I chase her and fuck her and train her?

That version of her is dangerous.

I'm already forgetting what this marriage is supposed to be. I told her we'd take it day by day, but I've spent my entire evening slipping into daydreams of what she'll be like in five, ten years. I imagine her and me in bed on a lazy Sunday afternoon, or her standing over me with that look of intense desire as she tells me what to do in her sweet, bell-chime voice.

She wants protection, control, and maybe a little fun. I can give her all those things, but eventually, she'll want more—she deserves more.

I pull up to the address Turi gave me and peer through the windshield. Even in the dark, I can see this place is a shithole. Sure, I've learned that looks can be deceiving, but I can't imagine anyone living like a king inside this cardboard-colored apartment tower.

In either case, I pat my gun and knife and jump out of the SUV. The two smokers on the front steps of the building take one look at me as I stride past and beat it.

Smart.

I'm breathing through my mouth as I pass through piss-stained hallways that reek of weed and sewage until I get to the door I'm looking for—lucky number 111.

I rap on the door and wait.

Several locks click on the other side of the wood, and the door cracks open just to the length that the thin door chain will allow. A sallow twenty-something-year-old man looks out at me. His eyes widen as he takes in my appearance, and I can tell he's fighting the urge to slam the door in my face. He must understand that it wouldn't help him, because he keeps it open.

I grin. I'd lean against the doorway, but I'm not touching anything in this hellhole that I don't have to.

"You know who I am?"

His Adam's apple bobs as he swallows. "No, sir."

His shirt, at least, is clean. I can make out the fast-food uniform logo stitched onto his chest through the crack in the door.

"It's probably best you don't, but you should let me in anyway."

Another bob of his throat. "Yes, sir."

He shuts the door. The chain lock jangles against the back of the door, and then it swings open.

"You just move in?" I ask as I step into his apartment.

Despite the disrepair outside, the inside of his apartment is nearly empty and about as clean as it could be in a place like this. A lone cup of instant ramen sits on his kitchen counter, a wispy tendril of steam curling out. The only pieces of furniture in the entire studio apartment are a metal fold-out chair, a plastic grey table, and a neatly folded pile of blankets next to a stained foam mattress.

"No, sir."

My first thought is that he's an addict, but he doesn't have a bong or needles anywhere. And anyway, he's as alert as a rabbit as he watches me from the kitchen.

Best to get this over with before I start feeling bad for the kid.

"Does the name Serafina mean anything to you?" I hate that I still have to say her name when that's not my wife's name.

"Y-you mean Mrs. Lombardi?"

And just like that, I like the kid a little better. I'm glad he's scared shitless—I won't have to do anything painful to him tonight.

"Yeah. Mrs. Lombardi. You owe her something, don't you, Neil?"

"S-she said, she said it'd be okay!" His face is already shiny with sweat. "She was gonna get me a piano. I told her I can't get the money back from my landlord."

A gifted piano? That seems like something my sweet little wife would do. I'll do her one even better.

"I don't really give a shit. You figure out a way to get her back that money, or when I come back later this week, I'll cut off a finger."

He goes completely pale, pressing his stiff body against his refrigerator.

"But I'm a pianist," he whispers.

I lean in, meeting his eyes until he drops his gaze down to my boots.

"Sounds to me like you have a pretty good incentive then."

18

DOM

WHEN I GOT HOME last night, the shooting target's paper heart was obliterated.

I stood there for a while, playing with the velvet box in my pocket while she finished dinner.

I've trained a lot of men over the years, and there are three things I've learned to look for that make them a good fit for the Family.

A man who takes initiative.

A man who keeps his fucking mouth shut.

A man who can be cruel when he needs to.

The last part is the easiest to find. Lots of people are cruel. I'm cruel. My dad and his dad, before him, were cruel. The tricky part is finding someone who can turn off their viciousness to be a normal part of society. Some people can do it. They can go home to their wives and kids and compartmentalize the rest. Others, like me and Turi, always have cruelty lurking underneath the surface, waiting for the chance to show its ugly head. It's easier for us to reach, but also harder to hide.

Annetta is the rarest combination—a person who uses

cruelty when she has to, but is also compassionate. It's not a malignant part of her personality—it's an evil necessity.

It's why she won't understand.

After my first bite of under-seasoned pasta, I knew something was wrong. I ate my entire plate anyway—no use arguing on an empty stomach, and even her half-assed meals are still pretty damn good. Once my belly was full, I turned to face my wife.

She looks like a painting tonight.

Behind her, the night sky is obscured by dark clouds and light pollution from the golden streets weaving through glittering skyscrapers. She's sitting at the dining room table, in black leggings and a flowing black top, her hair scraped back into a sharp bun. She snips at a rose stem with a violence that suggests she has castration in mind. She looks beautiful, though I'm not so stupid as to voice that thought aloud.

I'm already late to threaten some asshole city council member at his family dinner, but I'm in no rush to leave. If she's upset, it's for good reason.

She's supposed to be working on the arrangements for Aceto's party, but this doesn't look like any of the elegant white and cream designs I've seen her make before. A fan of black plant fronds stabs into the open air as she fills the rest of the vase with blood red flowers. Maybe this is an artsy outlet for what she's feeling—or maybe she's sending a message. In either case, I'm ready to listen.

"Let's hear it," I say, leaning back on my elbows against the kitchen island.

She huffs a heated exhale and points her snips at me in a way that has my balls tingling.

She shoves the rose into a terracotta vase. "Why didn't you trust me to get the deposit back for Valeria?"

That's what this is about?

I drum my fingers against my thigh. Sounds like that little worm Neil ratted me out—a shame, too. I liked the kid.

"No," she says, like she can hear my thoughts. "Don't bother him anymore. You already did plenty. I need to know why you went and threatened him."

I shrug. "I was following up for you. That's what I'm here for, *reginetta*. I back you up."

"*No*," she repeats with more force and drops the snips on the table. I'd guess she spoke with Neil this morning and has been letting anger fester the entire day until I got home. "You didn't back me up. I had it handled. What you did was undercut me."

"Is he not giving you back the deposit?"

"We live in a penthouse. I spend the same amount on his deposit on *flowers* every day! Would you have even noticed if I paid for his deposit with the card you gave me?"

"I already said you could spend whatever—"

"So then money is not the problem. The problem is that I had a solution. Neil is broke. I was going to buy him a piano, and he was going to play at the party. He didn't need to return the deposit. We had an arrangement worked out, but instead of getting to call Valeria up and let her know I took something off her plate, I had to spend the entire morning calming Neil down and promising him that no, my *husband* wouldn't break into his apartment and chop off all his fingers!"

Ridiculously, it's the thought that she was consoling that fucking kid all day that has me folding my arms across my chest. She shouldn't have had to waste her time fixing something I took care of for her, and she definitely shouldn't have had to emotionally coddle another man because of me.

"I wanted to help you—"

"Threatening some poor kid with violence isn't helping."

That's where the line is? Was I supposed to read her fucking mind?

"Where was all this morality when I had Mikey's life in my hands? Was it you who told me to hurry up, or am I just imagining that?"

"That's different, and you know it."

"Not to me. If a man tries to disrespect you, it's my *job* to fix it."

"Neil wasn't—" She sucks in a breath. "I am thankful you protected me from Mikey. You saved me. But I've been disrespected by men my entire life, and you being a big, scary badass won't change that. But you know what? I don't care. The only man I need to respect me is *you*, and last night you showed me that you don't."

Shit.

I stand up.

Annetta gives me a look of tired disappointment that buries a knife into the center of my chest. "Going out?"

I want to tell her no, just to prove her wrong, but I need to leave and think. "I'm late. I'll be back tonight."

Right on cue, Eduardo steps into the apartment. I stride out and Annetta's disapproval follows me like a dark cloud.

SOMETIMES, being a big, scary badass has its downsides.

The councilmember who hasn't been playing nice with us took one look at me as I stormed into his restaurant tonight, and he promised me the world on a silver platter. Hell, if I'd stayed a moment longer, I'm pretty sure he would have offered me up his brand new BMW, and the only reason I didn't stay to find out was because I'm not in the mood to fuck with people tonight.

I'm in a different kind of mood.

I've long since given up wondering if my need to hit things was a learned or born trait, when the answer doesn't change a thing. I get mad and I punch things, just like dear old dad. Except, unlike dad, I don't direct my fists at my wife and kids—generally, I prefer a target who hits back.

I park outside my favorite warehouse in Southside. It's frigid and dark, but it's Saturday, so there should be at least a few poor bastards inside. Hopefully, at least one of them is stupid enough to help me burn off this excess energy. I need to clear my head before I go back to Annetta.

My boots crunch across the gravel as I stride toward the muffled buzz of a crowd. Even in the dark, the lookout tonight—Devin—recognizes me enough to open the door for me without question.

About ninety people face the fighting ring in the center of the warehouse, most of them men and sex workers, watching the two fighters with muted interest. A haze of cigar smoke filters the harshness out of the overhead fluorescents. I take a deep inhale. This is the place I take all the wannabes to see what they're made of, and when I can't go to the woods for a week, I come here. I shed my coat in the sudden blast of body heat and scan the crowd for any sign that this might not be a waste of time.

Giovanni Russotto—our newest capo and almost certainly a spy for Turi's dad—stands a head taller than the rest. He's gotta be the only guy in the entire place who's wearing a full suit as he watches the fight, looking like he's bored out of his mind—which makes sense, given his unsavory reputation as Ottavio's former right-hand man.

There are about forty people between us, but somehow,

the sly bastard must sense that I'm looking at him. He glances in my direction.

The second we lock eyes, I grin and jerk my head toward the ring. For a while, he doesn't move as the crowd rumbles around us. Then he lifts one shoulder in a *eh, fuck it* gesture.

Turi's going to be stoked. He and I have been wanting to get Giovanni alone for a little one-on-one for a while now, and what better way to measure a man's character than when you're breaking his nose?

When I go to find the MC for the match, he nearly pisses himself with delight at my impromptu matchup and dives into the crowd to hunt down his bookie.

I search through the mix of faces who are stealing glances at me, and land on the gaunt, skeleton-face of my new best friend Riccardo. He doesn't seem to have noticed me come in yet, and I take great joy in sneaking up behind him and clapping a hand on his shoulder.

He startles, nearly slapping my hand away until he realizes who I am at the last moment.

"Riccardo!"

"Dom," he says in his mopey little voice.

"I got a job for you. Hold my coat and my phone for the next fight." My fingers linger around my phone. "And if *Serafina* calls, I want you to get the MC to stop the fight and let me know."

Riccardo gives me a solemn nod. "Yes, sir."

I slap his shoulder again. "I knew I could count on you."

The energy in the crowd tips into buzzy anticipation as the news of the next fight spreads. When the fight ends— with a knockout no less—only a few people cry out in disappointment. The rest are busy stealing covert glances at Giovanni and me.

The frustration I felt with my fight with Annetta tonight

fades into the background. I go to the meditative place inside myself that exists when I'm looking down the scope of a rifle or my bow, or when I've spotted something unusual across the street. Or when I'm eating Annetta out on the kitchen counter and she's giving me a look like I'm the answer to all her prayers. The MC's excited voice, the noise of the crowd, it all melts away as my gaze zeroes in on Giovanni. He slings off his coat and his suit jacket and carefully undoes his waistcoat and button-down until he's shirtless.

He looks strong and not the least bit scared as he approaches the ring. I bet he already knows *my* reputation, too, so he's either stupid or arrogant for agreeing to do this so casually.

The MC finishes ticking off the rules and looks between Giovanni and me. "We're gonna keep this nice and clean, right, gentlemen?"

"One more," Giovanni adds in heavily accented English. "Nothing above the neck."

A few people in the crowd boo, but I grin and smack a kiss in his direction. "You got it, princess."

Some men get pretty worked up about that kind of talk, but Giovanni doesn't react as he extends his knuckles toward the center of the ring for me to tap.

Time to dance.

When the ref whistles to start the match, we stalk each other in a circle with our fists raised. The sound of the crowd pumps through me, invigorating me even as it calms me.

I test Giovanni's reaction by throwing out a punch. He dodges it, but just barely. As we circle each other, Riccardo's somber face jumps out in the crowd. Is he trying to get my attention?

BAM!

Pain explodes in my kidney from Giovanni's brutal shot. I suck in a breath and brace myself, stepping back just in time as he swings for another.

There's no way he should have landed that slow-ass hit on me. Fuck. He's fucking *strong*.

I break out into a grin, and Giovanni smirks. He goes for another punch, but this time I'm ready. I dive under his defense to hook his arm, drag myself across his back, kick his leg out from under him, and slam his body to the ground. I'm on top of him in an instant—he's got some experience, that much is clear, but I can tell he's a better boxer than wrestler as I drag his limbs into position for an arm bar.

The ref blows the whistle for the end of the round, and I get up. The sound of the crowd chattering swells, as if someone has turned up the volume.

I stick out my hand to help him up, and instead of being a stuck-up pissant like his three-piece suit would suggest, he takes my hand and stands.

"That was a nice move," he says in Italian.

I grin, answering in the same language. "We'll see if you think so next time."

"I think you won't find it so easy the second time. Not when you're so distracted."

I don't get a chance to ask what he means when his buddy rushes up with water. Surprisingly, Riccardo found some water too, which I gratefully accept. I stick my hand out for my phone, and he passes it over.

No missed calls. Only a few texts, none of them from Annetta.

Normally, that would make me laugh, but right now, it's taking everything in me to pass my phone back instead of chucking it at Riccardo's head. If she's going to play hard to get, she's going to find I play to win. I have my secret weapon in case our talk goes south—all wrapped up in that velvet box in my coat.

I turn back to Giovanni for the second round, and frown when I spot that too-perceptive look on his face. This fucker's going to be a handful for us, I can tell.

The ref blows the whistle, and we break into our slow circling again. This time, each loop we make around the ring, I glance at Riccardo. After a few rotations, Giovanni seems to notice.

"We can end it here, if you want to be somewhere else," he calls out to me in Italian.

I snap my attention to him. "No fucking—"

Right as Giovanni swings at me, I dive.

Blinding pain sears my left eye and nose as he connects his fist with my face. For a moment, I'm dazed, stumbling back to defend myself, but he doesn't press his advantage as the ref blows a whistle.

"No headshots!" someone from the crowd calls out.

I raise a hand. "My fault!"

Giovanni approaches me, and despite the headache pounding into my temple and the beginning of a black eye swelling my left eye shut, I meet his gaze.

"You good?" he asks.

You're a good husband.

I grin and spit out a glob of blood. "Yeah. Let's go."

He shakes his head. "You have other business to attend to. I can see it in your eyes." He turns and walks to the refs.

After a moment, the MC calls out that Giovanni forfeited and I won, to the mixed reaction of the crowd.

I'm half-tempted to force him to finish out the fight, but

for once, I don't feel like fighting anymore. I'm hungry. Tired. I miss my wife.

After I gather my coat and phone from Riccardo, I walk up to Giovanni, the crowd parting around me like the Red Sea. He turns to face me, about halfway through the process of buttoning up his eightieth shirt button.

I put out my hand, and he shakes it with a powerful grip.

"You want to spar when you're in a better state of mind," he says with a knowing glint to his eye. "Let me know."

I grin. "Yeah, I will."

THE PENTHOUSE IS dead silent as I step inside. I'm almost certain Eduardo was dozing off on the couch, but I don't ride him about it when I send him away.

Feeling like complete shit, I make my way to the kitchen by muscle memory and the dim light of the skyscrapers through the windows. My fucking kidney hurts as I bend down to search the freezer for the old bag of peas I keep to give to the fish as treats sometimes.

I slap the bag on my brand-new black eye, courtesy of Giovanni.

I'm a colossal fucking idiot.

Now that I've had the fight driven out of me, I can admit it. She was right. Here I was, thinking I was doing her some great favor by helping her out with her pianist problem, and instead I made it worse for her.

Tomorrow, I'll talk to her. Maybe she'll let me stop by Neil's place again and fix things, or make a generous donation to her and Valeria's cause.

I drift out of the kitchen, still restless despite the fatigue settling into my limbs.

Normally, when I get home this late, I like to look out the windows—a whiskey in hand when it's been an especially rough day—and think about nothing in particular. Tonight, it's our little gun range that draws my eye.

She practiced more shooting after our argument, and she swept up the stray bullets after—Eduardo sure as hell didn't do it. She did well in the gym this morning before our fight, pushing herself hard to run sprints, lift weights, and practice her first basic fighting drill—a simple shoulder roll that I had her repeat until her form started to get sloppy. She never once complained. She never complains.

I tap my finger against the velvet box in my pocket. I wish I could take Annetta out on dates, or that she had more need for things. All I can give her right now is myself, and even if I'm fucking great, I can only coast on her need for protection and sex for so long. Eventually, we'll take care of the Chiarellis, and she won't need protection. The Barbara twins have never lacked options when it came to sex. She already has status and money, and doesn't care for it.

What can I give her?

I shift the bag of peas, grimacing through the pain. I thought getting the shit beat out of me would clear things up like usual, but this time, it's only left me a headache and a black eye.

"Dom?" Annetta calls out from the top of the stairs.

I blow out an exhale. I was hoping for a good night's sleep before we jumped back into our argument, but maybe my pathetic appearance will earn me a little sympathy instead.

"Yeah, it's me."

When she comes down the stairs, I take it as a good sign that she's wearing my T-shirt. She sets the gun—the real one from my nightstand—on the kitchen island, and pride tears through me.

"I would have texted you first, but I thought you were asleep," I say, nodding to the gun.

"What happened?" she asks, looking me up and down. The worry in her voice cuts into my ego. She shouldn't worry about me, not when she's got plenty to worry about on her own, and I'm some jackass who chose to do this to himself.

"I went to clear my head. Got myself into a fight."

She folds her arms across her chest. "Because of me?"

At least I'm capable enough to recognize a trap when I see one. "No. Because of me. You were right, *reginetta*."

She quickly smothers her look of surprise with one of suspicion. "Right about what?"

"I shouldn't have threatened your pianist. I made more work for you, and I'm sorry. I have a few ideas on how I can fix it if you'll hear me out."

A deep frown creases her mouth and sinks an ominous feeling into my chest. "That's *not* what I'm mad about."

A few hours ago, that would have made me frustrated, but I'm too exhausted to argue. My brain's barely online. My only goal is to get in the shower and fall asleep wrapped around her angry little body.

"Then tell me what you're mad about."

"Are you going to run away again if I do?"

"You're welcome to shoot me if so."

That earns me a tiny little smile. She uncrosses her arms and lifts herself to perch on the edge of the kitchen counter. With no makeup on and her hair pulled up into a messy bun, wearing just my shirt, she's fucking beautiful—maybe even more so than in the daylight. This relaxed side of her is the part of her that only I get to see. It's just for me.

I guess I've resigned myself to being a deeply possessive man, at least when it concerns her.

"I don't want you to solve my problems if I can solve them on my own."

I scoff. "What do you want me to do instead, sit on my ass?"

She smirks. "Sometimes, the only thing I want from you is support. You know what that is?"

I lean back against the opposite counter so I don't reach for her and piss her off more. "I want to say it's when I go out and kill whoever looked at you wrong, but I'm thinking that's not the kind of support you're looking for."

She crooks a finger toward me. "Come here. I'll show you."

Heat zips to my groin as I step to stand between her spread legs.

"Now you put your arm around me," she says, and I splay my hand across the small of her back, "And you ask me questions like, 'How are you feeling?'"

I grin. "How are you feeling, angel?"

She melts into me, pressing her face against my chest. "I was pretty upset you left in the middle of our argument."

"I know. I had to go punch something first."

"We have a punching bag upstairs."

I don't know if it's the exhaustion or the pain throbbing over my body, but right now, I just want to agree with her. "I can do that. What if I have to leave, anyway?"

She thinks for a moment in the center of our silent kitchen. "Then you should kiss me before you go."

"Even if we're fighting?"

"Especially when we're fighting."

My chest squeezes, and I kiss the top of her head. "Anything else, *reginetta*?"

"I'm going to fix things with Neil, because I want to and because I can. Can you let me do that on my own?"

All I have to do is squeeze her and listen to her talk? Sure as hell beats getting punched in the face.

I huff a laugh. "Yeah."

"Then let's get you cleaned up."

She's more patient than I deserve as she follows my slow, geriatric ass up the stairs to the master bathroom. I fall back against the bathroom counter and build up the will to undress for a shower while she starts the water. If I hadn't been watching her so closely, I would've missed it—her shoulders bunching and a tight smile as she turns back to me.

"You wanna talk about that?" I ask, nodding toward the water raining down behind the glass door.

Her smile turns into a grimace. "What do you mean?"

I suppress a groan as I reach for the hem of my shirt and tug it off. I drop my hand against the bathroom counter so my body language is as open and relaxed as I can make it. "I mean, you crying in the shower every morning. I can hear you through the walls."

She sucks in her cheeks, her eyes shining with sudden tears. I can hear the old Annetta, the one who was trained never to be a problem for others, when she whispers, "Oh, sorry."

"Why don't we try out that new support thing now?" I extend my arm out to her, and it's a minor victory when she comes willingly, tucking herself against my naked chest. "Do you want to tell me how you're feeling?"

"Mostly good," she murmurs. Her arm circles around my waist, tightening against a massive new bruise that I don't say shit about. If this is what she says she needs from me, then I'm going to do a good fucking job of it. "I like when you're around."

The implication—*but when you leave*—stings. I swallow down any protests.

"And then, sometimes, I feel bad. Really, truly awful, like I've gotten hit by a truck, and the only thing I can do is breathe through the pain and lie there. The worst part is that sometimes I can feel it coming on, and I let myself get like that on purpose. For some reason, when I feel like total garbage, that's when I feel closest to her."

I know what I'm supposed to say.

I'm so sorry for your loss. You should never say that. Serafina would want you to be happy.

But I'm not a stranger to grief. When I lost Turi's brother Matteo years ago, it felt like losing one of my own brothers. Sometimes the worst of that time was when the people who didn't get it acted like they did. You get tired of hearing the same thing over and over again from someone who doesn't really care and wants you to stop bumming them out.

Sometimes, though, you meet another person who understands all too well what you're going through, and talking to them helps you feel less alone. They're a part of the special grief club, too, the one none of us asked to be a part of and none of us gets to leave.

I kiss the top of her head and squeeze her against me, ignoring the pain in my side. "Do you want comfort or truth?"

She laughs bitterly, her breath puffing over my chest. "Can't I get both?"

"Of course you can. You already know the truth—this kind of pain isn't going away. People say shit like 'time heals all wounds', but this isn't the kind of wound that can heal. This will be more like learning to live after your arm got hacked off. Eventually, the people around you will get used to it, but for you, it will never be normal. It'll just be something you learn to manage, five years from now and forty years from now."

"So it won't get easier?" she asks in a miserable voice, barely audible over the shower.

"It will, but that's because you start to forget. The shitty part is that forgetting will bring a whole new cycle of pain and guilt."

She sniffles. "And the comfort?"

"There's no wrong way to go about this. You can try to be strong or let yourself be weak. We can do distractions, or we can talk about it every day. You do whatever you feel like until you can stand on your own two feet."

"And if I can't?"

"Then I'll carry you, or I'll sit with you."

"Tonight, you left." She's stating a fact, not an accusation, which might be why it cuts so deep.

"I came back. I'm not going anywhere, angel."

She pulls back to look at me as the steam from the shower curls around us. "Don't tell me things like that if you don't mean it."

Her slender face is guarded, her dark eyes closed off.

And I realize, despite all my fighting, all the ways I tried to push her away, I'd already lost a long time ago. I just had to have some sense knocked into me first before I could accept the truth.

I reach into my pocket and pull out the velvet box. I meant for this to be a gift, a flashy display of my affection and wealth, but as I look at her with one good eye and a battered body, I want it to promise something else.

"I'm here, Annetta. I'm yours."

When she sees the engagement band that matches the

ring I'm wearing, and the gold wedding band with a heavy, princess-cut diamond cushioned in the center of the box, the tears that have been threatening to fall finally break free.

She slips off her mom's engagement band and slides on her new one—a perfect fit—throwing her arms around me. I want to call it blind trust or naïve optimism that she accepts the ring so easily—she's so young—but Annetta's gone through a lot in her life. Maybe it's something else. Maybe she sees something in me that I don't yet.

I hold her in my arms, and I don't say a word about the rest of the promises that are taking root in my mind— promises like forever and commitment and love.

Instead, I tell her to rest in bed while I get myself cleaned and patched up.

And because she's Annetta, my defiant, compassionate wife, she waits while I shower so she can stick Band-Aids on me.

When we finally go to bed, we go together.

19

ANNETTA

After that night, Dom kept his word.

The first morning I slid out from under his sleeping body to shower, Dom joined me moments later, slipping behind me without a word. Neither of us spoke as he wrapped his arms around me and let me finish sobbing onto his chest until my timer ran out.

After, when he asked me how I was feeling, and I told him I was hungry, he laughed and took me downstairs to cook eggs for breakfast.

Each morning, he's put me through a grueling—at least for someone who hasn't worked out in months—workout routine that mostly consists of me beet-faced sweating as I sprint on the treadmill in his personal gym and cycle through a calisthenics circuit, before he teaches me basic grappling moves on his wrestling mat. When I called Neil the next day to make sure his piano came in, he didn't mention any new visits from Dom.

The biggest change has been the way I'll sometimes catch Dom looking at me—in the mirrors in our upstairs gym or over breakfast when I pass him a cup of coffee—a significant, intentional look like he's about to deliver serious news. He never does, dissolving the tension to crack a joke or wrapping himself around me for a kiss.

I would've been happy to let our new routine of training, eating, and making love go on forever, but after I missed Thanksgiving dinner with the family, Mom decided enough was enough.

"It's a good idea," Dom told me when I showed him my mom's text invitation to a family dinner. "If anyone's watching you, they won't attack at your dad's house, and seeing you out and about will keep them from getting desperate enough to try getting into the penthouse again."

I spent the better part of the evening picking out an outfit, applying a full face of makeup designed to look like no makeup, curling waves into my hair, and stalling until Carlo texted me to get our asses over before he starts chewing on the furniture.

As I make my way to the living room, walking as gracefully as I can with every single muscle feeling like old chewing gum from our workouts, Dom's attention pans to me like the beam from a lighthouse. He gives me that look again, and a shiver rolls through me.

He has a small yellow cloth, a bottle of oil, his arrows, and his phone playing a video about a guy in the wilderness scattered over the coffee table. He sits up on the couch, an empty bow pulled tight in his hands until he relaxes the string back to rest.

His beard is trimmed, his hair's tamed into a bun, and only a small bruise remains on his left eye. His dark, rust-colored button-up is tucked into black jeans, and his heavy boots suit him perfectly. I've never thought much about cowboys, but if Dom had a cowboy hat and a big belt buckle, he'd blend right in with a roster full of bull riders.

Dom stands, dropping his bow on the couch, and takes a step toward me, filling my vision with broad, masculine features, high cheekbones, dark brows, and gentle brown eyes. He glances down at my hand, where my new engagement ring glitters on my finger for the first time.

He gives a wolf whistle and takes my hand, drawing me to him. "You look beautiful tonight, Mrs. Lombardi."

A strange fluttering starts in my belly, spreading quickly to my chest. The past couple of weeks of spending time with Dom, chatting in the mornings with Valeria, working out, and practicing my shooting have all propped me up in little ways, like extra poles for a drooping tent.

That feeling of happiness sours to nausea. How can I be girlish and carefree when it's my fault Serafina never got to feel anything like this?

Dom takes my shoulders, his fingers spreading long over my shoulder blades. "Stay with me, Annetta."

My name sounds as soft and sensual as cashmere when he says it.

I smile, gazing up at him. "I'm not going anywhere."

In the parking deck, he tosses me his car keys—which by some miracle, I manage to catch.

I give him a dumbfounded look. "What are these for?"

My voice echoes against the concrete walls.

He tucks one big hand into his pocket. "Generally, to drive."

"I'm not driving that." I glance at his massive SUV, and my chest constricts like it's caught in one of those medieval screw torture devices.

He rocks back on his heels. "You should."

I go to smack him, but he catches my hand and kisses my knuckles. I watch him with parted lips and wide eyes. Everything inside me tenses. When will I get used to this? When will he stop making me feel so light with only a touch or a glance?

"Light's green," he says, right before the driver behind us honks.

On the way there, he fiddles with the radio, stopping at a pop-rock station, and we both hum along to the songs that pour in while he drums his fingers on the center console, somehow making even this awful experience fun and light-hearted. When I roll to a stop in my parents' driveway, I give him a grateful smile.

He grins back. "You did amazing. Now let's go, I'm starving."

"Are you ever not?"

As we walk up to the front door, I take his hand in mine. He glances down at me with a look of flirty amusement that has butterflies swarming in my belly all over again.

"For my parents," I say.

His fingers tighten over mine.

The moment we step inside, Mom comes rushing up to greet us. "Domenico! I saved a whole *crostata* just for you!"

Dom laughs and answers my mom smoothly, "Ricotta filling?"

"Of course!"

As usual, Mom's stuffed every spare corner, banister, and surface with Christmas knick-knacks and fake snow. I used to think it was cheesy, but now it's nice to see that some things are still the same in my childhood home.

Dad, Rafa, Carlo, and Cousin Red are all at the dining room table, drinking whiskey. The skin on Dad's knuckles from Don Salvatore's basement is healed, not that he gives any sign of that night as he snoozes in his chair with his hands resting on his belly. Carlo's slumped onto one hand, swirling his nearly empty glass of whiskey with his other. Rafa's tapping something out on his phone under the table.

Red's gaze skates all over me, lingering at my hips like always, as we approach. Dom's hand tightens over mine.

"Serafina, will you help me get the first course?" Mom asks and steps off to the kitchen. I hate that it's always me and never my brothers who have to help.

Dom releases me easily, waltzing over to sit next to Red. He slings an arm over the back of the other man's chair.

"How's it been?" he asks Red, who's slowly wilting into his seat.

In the kitchen, Mom makes a beeline for her Pinot Grigio. After a few gulps, she motions to the cabinets. "Serafina, can you plate everyone's food and take it out to them?"

And just like that, I feel like a kid again in my parents' house, doing exactly as I'm told. "Sure, Ma."

I open up the nearest cabinets and pull out a stack of plates.

Mom leans one hip against the counter as I pile up a ceramic plate with sauced pasta and fillets of fried eggplant. The breaded eggplant is burnt on one side—normally something Mom would never let slide. I almost hesitate to plate it, but it's best to shut my mouth.

"When did you start wearing your hair like that?" Mom asks about the waves. Serafina always kept her hair pin-straight.

"Just thought I'd try something new."

"Now's not a good time to be trying new things."

"Dom likes it." I turn with my full plate.

Mom's mouth twists down.

"I'll go bring this out to Dad."

When I return, Mom's moved the wine bottle closer to the stove, and she's got that look in her eye like she wants to offer my diet tips or ask me about my grades. I load up the second plate a little faster. My calves burn from the effort of standing in heels after working out.

"Did Dom like the wine I sent over?" she asks.

"Yes, thank you."

"When was your last period?"

"Ma!" The eggplant I was balancing on a serving spoon slips back into its pan and splatters oil onto my dress.

"Honestly, Serafina!"

I blow out an exhale and reach for the paper towels, but Mom's closer and snatches a handful off the roll to dab at my breasts. Without thinking, I slap her hand away.

"Serafina!"

"Ma!"

A burst of masculine laughter erupts from the dining room. Mom's gaze flickers from the doorway to me.

"Your dad is going to Florida next week to meet with the Chiarellis." She levels a serious, sober stare at me.

I'm as stuck as a fly in honey. Guilt coils in my belly.

This was all your fault, her look tells me.

I lower my eyes.

Mom wrings the damp paper towels between her hands before sighing and setting them on the counter. "I know it might take a few tries, but you know me and Aunt Karen got pregnant young. The sooner you can get pregnant, the better."

"Dom will stand up for me." My mind flashes back to Don Salvatore's basement. I load up another plate. "He's not Dad."

"Serafina, do not be rude!" she calls after me as I walk to the dining room. Like it's *rude* to remind her she only got

Dad to stop cheating on her so much when she baby-trapped him with Carlo, instead of thinking it's *rude* to send ovulation tests to her grieving daughter.

When I come back, Mom's loading a plate for me, taking her time to arrange everything beautifully. She finishes, sets it on the counter, and reaches for my arm to rotate me toward her.

"Serafina." She cups my face, and I have to shut down the urge to pull away. "Dad and I are doing everything we can to keep you safe. You need to be doing your part."

I'm training, I want to tell her. *I can use a gun.*

I know it's not enough, but it's *something*. It's at least more than waiting around at home for my husband to shoot his load into me.

I swallow my protests, resisting the urge to argue with her—like our arguments have ever done me any good anyway. Mom will just cry about what a terrible mother she is, like she always does when she's against a wall.

Instead, I jerk off her ring from my right hand, and her eyes widen when she spots my new engagement ring on my left. Without a word, I drop her ring on the counter, take the plate, and walk to the dining room.

I don't return to the kitchen after I sit down between my brothers. Mom brings the rest of the food out, with a smile plastered across her face.

"*Buon Appetito!*" she exclaims. She sits and pours herself a glass of wine to the absolute brim.

Carlo immediately points his loaded fork at Red. "What'd you think of the Bulls' game?"

Dinner passes quickly while Carlo and Red get into an argument about the latest game, which Dad eventually settles by telling them to shut their yapping. Mom and I clean the dining room table in silence, and the guys leave to start a game of poker. Once the kitchen's cleaned, I feign the need to go to the bathroom, leave Mom with her bottle of wine, and go upstairs.

The day I'd moved out to live with Frederico, Serafina had told me Mom and Dad had all my things packed up from my old room. She'd rescued a few items, but most of my stuff got thrown away or donated. What was the point of a young, virginal bride if she brought literal baggage with her? I was supposed to be shiny and brand new. If I needed dresses or equipment for hobbies, my new husband would supply what he thought I needed.

I pass by my room and slip into Serafina's old room, shutting the door softly behind me.

Her room is like a time capsule.

I run my finger along the top of one dresser, and it comes away with a light coating of dust. The housekeepers haven't been allowed in here. A pang of guilt strikes my chest at how I spoke to Mom earlier—she's grieving too, even if it makes her a bigger pain in the ass. Does Dad hold her in the shower while she cries like Dom does for me? Somehow, I doubt it.

The empty wine glass next to Serafina's bed confirms my suspicions and twists the knife in a little deeper. I hate that I have to be the one who has to be gentle with Mom, and not the other way around. I know she's trying her best. She just can't imagine a relationship that's not built on babies.

A hint of dried flowers permeates the stale air as I kick off my heels and walk through the room. I don't think Serafina would've understood either. She loved thinking about the little family she'd have with her future husband.

I swallow past the ball of wool in my throat. She would've made a great mother.

I wipe away an errant tear as I open her closet, a little

smile twisting my lips. She would always share any of her clothes with me, but she never liked anyone to be in her closet, even the housekeepers. The one time I teased her about hiding her nonexistent vibrator in there, she got red in the face and refused to talk to me for the rest of the day.

That memory used to make me so mad, and now I'm smiling and a little heartbroken thinking about it.

The plastic bins I'm searching for are stacked in the far corner of her walk-in closet, and I pull off the top one with a grunt. Most of my cookbooks are in here, and another one I haven't seen before, about vegetarian cooking. I pop off the plastic lid of the storage bin and reach for it. As far as I know, Serafina had never taken an overt interest in cooking. She used to tell me that if she hadn't married a man who didn't give her a personal chef, she hadn't done her job right.

Did she want to be a vegetarian? My stomach sours. She never told me.

The book's much lighter than it looks, shooting upward when I misjudge its weight.

"What the...?"

Pill bottles tumble out from a hollow center. I don't know why my heart's racing as I pick them up and read the labels.

One of the bottles says it's Xanax, prescribed to Serafina. Since when did she take Xanax? She never told me about that. Why would she even hide this from me? I knew she had panic attacks, but I wouldn't have judged her for the Xanax. The bottle's nearly empty, with only a few white pills at the bottom. The other bottle's nearly full to the brim with tiny blue pills. The label says it's Adderall for Russell Wilson.

So that loser was giving her drugs?

A knock at the door has me scrambling to hide all the pill bottles back in the book and tucking it away.

"What's up, creeper?" I ask as Rafa comes in.

Once, I overheard some of Dad's coworkers calling him their keeper. They were talking about bookkeeping, but they could've been calling him a creeper—one can never be certain.

"Shrimp," he says by way of greeting.

I wait to see if he has a good reason for coming in here, but when he starts doing his Rafa thing and feigning disinterest by picking up and setting back down some of the perfume bottles on Serafina's dresser, I turn back to the rest of the boxes.

It's oddly comforting to hear my brother rustling around while I do my own search until I find what I need—my old camera equipment. Spending all that time overlooking the city in Dom's penthouse has been making me itch for my DSLR. I had a few more pieces, but it looks like Serafina didn't know they were worth saving. I sigh.

"Do you know where Mom and Dad put my tripod?" I ask, hauling the box with my equipment out of the walk-in closet.

Rafa shakes his head as he peers into a collage of Serafina's and my pics for our graduation trip to Europe.

"What're you doing here?" I ask, perched on top of the box.

"I'm moving."

The statement hits me like a bag of rocks.

"What?" I ask, my voice pitching high.

I know it's ridiculous to expect Rafa to stay here, especially when I've already moved out. He's twenty-eight. I can't expect him to live with Mom and Dad forever—although Carlo probably will. Rafa, on the other hand, has more money than God. He could afford a nicer place than our parents if he wanted.

I just thought he'd stay.

Rafa exhales, stuffing his hands in his pockets. "I stayed for Serafina. Now there's no point. I'll stay in town. I just want my own place."

"For Serafina," I say, dully.

He gives a short exhale. "You know she needed protecting. She's delicate."

"So am I."

Rafa smirks. "No. You're tough, sis."

That takes me by surprise. Has he met me? "It doesn't mean I didn't need protecting."

His smile falls. "Yeah, I know." He scans over the room again before landing on me. "Dad said you wanted to marry Dom. Is that true?"

I nod.

"Things are good?"

I flush. "Yeah. Really good."

"Glad to hear. Just so you know, the place I'm moving into? There'll be a room made up for you. It'll always be there for you, too. You know, just in case you—*oof.*"

I cut him short with a tight hug.

"Thanks, creeper."

"Sure, shrimp." He rustles my hair, and I step back with a shriek, slapping his hands away. He grins and walks out of the room, leaving it a little brighter than when he came.

I glance back at the boxes in the closet, filled with a new sense of purpose. I'm going to need to get to the bottom of those pills, and I think I have a good idea of where to start.

The door opens gently. Footsteps shuffle in, then the door shuts and locks.

Still smiling, I turn to tease Rafa.
Except, it's not Rafa.

20

ANNETTA

I SCRAMBLE TO MY FEET, ignoring the soreness in my thighs as I put on a scowl despite the fear thrumming under my skin.

"What are you doing here?" I ask.

"Don't be a bitch," Russell says without any heat. Has he slept at all since I last saw him? His eyes are red-rimmed, and his grey clothes hang off his skinny frame like an elephant's skin. He looks over at the perfume bottles on Serafina's dresser and steps over to pick up *Rêves de Pensées* —her favorite.

That's when I know, without a shadow of a doubt, that he was telling the truth.

The pills in her closet, a hidden boyfriend—Serafina was keeping *secrets*, from me, from the whole family.

I can't breathe. A sick, foul scent like rotting flowers coats the back of my tongue. My stomach lurches, and I swallow the horribly familiar nausea rising in my throat.

The image of Frederico in bed with that girl through the crack in the door, of my Prince Charming husband finally exposed as a disgusting monster—and now, Serafina? How could my sweet, perfect, innocent sister have lied to me? Why didn't I know?

Russell ignores me as he takes the perfume, sprays it onto the collar of his shirt, and lifts it up to smell. He turns his bloodshot eyes toward me. "You don't smell like her."

He knows.

My blood runs cold.

Even as I'm reeling and the edges of the room go blurry, a desperate, animal instinct for survival has me blurting out, "I don't know what you're talking about."

Russell scoffs. "It's your fault, isn't it? Carlo said that the guy we cleaned up was supposed to kill you, but he got Serafina on accident."

I want to cry. *Fucking Carlo.*

"You shouldn't believe everything my brother says." My voice is distant, like it belongs to someone else.

He strums his fingers through Serafina's jewelry display until he touches the gold cross necklace she used to wear every Sunday. He pockets it.

Righteous anger swells inside me. "Put that back."

"You know they asked me to kill you."

My anger dissolves into chilling fear.

I don't have to ask who he's talking about. He takes one long step forward, placing himself halfway between me and the door.

Once, when we were little, Serafina and I were redecorating her room. I jumped from her bed to the floor, and Mom came running up to whisper-hiss at us that we needed to be silent when Dad had guests.

If I stomp loud enough, as a last-ditch measure, someone downstairs might hear me, but Dom will notice I'm gone first... won't he?

I just need to stall.

"You wouldn't get out of this house alive," I say, and a vicious part of me hopes he doesn't. He's ruining Serafina's memory when she's not here to defend herself, and all for what—to scare me?

Except he doesn't seem all that concerned with me as he walks to Serafina's bed, pushing aside the canopy to sit down.

He's got a gun stuck in the front of his waistband, the outline faintly visible behind his shirt. I avoid looking at it, trying to meet his eye, but he's looking everywhere in the room but at me.

"I don't give a shit about that anymore. Your sister was the one good thing I had, and some fucking bastard killed her by *accident*." He runs his fingers across her pillow in a caress so tender that I look away.

There has to be another explanation, something I'm missing, even as the truth stares me in the face. Serafina was *good*—she wouldn't have spent time with some loser like Russell without reason.

"You sold her drugs," I snap, latching onto the most logical explanation.

Hurt crosses his face, and his fingers dig into the pillow. "She never paid for those. She asked for them, and I brought them to her—you knew the pressure she was under." He finally meets my eye, his gaze hard and accusing. "You knew her better than anyone."

"I didn't know about *you*," I choke out before I can stop myself. I slap a trembling hand over my mouth, and the bastard has the fucking gall to look sympathetic as I compose myself. "Why would she hide all this from me? Why would she lie to me?"

He stands but doesn't move again, staring at her pillow with a lost look in his eye. "She wanted to tell you, but she was suffocating even before you left. When you married Frederico for her, she thought she had to be perfect to deserve your sacrifice."

"She didn't—"

Russell laughs bitterly. "I told her. Trust me. I told her all the time." He touches a picture of her on the wall. "Why didn't you stay in Florida, Annetta?"

He turns toward me, the blame and loss in his eyes like the glare of the sun—too bright to look at directly.

I hate him. After everything I've done for Serafina—helping her with school, piano, dance, and even marrying Frederico—she repays me with this. With drugs and a secret lover.

Serafina was the one bright spot in my life, the one good person in our family. I always thought that living in her shadow, my horrible marriage to Frederico, and his mom—all of that was *worth it* for the only person in my life who deserved those sacrifices. All I'd been doing was putting more pressure on her, making her feel like Russell was the only person she could turn to.

I hate her. I hate that she didn't love me enough to sacrifice for me, that she thought my life could be thrown away to Frederico while she got to stay and live hers. And I hate that she didn't trust me enough to believe I would've made that sacrifice anyway, if she'd told me the truth.

I take a step back, bumping into the wall behind me, and Russell pushes forward.

"I would've." Hate and love and grief for my sister twist together, writhing in my belly like snakes. "If I'd known what was going to happen to her, I would've stayed."

Even if she wouldn't have done the same for me.

He takes another step forward until he's breathing down

my neck, his hand rising toward my face. "I can't forgive you for what you took from me."

SLAM.

The door crashes open.

"What the *fuck* are you doing?" Dom stands in the doorway, imposing and *furious.*

I'm standing with my back against the wall, tears on my cheeks, and Russell's too damn close, snatching his hand back from me like he's guilty of something. Dom surges forward.

"We were talking—" Russell starts, but Dom's already on him, squeezing his neck and shaking him like a puppy.

"Yeah, that's the problem. You don't talk to my wife." Dom slings him to the ground and lands a swift kick to Russell's belly.

Russell rolls over and throws up.

All over my sister's carpet.

"Dom!" I shove his massive body, but he holds me away by my shoulder like I'm nothing as he lands a brutal stomp to Russell's extended hand. Dom looks over to me as Russell screams in pain.

"What the fuck were you two talking about?" Dom asks.

I wrap my hands around his wrist. "What's that supposed to mean?"

"Why the fuck were you crying?"

Russell groans from the floor. "It wasn't her fault, she—"

"Shut up, Russell!" Dom and I shout at the same time.

Dom pulls his knife out from his waistband, and Russell scrambles for his gun. Dom kicks his hand, launching the gun across the room, and bursts out laughing when Russell groans, clutching his broken hand to himself.

"You have balls, kid, I'll tell you that much. But you gotta be a real dumb fuck to talk to my wife in a room alone like this. How much did they pay you? Because, I'll tell you now, it wasn't nearly enough for what I'm about to do to you."

Hate for Russell shocks me with its intensity.

I want all of this to go away—back to how it was before I found the pill bottles in her closet.

I want Dom to hurt him.

I want to punish Serafina for choosing Russell over me.

But when Dom drops to kneel over Russell, the movement kick-starts me into action.

I can't punish the dead. There's nothing left for me in this room.

"Dom, I want to go home," I say, hearing the ineffectual whine in my voice.

He barely spares me a glance as he grins down at Russell, who, strangely, has gone completely limp and expressionless. "Go wait in the car, angel. I'll be right down."

"No," I whisper.

Dom's head snaps toward me. Russell's eyes flick from Dom to me.

"I want to go home. *Now*."

I peer at the man my sister chose. He watches me impassionately.

He's not asking for my mercy. He's got nothing to lose. And even though I hate him, for a moment, I understand him completely.

I turn and walk away.

I think Dom will go through with it anyway—kill Russell, because why not? It's what he does. But once I step into the hallway, heavy footsteps sound behind me. We walk through the house like that, with him several steps behind me, until we get to the bottom of the stairs and he finally catches up. For once, he's not smiling as he snatches my hand in his.

"For your parents," he says.

I dig my fingernails into his hand, and the corners of his mouth twitch.

The living room explodes with drunken laughter as Dad, my brothers, and Carlo's friends play poker in the sitting room. Mom's in the kitchen, preparing drinks for them.

"Serafina, help me get these drinks out to the guys," she says.

Dom waves Mom off, a luxury I've never been afforded. "We're heading home, Debbie. Thanks for the dinner."

IN THE PENTHOUSE, Dom and I step off the elevator into his foyer. I take off my heels and pass them to him before striding into the living room. The tall, open windows that once felt like a little slice of the outside world are now like the pane of a glass case. I look down at the cars passing below, taillights glowing red against the black streets, and into the golden windows of the other apartment buildings. None of what happens in our penthouse matters to those people. None of this matters at all.

When I turn around, Dom's looming over me with barely contained anger.

"Did he touch you?" he snarls.

"No."

"What did he say to you?"

I wait for the tears to come again, to feel anything at the memory of what happened in my sister's room, but they don't. There's only a quiet, simmering anger, suffocated by a blanket of apathy. I thought I was the only person who could protect the memory of her, but all I've been guarding is a hollow box.

The girl I knew never existed.

"He told me Serafina had been lying to me. She loved Russell, and she let me get married to Frederico to be with him."

When his expression softens with something like pity, I turn away, watching the cars.

He steps behind me and circles his arms around my shoulders, but instead of feeling comfort, I'm irritated.

"Can you tell me how you're feeling?" he asks.

"No," I answer sharply. I blow out a long stream of air and turn, placing a hand on Dom's arm as my ribs distend outward from the malignant anger inside. "Tonight, I want a distraction."

The city lights create a glittery illusion in his dark eyes.

When I'm finally sick of the sad, pitying look in his eyes, I decide for him, shouldering past him and setting off toward the stairs. "Let's go."

If he hesitates, I don't turn back to check as I go to our shared bedroom, standing in front of the ottoman at the foot of his bed. I count to three and turn.

I smother the relief that sparks through me at seeing he followed. He stands in the doorway, the only light comes from the half-closed door in the bathroom, giving him the ominous shadowing of an intruder in a horror film.

He said I could tell him what to do, any day of the week —time to test that.

I nod toward the cushioned seat. "Sit."

He doesn't move. "I don't think this is what you need right now. We can talk—"

"You said you'd give me a distraction if I asked for it," I snap. "Was that a lie, too?"

"I never lied to you."

I scoff a laugh. Everyone lies. I jerk my chin to the ottoman. "Then sit."

His jaw ticks, but finally, he listens, brushing past me to sit on the ottoman and clamp his hands on his knees.

I slip one leg over his and then the other until I'm straddling him, my hips already aching from our workouts and his width. When my pussy presses against his cock, through all the layers of clothes, we melt into each other—the natural reaction of two people who are attracted to each other.

Dom leans back, resting his elbows on the mattress behind him, watching me expectantly in the darkness. I can't stand the way he looks at me, like he's seeing past my skin and bones into something deeper.

I don't want him to discover me. I'm trying to get lost tonight.

"I want you to make me feel good." I flick his top shirt button, and his eyes spark with interest. "And I'll take a button off for each time you do."

This, at least, is simple. Dom knows how to follow orders, and I know perfectly well how he can please a woman. For the rest of the night, I'm not a daughter or a wife or a sister—I'm just a woman who wants to forget herself in a man.

He lets me push his hand down until his finger brushes against my slit. Like a switch is flipped, he spurs into action, stroking two fingers against me and slipping down enough to rub gently against my clit. Simple, straightforward pleasure rolls through me at his soft touch. I unbutton his top button, and he thrusts me into the air with his hips as he adjusts his seating.

Tugging my bra down, I shove my breast forward. "Suck, and I'll take off another button."

If he thinks I'm too demanding or cold, he doesn't show it as he scoffs a laugh, opens his mouth, and latches onto my breast. I groan and arch against him, filling his mouth as I work down two more buttons of his shirt while his tongue laves my nipple.

"I need another finger," I moan in his ear.

He grunts in response and slides his fingers through my slick to press into my entrance. His other hand travels eagerly along my body. Squeezing my hip, rubbing against my back, sliding down my hair. This, at least, is real—the way he makes my body feel.

"Now," I say harshly and buck my hips up to swallow his finger. I barely remember to unbutton another button. Two more to go. "Ah, *fuck*. Just like that."

He pumps into me as his hips chase the same movement beneath me, rocking me up and down like the swells of a boat on the ocean.

"I want you to work another finger into me," I hiss into his ear. "And then go hard. I'm close."

"*Reginetta*," he says in a strangled voice.

"Don't call me that," I snap. I can't meet his eye as he slows to a stop. I grind against his hand, frustrated. "Just— just Annetta tonight. Please don't stop."

He kisses against my neck, and I'm grateful I can't see his expression as he murmurs without resentment, "Whatever you say."

His confident, liquid compliance helps build the pressure mounting inside me until it reaches its tipping point. I grab his wrist, cant my hips back for more friction on my clit, and explode onto his palm.

His big, powerful arms coil around me as a hot, almost

painful orgasm tears through me. I suck, moan, and bite his neck while I ride his fingers. The strength in his arms makes me feel like nothing could ever hurt me. Once the aftershocks pass through me, I slump against his chest, heaving like I've just sprinted a mile.

Dom chuckles. "Feeling good?"

Against my languid body, his soft, muscular chest under mine is a familiar comfort. I'm tired and sated, but when a low buzz of thoughts of Serafina, of Frederico, returns to swarm into my mind, I sit up straight and unbutton his last two shirt buttons.

"Take your clothes off now." I need to be so exhausted that I'll pass out after. I can't think right now. I don't want to.

I step off of him less gracefully than I would've liked, with sex-drunk balance, but he doesn't seem to mind as he tears the stitching on his shirt to yank it off.

He stands suddenly, looming over me with a single movement as his hands reach for his belt. His pants and boxers drop, and his heavy cock springs forward, foreskin drawn back over the almost purple head. My mouth goes dry. For tonight, his body is a promise of pleasure and safety I can sink into.

His dizzying height disappears as he kneels before me. He presses his mouth against my panties, and I would've stumbled if it weren't for his hands supporting my weight.

"Can I take these off?" he murmurs, his voice muffled. He rubs his face against my pussy with a dangerous sincerity of affection, and right now, it feels so good that I don't care. I need what he's offering.

"Please."

He hooks into my panties and throws them to the floor with the same eager violence he used to tear off his shirt. But he's tender when he slides his fingers under my feet, lifting them high enough so he can kiss the ball of each foot with so much reverence that I have to grit my teeth together and look up to the ceiling so I don't cry. I'm on the cusp of demanding he stop. Then the pendulum swings back to ferality as he scoops up my panties off the ground, crushes them to his nose and mouth, and inhales deeply like it's a hit of his favorite drug.

"*Fuuuuuck*," he groans.

Heat plunges through me. I barely manage to get my bra off before he's standing and lifting me into his arms. I wrap my legs around his waist and we're kissing—fast and brutal. I can't remember ever being so hungry for a man.

"Lie on the bed," I whisper.

He groans and strokes himself once before sliding onto the bed, the mattress dipping under all that glorious weight. His muscled thighs and wide belly invite me to sit.

I crawl over him, swinging one leg over his thighs. His hands move to my hips, his thumbs tracing over the bones there. We're mismatched, but I'm glad for it now, glad for the promise of forgetting anything that isn't the burning stretch when I take him in me.

I lower myself until his thick cock's pressed between my thighs, and the point of our connection is molten hot. The tendons in Dom's neck are harsh lines before they disappear into his beard. I avoid his watchful, piercing gaze as I reach down for his length and press it against my entrance. Taking several deep breaths, I drop onto him, taking him into me faster than I have before.

Dom's fingers press against the underside of my thighs, slowing my descent.

"Hands above your head," I say.

"You'll hurt yourself."

"Should I go get in a fight with someone, instead?"

For a moment, we're locked in a silent standoff in the dim light of the bedroom.

Of all the people in my life, Dom should understand why I need this right now—why I don't want to think about all the hard decisions in my life and how little they meant to the people I loved. How little I meant.

Just as a fight sounds like a good alternative, right when I decide Dom won't listen—like always, he surprises me. He stretches his arms above his head, joining them as he grabs his right wrist with his left hand, and watches me with a taunting look behind his half-lidded eyes. That familiar thought crosses my mind—how can a person be so strong and vulnerable at the same time?

"Thank you," I murmur.

"Anything you want."

I swallow the lump in my throat and lean down to lie across his broad chest so he can't see my face as I work him into me. He's good—he's been so good to me, but it hurts to believe that right now.

I squeeze my eyes shut as I grind against him, crowding out my thoughts with the heat building inside me until I hit the right point, and the first wave of my orgasm crashes through me. His belly flexes under me, he jerks his hips up, and his cock twitches as he comes, filling me up with his hot seed.

I forget, for a moment, that tonight is supposed to be about the physical act—his desire is thrilling, it's always *sublime*. I can't help but get carried away with the heightened pleasure of our orgasms until we're both curling forward into the other, gripping and squeezing like we're fighting a rising tide to stay together.

As the pleasure recedes, I come back into myself, curling against his chest and staring at the far wall. Dom drops his arms to stroke a lazy path up my spine, the movement relaxing enough that my eyelids grow heavy.

His fingers trail down my arm and brush against my wedding ring. "You know I'm here for you."

At the edge of consciousness, I don't make a sound. He can think I'm asleep.

Whether he believes that or not, he continues talking. "When I saw you with... when I saw you in the bedroom, *crying*, I was scared. I don't ever want to lose you, Annetta."

My heart fills with misery as he squeezes me gently to his chest.

21

DOM

"Y ou ready for a break?"

Annetta's face is flushed, and her newly developed muscles glisten with a thin sheen of sweat. She drinks from her squirt bottle, the elegant line of her throat working to suck down the water. My arousal stirs.

She braces her elbows on her knees and stares up at me. "No."

I had to catch her last curl attempt, and that's the third save this session. She's exhausted.

I've already pushed her further than I would anyone else —not that I needed to. She's a fucking machine all by herself. She pushes herself like Matteo used to.

Thoughts of Turi's little brother always catch me at the strangest times, like when I'm at the deli and I can practically hear him complaining about how disgusting cut meats are, or the few occasions when I drive with the windows down and laugh to myself, thinking about how I used to be the one who always told him to roll the windows up so he wouldn't get a sore throat.

Then the Colombians cut him up into a hundred pieces,

and Turi lost it. The shit he did on that rampage earned him the fear of every man in the city. His little brother, who had somehow become my little brother over the years, fueled us both to do unspeakable shit.

Violence and revenge were our way to grieve for Matteo's death.

I cup Annetta's cheek, and she closes her eyes and leans into my palm, her breathing slowing.

After that dinner at her parents' house, she's become relentless. She pushes herself in our workouts until she can't lift her arms anymore, and Eduardo tells me that when she's not helping Valeria, she stands in the living room and shoots at targets all day long. There's only one thing on her mind when I come home—in the bed, along the stairs, against the kitchen counter.

A part of me knows I should be thrilled. She wants distraction, and I'm the perfect man to give it to her.

I've always been good at stealing attention. When Dad would get that look in his eye—like factory work with five kids and a sullen wife at home wasn't everything it was cracked up to be—that's when I'd step in, bringing him beers and joking around louder than anyone else in the house. Sometimes, that was enough for him to settle down for a few days, but usually it was a straight shot to getting the shit beat out of me, and Mom coming by to my room an hour later to silently offer me a plate of food for my troubles.

I tried following in his footsteps when I got older. I fought anyone who looked at me wrong and spent more than one night getting plastered at a bar with a stranger. That shit gets old as soon as you wake up and realize the road you're headed down is a dead end.

Annetta isn't me. She's a hell of a lot smarter than I was

at her age, and I know she'll figure it out. The real her is still there, buried deep under all the hurt she's carrying around. Sometimes, I'll manage to fuck her so thoroughly that she's too exhausted to hide herself, and I'll catch a glimpse of that connection we were building before—the one that felt like our fucking souls were touching—until she shuts down again and the only thing she lets me do for her is hold her.

"Well, you need it," I say, pushing myself to standing.

She captures my wrist with her hand, opening her eyes and zeroing in on me. "Do you want to know what I really need right now?" she asks in a suggestive tone.

"Oh, I already know." I grin despite the cold, unsettling look in her eyes. "Coffee."

WHEN SHE COMES downstairs after her shower—a quick, efficient rinse—I have her cup ready.

She won't let herself cry anymore, either, and that's the shit that worries me more than anything else.

She tips forward on her toes to kiss my cheek and takes her mug. "Did Don Salvatore say if I could leave yet?"

"Getting bored, angel?"

She looks into her cup. "A little."

"He said they're making progress. We just have to hang tight."

The Chiarelli *consigliere* has been making regular trips to New York, painting a tragic picture of a family grieving the loss of Frederico to the rest of the Mob families, especially those who are part of the Commission. Apparently, they're all falling for it. Despite Turi's spying, he can't dig up anything damning enough to take the Chiarellis down, though I suspect getting Annetta out of my penthouse isn't all that high on Turi's list of priorities. He practically sealed his wife in his home, and because she's such a little freak, she likes it.

The problem is that my wife is nothing like his. Annetta is grasping for a purpose—something outside of making me dinner every night. If she doesn't find it soon, she's gonna turn reckless.

She takes another sip of her coffee, looking at me over the rim of the cup. "If the Chiarellis were going to try something else, don't you think they would've already?"

"We've talked about this. There's no set timeline for these things. You might be waiting years."

I expect more of a fight, but she only smiles up at me and touches my arm. "I'm glad you're here to help me through this, at least."

I feel like I'm grabbing at a fish that's wriggling out of my fingers.

"What if we got you a dog for Christmas? And I've been thinking about converting the downstairs bedroom into a darkroom for your photography. You could keep busy. It wouldn't be so bad." I grin. "You might even like all this time to yourself."

She smiles back, but it doesn't reach her eyes. "Yeah. That sounds like a good idea."

Annetta stirs under the blankets as I reach over her to grab my phone off the nightstand.

"What?" I snap, answering the call. They better have a good fucking reason to wake me up at five in the morning.

Annetta murmurs something in her sleep, and I run my hand along her shoulder blades while Riccardo blathers on about some sex workers he found in a shipping container.

"I don't give a fuck," I hiss in a low voice.

Annetta's already waking up, blinking at me in the dim light. Returning to sleep is becoming an increasingly distant possibility with each passing second.

"Where's Aceto?" I ask, stroking my beard.

Riccardo reports to Aceto, so he should be waking *him* up, not me.

"That's what I'm saying, boss," Riccardo says in his mopey voice. He drops to a whisper. "The women are saying they *know* him."

Fuck me. I exhale and tug on my beard.

"I can bring them to Don Salvatore's?"

"Fuck no." Not that he could anyway. Turi's on a honeymoon to Italy right now with his little hacker wife. "Bring them here. I want to talk to them."

"On our way, boss."

The moment I hang up, Annetta sits up in the darkness, the white sheet pooling around her waist and exposing her sweet little breasts. I want to so badly to touch her, but she's got that look on her face like she's got something to say first.

"Let's hear it," I say grumpily, leaning one arm against my knee.

"Who was that?"

"Just some guests. One of my guys found some women in a warehouse. Supposedly, they recognize Aceto. They're gonna swing by, and I'm gonna talk to them."

Her dark eyes glitter in the darkness. "Let me talk to them."

"Fuck no."

"Dom."

"You ever talk to a sex worker? They're not gonna take

too kindly to some spoiled rich girl. They'll be comfortable speaking to a man—more comfortable, even."

"I'm not spoiled." She pouts adorably. "And just because they can speak to men, doesn't mean they want to. When are they going to be here?"

When she rises from the bed to pull on clothes, I'm truly fucked.

Annetta already has a few grilled cheese sandwiches sizzling in a pan by the time Riccardo brings up the two women—or the *girls*.

They must be no older than fifteen, and they must be sisters. They huddle close together, staring around my penthouse with wide eyes. Despite the snow outside, they're both wearing flip-flops and loose-fitting dresses. No visible bruises, I note with a tiny measure of relief.

"They were naked when I found them," Riccardo says in Italian.

I'm nearly vibrating with the desire to hide all of this from Annetta. I know her. This isn't the type of shit she needs to find a purpose in.

Like she can read my fucking mind, she approaches the girls with two plates of the fresh grilled cheese sandwiches.

They accept the food nervously.

The younger-looking one whispers, "*Gracias.*"

Riccardo watches the steaming, cheesy sandwiches go to the girls with a droopy frown, then turns to me. "They're from Cuba," he says in Italian. "They said some guy just pulled them off the street on their way to school and took them here."

I glance at Annetta, who looks like she's following this conversation way too closely for someone who should only know a few words in Italian.

"How long have they been in the States?"

Riccardo glances at them. "They said they woke up, some guy came and inspected them, and they traveled in a truck to the warehouse I found them in. Another guy looked them over, and then I found them."

"How'd you know they were talking about Aceto?"

"They said he had a mustache. Then I showed them his picture, and they freaked out. I don't know if he touched them or what, but they basically wouldn't talk after that."

I stroke my beard. Guess I figured out why Aceto was being weird about his warehouses when we met for lunch ages ago. This also explains why he was so *supportive* of Turi's ascension to Don—he saw the way the tide was turning, and thought he'd ingratiate himself with the new boss so he could hide this shit in plain sight.

If he's trafficking girls, he's going to be enjoying a nice, long vacation in Turi's basement. Pretty much anything goes in the Family, except the skin trade. It brings way too much heat on us. Aceto's even dumber and greedier than I thought, which is saying something when he'd sell his daughter for two shiny quarters.

"What did the man who took them look like?" Annetta asks in English.

Riccardo blinks a few times before glancing toward me for permission.

I shrug. The cat's out of the bag now.

Riccardo speaks in a low, respectful tone to Annetta, which raises him several notches in my book. Maybe I'll recommend him for a promotion after we off his capo. "They wouldn't say anything about it, *signora*. I think they're a little afraid of men right now."

I roll my eyes when Annetta shoots me an "I told you so" look.

"What are your names?" she asks the girls in a clear voice.

The younger one answers, pointing between them. "Maria. Lucia."

"Okay, Lucia. The man who took you, what did he look like?"

Lucia thinks for a few moments. "Small *barba*." She points to my beard—the word for beard in Spanish and Italian being the same, making her meaning clear.

Riccardo swears under his breath. "They speak English?"

Annetta approaches me. "Taller?" she asks, holding her hand to indicate a height taller than me. "Or shorter?"

The girls confer for a moment. Then Lucia answers in a stream of Spanish.

"Hold on," Riccardo says, and fishes out his phone for the translation app.

He has the girl repeat herself, and she tells us the man is about Riccardo's height, with green eyes and a very short beard.

Annetta frowns. She asks the girls several times through the translator, "Green eyes? Are you sure?"

I have a bad feeling when she turns to me. "I need to speak with you. Privately."

"Watch the girls," I say to Riccardo.

Upstairs in our bedroom, Annetta paces around the room like a caged tiger.

"Since when do you understand Italian?" I ask.

"Since Frederico's mom refused to speak to me in English. She thought it was embarrassing that I didn't understand."

"*What?*"

She waves me off, an urgent brightness to her face. "Dom, it's *Marco*."

The name tugs on a hazy memory. The last time I saw Frederico's younger brother was at Annetta's wedding, as I watched the whole thing unfold from a far-off distance. Marco was the best man. I remember thinking he looked like a bastard, like all of Frederico's family.

"I thought I was just going crazy, that I saw Frederico outside the church, but I think it was Marco."

"What the fuck do you mean you saw him outside the church?"

"I mean, I saw him outside the church after our wedding. I thought he was Frederico because he shaved and was wearing Frederico's clothes, but now I'm certain—it's Marco."

"Why didn't you tell me that?"

She raises an eyebrow at me. "So you could've told me I was seeing things? Like with the elevator?"

"Fuck." I groan. "Alright."

"He was always taking trips to Cuba. He"—she presses a hand to her mouth—"he used to bring me souvenirs when he came back. I never knew he was snatching girls off the street, and I never would've guessed they'd bring them as far as Chicago."

"Did they ever find out that you knew about the girls?"

"At the end, yeah."

So, the Chiarellis have more than one reason to hunt Annetta. If she knew about the girls they were trafficking, her running back to Chicago could fuck up their whole cash cow operation.

I'm going to enjoy killing off that damn family one by one.

She bites her lip and looks away from me. "Giulia told

me Frederico would never cheat on me with another Italian woman, and that I should count myself lucky that he was *only* sleeping with foreign girls."

"What?"

Her voice comes out as a near whisper. "She gave me pills to induce ovulation, and she said they were gonna use one of those girls as a surrogate if I didn't give Frederico a baby soon."

Rage burns into my chest like a hot poker through the heart. Before I can think, I grab Annetta and crush her against me.

Useless. I'm useless. I keep thinking I can fight her enemies, that I can kill anyone who wants to hurt her, but I can't undo all the shit she's had to go through. There's no protection from the past.

She mumbles against my chest, but the blood pounding in my ears is so loud that I have to draw her back to arm's length to hear her.

"We have to help them."

The girls. She's talking about the girls.

"We'll get them a hotel tonight," I promise. "I'll go have a word with Riccardo."

"No." Her voice is firm. "I mean, the rest of the girls. All the other ones who are being trafficked."

I bark out a laugh. "You can't be serious. That's gotta be hundreds of thousands of people."

"We can help some of them."

"You need to focus on yourself. How are you going to help those people when you can barely keep yourself alive?"

She pushes against my hands on her shoulders and plants her feet in a wide stance like we're about to spar. *Fuck.*

"Annetta..."

"Dom." The corner of her mouth spasms like she's

holding back tears, but her eyes are clear and dry. "I waited three months to kill Frederico after I saw him in bed with a girl. I let that go on for three goddamn months. And in the end, the only reason I did it was to save myself, so I wouldn't get pregnant. How many girls did I let get hurt because I was too scared to do anything?"

"None of this was your fault. You got him, didn't you? You did more than anyone could've asked of you."

"No. I can't lie to myself anymore. I can do something to help Maria and Lucia. *We* can help them."

She gives me a firm look that makes my heart swell and my stomach sink. "Promise me you'll get those girls the best hotel money can buy, and then promise me you'll get them home."

She's stealing a piece of my heart every time she rips another promise out of me, but I do it anyway, because *this* is the Annetta I know.

If saving the entire fucking world is what it'll take to bring her back to me, then she's going to learn I meant every word of my vows. I'm not letting her do any of this alone.

I cup the back of her neck and press forward until my forehead touches hers.

Her eyelashes flutter shut.

"I promise."

22

ANNETTA

"Wow, Mrs. Lombardi, those look real nice," Eduardo calls out from the kitchen as I step back to survey my work.

Flower petals and pine needles are scattered around three arrangements in the center of the dining table, each one designed as a mix of rustic elegance with birch twigs, roses, anemone, berries, and pinecones.

I know they're at least as good as something my sister could do on a lazy Sunday afternoon, but when I wait for a sense of satisfaction to wash over me, there's nothing. It's just a few handfuls of tiny, delicate *flowers*—existing only to look pretty and give you something to fuss over until they promptly wither and die.

At least they don't look drunk.

"Thanks, Eduardo," I say.

"You're welcome. Also, we're out of salami, Mrs. Lombardi."

I roll my eyes. "Thanks, Eduardo."

He flops onto the couch and pulls out his phone. To the soundtrack of revving motors and giggling women, I snap a picture of the arrangements and send it to Valeria.

As the last pieces of her dad's dinner celebration fall into place, we've met less and less, which suits us both just fine. I haven't wanted to chat lately, and the dark circles under Valeria's eyes are more pronounced every time she comes by to drop off groceries. Whenever I ask her about it, she yawns, claims she had another late night at work, and swears to me that she wants to keep bringing groceries, because Mom pays her well and she's saving up for a new car.

In the kitchen, I pull out the chicken I've been letting brine all day and pat its pale flesh dry with paper towels before sliding it into a stoneware baking dish. As I wash my hands with thorough, mechanical movements, I stare out at the flickering city lights cushioned against the night sky, my thoughts drifting to the same place they've been going for weeks.

Dom said he was going to make sure Maria and Lucia were getting sent home, but every day, I ask, and every day, he tells me Salvatore hasn't given him an answer yet.

Every night, he crawls into bed and tells me he won't break his promise, to give him time.

How long am I supposed to wait?

My old family stole those girls from their homes, and my new one won't send them back. Maybe I can barely keep myself alive, but here, I have some influence. I can at least try—this, at least, matters.

I've just gotten the chicken in the oven and returned to the kitchen table to tidy up before I practice shooting when the elevator door beeps.

"It's just Valeria," I say to Eduardo.

But when he sees the newcomer, he tucks his phone away and stands at attention.

"Hi, Eduardo. Can you wait in the foyer for me? I want to have a little chat with Serafina," a woman's voice says.

I freeze, trying to place the vaguely familiar voice.

"With all due respect, I was told by the don himself not to leave this penthouse until Dom comes home."

"The don knows I'm here. Feel free to call him while you wait downstairs."

It takes me a moment to place the voice, but I'm certain now.

Marisol Luporini. Don Salvatore's wife.

"I'll be right next to the elevator in the foyer."

"Thank you, Eduardo."

Eduardo disappears into the hallway, and Marisol Luporini walks around the corner, holding an armful of flower bouquets. She's a little taller than me—even taller with her black heeled boots—with dark hair secured by a black headband and a burgundy wool coat.

I consider hiding upstairs, but before I can act on it, she spots me and smiles.

"Hi there. I saw your delivery girl downstairs and thought I'd save her the trip." Marisol's heels click as she picks her way across my home gun range like it's the most natural thing in the world and drops the bouquets on my table. Her gaze ticks over the roses and eucalyptus like she's searching the fresh leaves for blight, before she looks to me. "These are quite beautiful. Are you doing all three for Aceto's celebration?"

My brain finally kicks back online, and I stand. "Valeria and I will pick just one, Mrs. Luporini. Can I get you something to eat?"

She waves her hand at me to sit. "No. I won't stay long. Salvatore doesn't like me to stay out late."

Instead of resentment, she says it with a certain amount of pride.

My thoughts must be evident on my face, because she laughs as she shrugs off her coat and sits down at the head of the table.

"It won't surprise you to hear the don is a bit of a control freak."

I settle back into my seat. Marisol picks up the snips, turns them over for inspection, grins at me, and sets them next to my hand. My pinky twitches.

"So how are you liking married life?" She turns to her bag and rustles through the contents.

"I... Dom is a good husband."

That's true, at least. He treats me kindly, listens, and makes time for me. He's funny, charming, and an enthusiastic eater in and out of the bedroom. I know he's trying so hard to be patient, but the part of me that used to be able to open up is so faded now, like the impression of an image after it's been passed over with an eraser a thousand times.

"Sounds like you couldn't be happier," Marisol says with a snort. She pulls a card-sized speaker out of her bag.

"He's a *great* husband," I correct, before considering that maybe talking to the don's wife like this isn't especially wise. When Aldo used to bring his girlfriends, wives, even his "lady friends"—which was just code for mistress—to my parents' house for dinner, Mom made sure we always spoke to them with the utmost respect. "We're just in a bit of a rough patch, Mrs. Luporini."

She switches her speaker on, and it fills the room with the sound of people chatting and clinking silverware against ceramics.

"Salvatore and I had plenty of rough patches ourselves,"

she says, without addressing the crowd noises. "I'm sure you'll come to an agreement soon enough."

I roll a fallen pine needle back and forth on the table.

"You must be wondering why I'm here."

"The thought had crossed my mind."

She lays her hand over mine, and her skin's soft and warm. Her nails are perfectly manicured and ruby red. "I was actually hoping you and I could be friends."

I blink at her a few times. "Friends?"

She nods, her dark eyes wide and childlike. She has a strange sort of fae-like beauty about her that makes me nervous, like she's going to ask me to dance or try to drown me in a lake.

"You tried sticking up for me, back at the house," she says. "You thought everyone was going to sell me out to Junior, and you fought for me, anyway. That means more to me than you could know."

Everyone? She couldn't be talking about Dom as well.

I stumble over my words to defend him. "Dom only took me out of the house because he said Salvatore would sooner cut off his arm than let harm come to you."

"Oh." She looks surprised for a moment, then smiles. "That's nice to hear. Regardless, you didn't know that, so thank you."

"Um. You're welcome."

She squeezes my hand and settles hers on her lap. Even her smile gives me the oddest sensation that she's a cat, and I'm a little bird on her windowsill.

"You know, I think you and I have a lot in common."

"Like what?"

"We're both brave women married to dangerous men."

I snort. Brave is the last word I'd use to describe myself.

Scared and pathetic, more likely, with a heavy shot of depressed.

"And we both want the same things. You want to help those poor girls, don't you?"

The pine needle shoots out from under my fingertip. I swallow. "I want to help get them home."

"Yeah. I know. Dom's been bothering Salvatore about them every day." She wrinkles her nose. "It's pretty annoying, actually."

Affection for Dom clashes with cold distrust for Marisol.

"He said when Don Salvatore got back from his trip, he'd make sure he'd send the girls home."

"Yeah, well, he made a promise he couldn't keep. They said you spoke to the girls, so you already know—they saw Aceto's face. And, unfortunately"—she draws out the word with distaste—"that's the only evidence we currently have of Aceto's involvement, so for now, we need those girls."

"What about street cameras to Aceto's warehouse?"

She scoffs. "Everything was cut. And Aceto is being very cautious about whatever he was using to talk with the Chiarellis. Which is great." She rolls her eyes. "But, there are other ways to nail him."

She reaches into her bag and, after a few moments of muttering and shuffling around, pulls out a tiny, white smart plug.

She places it on the table between us and taps it with one red nail.

"Do you know what this is?"

I stare at it without comprehension. "A smart plug?"

"That's not all. It's also a recording device. You plug this in, and it streams audio wherever you want. Easy."

I flick my gaze up to Marisol's innocently smiling face.

Does she have anything like this in *our* house?

"I have a proposition for you," Marisol says, like she doesn't know or care about my suspicion. "If you plug this little device into an outlet in Aceto's office, I'll get the girls sent home."

She watches me expectantly. Hungrily, even. It dawns on me slowly that the doorman never called her up—she let herself in.

Maybe it wasn't her soft innocence that drew Don Salvatore to her.

"So, you're not already tracking him?" I ask, if only to buy myself time to process.

"We have plenty of equipment to watch him, but it's not a perfect science. He's still figuring out a way to evade us, and I'll be honest, I'm getting a bit impatient. If he's a rat, he needs to be gotten rid of. And if he is working with your late husband's family, that's something I'd like to know now. You know the Chiarellis will be visiting Chicago next month? The whole family."

She watches me as the news settles in.

"Why?" I ask with a breathless voice. In all the time I'd lived with them, they'd only visited Chicago a handful of times, for business.

"They say it's to meet with your dad to talk about increasing his number of warehouses, but my guess is that it's to see you and confirm what they already know about your identity. They've been cautious over their phone calls and even in their homes, but no one's perfect. Giulia Chiarelli blames you for her son's death. She prays for your suffering every night."

The image of sweet, kind-faced Giulia praying for my suffering slices through my mind, but not out of surprise. She always told me you had to make your own justice in this world.

"If Aceto's really working with them, won't he hurt me if I go to his house?" I ask slowly.

"Doubtful. He needs to protect his own ass, and hurting the wife and daughter of two powerful men doesn't bode well for him. Better to let some hitman take the fall. I won't lie, though, it'll still be risky." Marisol smiles. "But like most things in life, this is worth the risk. Once Aceto figures out those two sweet girls know his face, he *will* kill them."

My stomach drops. I touch the outlet's cold metal prongs with the tips of my fingers. "But if I put this in his office, you'll send them home?"

"I will."

"When?"

She gives me a calculating look. "I'll make sure it happens the same day."

I know Maria and Lucia want to see their families. They want to return to the lives that were stolen from them. If we buy them a plane ticket and send them on their way, how much help will that be?

"Can you give them assistance if they need it?" I ask tentatively. "After you get them home?"

Marisol considers this. "I'll support any decision about them as you see fit. You've done charity work, right? I'll put you in charge of this."

Yeah, like running a cookie stand. I don't say it aloud. Being in charge for once sounds nice.

My hand closes around the smooth plastic of the smart plug. "When do I need to do this?"

"That's up to you," she says, standing and gathering her things. "But the sooner you do it, the sooner you'll be a little safer from the Chiarellis, and the sooner those poor girls are back home." She brushes invisible lint from her coat. "And, just so you know, Dom will be out for the rest of the night.

Aceto, too, though his kids are home. That shouldn't be a problem for you since you're such good friends with Valeria. Tonight could be an *auspicious* night for a visit."

She takes one last glance at the flowers on the table. "You really did a beautiful job with the arrangement. Your sister would be proud."

And then she leaves me completely alone in the house.

For one long moment, I sit there with my eyes squeezed shut. This is a small thing, isn't it? Visit my friend. Push a smart plug into an outlet.

And if I do it, Maria and Lucia go home.

Marisol could be lying. She probably is, somehow. She might not have the authority to make her offer, or there could be more conditions to this deal, but what else do I have to go on?

Aceto will be out tonight.

I've been so bitter lately. I'm impatient with Dom's promises, betrayed and heartbroken from Serafina's secrets, and angry at myself for being totally helpless and completely useless.

I roll the outlet in my hand. Maybe I can change one of those things.

It's hidden in my pocket by the time Eduardo returns to the penthouse.

We eat dinner, and I tell him I'm going to have an early night.

Upstairs, I change into jeans, a comfortable pair of sneakers, and a tight-fitting top. Then I stare at the gun in Dom's nightstand drawer.

I don't want to use it.

But I could need it.

And what have I been practicing for, if not for this?

The girls' faces flash in my mind. They'd need me to

take it. I take the weapon and its holster and shove it in the front of my jeans like I've seen Dom do. And then I throw a big sweater over that and a coat for good measure.

I glance at my phone. The last message I sent to Dom was about dinner. He responded a moment later.

DOM

Goddamn angel, I'm dying to get home for a taste

Guilt prickles my skin, but it doesn't stop me from taking Dom's keys and standing next to the second-floor elevator.

Eduardo has his show playing loudly in the living room downstairs. Maybe he won't hear the elevator. I press the call button, waiting for several long seconds with my lungs frozen, straining my ears to pick up any sound. Guilt burns into my chest. Dom will punish Eduardo if I leave without telling anyone.

I'll be back before they know. Dom will understand.

The doors open with a soft beep. When I don't hear any movement downstairs, I step inside and descend.

23

ANNETTA

I DRIVE EXACTLY at the speed limit, just like Dad and Rafa do. Even so, when I stop next to a cop at a red light, anxiety bleeds warmth from my fingertips until the light turns green again.

No one's called or texted me except for an unknown number, which I assume was Marisol, because she sent me Aceto's address and a cryptic smiley face.

That woman has a few screws loose.

Aceto's house isn't so far from my parents' neighborhood. He lives in a slender three-story building with a half dozen well-lit windows and what looks like a garden on the roof, though it's hard to tell against the darkening sky.

I park on the street and drum against the steering wheel for a few moments.

My palms are sweaty and my heart is pounding, but I unclip my seatbelt and walk silently up to the house. The gun digs into my belly as I knock on the front door. Out of the corner of my eye, two old men walk their mini Schnauzer along the sidewalk. I wipe my palms against my jeans and exhale little white clouds into the chilly air.

Just when I start to seriously regret not calling Valeria ahead of time, the front door opens.

It's Valeria.

And she has a black eye.

She's done a good job of covering it with her makeup, but there's a bright red patch on the white of her eye that can't be hidden, even with her hair pushed forward against her face.

"Serafina? What are you doing here?" she whispers. She raises a hand self-consciously to her right eye, but corrects the movement at the last second and traces a strand of hair around her ear.

All of my grim determination flees at the sight of my friend. "What happened to your eye?"

She blanches. "You need to go. My dad isn't here and—"

"Valeria, who's at the door?" a young man's voice calls from behind her.

Her brother steps into view. He gives me a once-over and smiles. "Well, hello, Serafina."

I've never spoken to Valeria's brother, but I've seen him at family events, and he's hung out with Carlo a few times. He's got a cruel glint to his eye that I don't trust. His black hair is perfectly coiffed with not a single hair out of place, and his button-up and trousers look like they're freshly ironed.

"Hello, Stefano."

"Come in. You missed dinner, but Valeria and I were just about to enjoy a smoke."

Valeria glances toward him with a guarded look.

"I was hoping to work on the dinner plans with Valeria tonight," I say.

Stefano's smile falters. He places a hand on my upper back and shuts the front door behind me.

"Aw, come on," he says. "The Serafina I know would never say no to a smoke."

The effect is like a fist to the gut. Stefano guides me through the living room to the first set of stairs. We pass by a friend of his, a portly guy I haven't seen before. He leers at me and Valeria over his phone in his cushy armchair as we pass.

Stefano claps his shoulder. "Sit tight, Lasso. We'll be right back."

Out of the corner of my eye, I can see Lasso watching us until we move up the staircase.

Acrylic paintings of landscapes, and not a single family portrait, press in on us from both walls in the narrow stairwell. Valeria bows her head with her shoulders pulled in as Stefano leads us between a massive stone coffee table and a leather couch. Behind the sofa is a door, opened just a crack, and there's a glimpse of dark wood furniture inside that could be their dad's office.

Stefano slides open the glass door to the balcony.

"Where's your husband, Serafina? I'm surprised he'd let a girl like you walk around all by herself."

"He's very progressive."

At this, Stefano laughs, a sharp sound that makes Valeria flinch imperceptibly at my side.

"Ladies first," he says with an easy grin.

The balcony is intimate, with string lights and a few potted junipers around the perimeter, each with a little fleece blanket tucked around its base. Exhaling a great white plume of warm air, Stefano slips into a coat hanging by the back door and swipes a pack of cigarettes off one of the outdoor tables.

Valeria also wraps herself in an oversized coat, and her

legs press together for warmth. She studies me from the other side of the balcony.

"I'm sure that husband of yours won't mind, seeing as how he's so progressive," Stefano says with a wink as he passes me a cigarette. When I don't immediately grab it, he wiggles it in my direction. "Your favorite."

Despite the cold, my thick coat and the cocktail of nerves in my belly are melting me. My hair sticks to the back of my neck with sweat. I need to find Aceto's office and plant this before he gets home or before Dom finds out where I am. And where the fuck did Valeria get her black eye from?

I take the cigarette from him. Was this really Serafina's favorite?

He cups his hand over his mouth, lights his cigarette, and steps forward to light mine.

"It's been a while, hasn't it?" he asks, squinting one eye against the cigarette smoke. "You still 'friends' with Russell? Probably not, since I heard he's still walking around with his balls attached."

I hold the slender cigarette between my fingers but make no move to raise it.

Stefano glances down and frowns. "Smoke the damn cigarette, *Serafina*." He chuckles darkly. "You're making me feel like I hardly know you."

My throat goes dry, and I lift the cigarette to my mouth. Carlo let me try one of his once. I can do this.

My lips touch the paper wrapper. I inhale, tasting ash.

And I *cough*. Violently, in wracking gunshot bursts. It's more intense than I remember, and the more I try to stifle the coughing, the worse it gets.

Valeria rushes to my side, patting my back. When I

finally stand, eyes watering, I meet Stefano's grinning expression.

"I think I'm done here," he says and crushes his cigarette into a nearby smoke tray. "You ladies enjoy your time together."

Valeria waits until he walks out and starts back down the stairs to hiss at me, "What are you doing? You shouldn't have come here."

The truth presses at my tongue, desperate to be free.

"Valeria," I say, dropping my cigarette into the tray.

She glances from the cigarette to me, before her eyes go wide. "Absolutely no way."

A world of meaning passes between our shared look.

She knows I'm not Serafina.

I move slowly, like you would in front of a wounded animal. "Valeria..."

She takes me by the shoulders, her gaze flicking back and forth between my eyes. "You aren't her, are you?"

I close my eyes for a moment. I shake my head.

"Why—"

"I can't explain right now. I promise you, it's for a good reason, but I need you to trust me. Please. I promise I'll explain everything when I can."

She continues looking between my eyes, her brows pinched together in worry, until she seems to accept what's happening as she stands tall.

"Okay." A pause. "Just tell me. Is it because of Dom? Is he hurting you?"

My heart warms and breaks for her at the same time. "Dom is wonderful."

And the girl with the black eye sighs with relief. "That's good to hear. He scares me."

I laugh. "I think *I* scare *him*."

Valeria smiles, then glances behind her. "I think my brother knows, too."

"If he didn't before, he does now."

"Why are you here? Was it really to work on the dinner plans?"

I shake my head. "I can't tell you why I'm here either. It's best you don't know, but I need to know where your dad's office is."

I half expect her to object, to rightfully deny my entry into her family's home. But she only looks behind her again. "You have to be silent or Stefano will come back upstairs."

I take her hand in mine. "Thank you."

She grabs my shoulder and pulls me into a quick, fierce, perfect hug. Then she slides the glass door open and points to the room I noted earlier with the wood furniture. I tiptoe across the carpet while she stands guard outside the door.

The inside of Aceto's office is small and dark, with one lamp lighting up the far corner. Tall, heavy bookcases line one wall, and when I take a step closer to scan the titles, they're all books about business or ancient Roman history. I suppress the urge to roll my eyes as I creep further inside.

There's one outlet behind his desk, but it's too accessible and probably one he uses regularly. There's got to be an outlet behind one of those bookcases, but they're so heavy and close to the wall, I don't think I could fit my arm behind any of them.

A dark brown wine cabinet winks at me from one corner of the room. I creep toward it, crouch down, and peer along the wall. My phone buzzes in my pocket as I spot the glimmer of white plastic behind the cabinet.

I slide my open palm against the wall, feeling blindly for the outlet until my fingertips brush against the open socket. One steady push tells me I won't be able to move the cabinet, at least not without moving the dozens of alcohol bottles and glass cups on top.

I glance back at the door of the room where Valeria has her gaze fixed on the stairway, her back turned to me.

"Val," Stefano barks from below, startling me and making my blood run cold. "Bring me the good whiskey!"

"Coming!" she calls back. She approaches me, but pretends she doesn't see me as she reaches for a bottle of whiskey.

"Hurry," she whispers and makes her way downstairs with the bottle.

I'm completely exposed without her as I pinch the smart plug between my forefinger and middle finger, guiding it toward the outlet. My phone buzzes again and again against my ass. I just hope it's not Dom getting home and realizing I'm not there, because whatever he does won't be good for anyone.

The plug slips from my fingers once, and I swear a blue streak in my head as I search for it among the dust bunnies, capture it, and bring it back up to the outlet.

Bzzz.

Bzzz.

My heart's pounding so hard, I might die of fright before I manage to do anything.

I catch the edge of the outlet with the prongs of the plug and push down with enough force to press it into place. The glasses on the cabinet tinkle, but nothing falls over.

I scrape my arm against the cabinet as I jerk my hand out from that gap and stand. No one's come upstairs yet, thank God. I walk out into the waiting room, wipe my sweaty hands against my jeans, and pull out my phone.

A missed call from Marisol and a few texts.

C is on his way

10 minutes

Leave now

C? My fingertips are numb. Aceto?

I approach the stairwell, but when I hear footsteps stomping up, I back away. They sound heavy, nothing like Valeria's silent tread, and there are two sets. I spin around and dart to the second stairwell to the last floor of the house, creeping up the steps as silently as I can.

"Serafina," Stefano calls out. "Come downstairs. We're taking shots."

I pause at the top of the steps, my hand clasped over my mouth so he can't hear my wild breathing.

"Serafina?"

I don't move a single muscle.

"Fucking bitch," he mutters. "Bring her down."

"On it," Lasso says.

On the last floor, I race past the leather furniture to a glass door leading to a large balcony outside. I slip outside and tuck myself next to a storage shed, listening for Lasso.

If he catches me up here, I'll pretend I came out to smoke another cigarette. Maybe I can find a fire escape before he does. I scan the edge of the roof for a ladder. The memory of scaling down my parents' house on a ladder to go to that bar on my eighteenth birthday bursts into my mind. Serafina held the top of the ladder so I wouldn't fall, even as she begged me not to go.

For several long seconds, I can barely hear anything above the wild beating of my heart. I turn my head to peek for Lasso.

He's right next to me.

I jerk back, stifling a scream as he throws a hand out and slaps my head like a fly against the plastic sliding of the storage shed.

I stumble backward as he laughs. A gush of heat drips from my nose, and I taste blood.

"You trying to run?" He shoves me.

My back crashes against the table behind me, and I scream out as the table tips. I go with it, the night sky careening over my head.

I land hard on my back, all the air punching out of my lungs, and I groan.

"You think we wouldn't know who you are?" Lasso asks from behind the table. "Aceto's telling everyone the truth."

My head is pounding, but I force myself to my knees, reaching for my belly.

"I can't believe you'd be so fucking stupid as to come here," he says with a disbelieving laugh. "But I'm not surprised when Valeria's a fucking dumb—"

He chokes on his last word as I whip my gun around to point at his face.

After all of my practice with Dom, the shape and weight of the gun in my hand are as familiar as a lover's body.

Lasso's face reddens. His jaw clenches, and his hands flex. He chokes out a laugh. "Stefano didn't say you'd have a gun."

I rise to my feet using just my leg strength and flexibility, another gift from Dom's workouts. "Who gave Valeria her black eye?"

He gives me a look of genuine confusion. "What the fuck are you talking about?"

I spit blood onto the cement. "Was it Stefano or their dad?"

My phone buzzes with a call. Lasso tilts his head. "You gonna get that?"

Aceto will be here any minute. I'm running out of time.

"If you move, I'll shoot you."

Shit, he's right in front of the door.

I wave the gun. "Walk to the edge of the balcony."

He gives me an obtuse look. "Well, which is it? Stay still or move?"

My phone buzzes in my pocket.

"Move!" I shout.

He scoffs and takes a few steps back. With my gun trained on his face, I open the glass door and shut it, locking it from the inside. He scowls at me through the glass.

I hold the gun close to my chest and race downstairs.

When I get to the first floor, I crash into Valeria and swallow a scream.

She looks horrified. "Your face!"

"I gotta go," I say, wrenching on her arm. "Come with me. I can't leave you here."

She twists out of my grip. "Go! I'm fine. Just go."

She runs upstairs before I can grab her. I hesitate for a split second until I hear Stefano cursing upstairs, then I dash out the front door and throw myself down the porch steps toward my car.

The keys slip in my hand over and over until I finally shove them in, start the car, and drive off, tires squealing.

24

DOM

I HAD A WHOLE THING PLANNED. I'd sit in the living room with Eduardo standing guard and wait for her to come in, soft and contrite.

But I forget all of that when Annetta steps into the penthouse with blood on her face.

I leap up from the couch, ripping past Eduardo, and cup her face in my hands. Blood is smeared under her nose, and the right side of her face is scraped. Did she get in a fight?

I'm going to have to kill someone tonight.

Her first thought, annoyingly, is not for me but for Eduardo.

"What happened?" she asks, pushing against my hands.

Eduardo's mouth is set in a grim line as he cradles a stained bandage around his left hand. He silently looks at me. He's smart enough to let me answer.

"He failed in his duties."

Understanding dawns in her eyes before she hardens her face into a furious expression. "What did you do?"

"What did *you* do?"

Of course, I know exactly what she did. I had a nice, long

275

chat with Turi about his wife's decisions, which fell on deaf ears. He'll never accept criticism of his *perfect* wife.

"I went out," she says.

"Go home, Eduardo," I grit out. "Mommy and Daddy need to have a little chat."

"Yes, sir." Eduardo exhales, giving us a wide berth as he runs to the elevator.

"What happened to his hand?" Annetta snaps once the elevator doors shut behind her.

I'm torn between grabbing her by the shoulders and shaking her until some sense falls into that pretty head of hers and cradling her against my chest and making her swear never to leave without telling me again.

So, I act like a jackass instead.

"*You* happened. You left without telling anyone except your new best friend, Marisol. When I came home to a guard who had no idea you had left, I had to take matters into my own hands."

"What does *that* mean?" she asks with deadly slowness.

"That means I cut off two of his fingers. One for each hour you were missing."

Which I know she'll disagree with, but I was incredibly generous. If he's smart, he'll run his ass to the Family doctor and get them sewn back on, and if not, I hope he's at least smart enough to have learned his lesson. I don't give a shit if she cuts into the glass window like a goddamn international spy and belays down the side of the apartment building—there's no fucking excuse for letting her out of his sight.

"That's horrible."

I give her my most roguish grin, the kind that usually has men clutching their rosaries and whispering their final prayers. Blood smudges my hand as I cup her face in my palms, and she glares up at me without blinking or pulling away.

I've always liked that she's never been afraid of me, but right now, I could use a little fear. She needs to understand she can never do this again—that she can't make me go through this. How the fuck will I ever be able to focus if I have to worry that she's going to run out of the penthouse and get herself hurt at any moment?

"Who the fuck did this to you?" I ask as softly as I can while my wife's blood mars my skin.

"It doesn't matter."

"It matters to me." When she doesn't give me an answer, I lower myself until we're almost eye level. "Annetta, if you don't tell me, I'm going to kill everyone in that house. I need a name, angel."

Her eyelashes flutter.

"Lasso," she breathes.

I file that name away. I know a Lasso who hangs out with Aceto's kid. I'm about to dump a can of gasoline on him and burn that little shit alive.

Annetta grips my wrists like she's reading my mind. "Dom, you shouldn't have done that with Eduardo. He didn't deserve that."

"And you shouldn't have gone to Aceto's." I meet her gaze so she knows I mean every word. "But you leave the house, and your lapdog might shit on the rug."

She scowls, twisting her face to wipe her blood on my palm like she's a cult leader marking me as her disciple. Heat travels south. I crowd her, inhaling her sweet shampoo and the metallic scent of her blood. My neck throbs. For all her baked bread and soft smiles, this is the woman who bit me hard enough to leave a scar.

"I'm not responsible for what you do when I leave," she

murmurs defiantly. She looks so fucking beautiful with her wild, golden hair framing her furious gaze.

Anticipation thrums through me, but for what? A fight?

I don't want to fight with her. I want her safe, alive, and happy. The rest doesn't matter.

I cup her waist, my thumb brushing against the bulge of her holster tucked in her pants, and drag us together until our bodies melt together. I rest my cheek on the top of her head.

"Yeah, I know." I glance at our homemade gun range, where she's worked on her shooting more than I've seen anyone practice. "Do you feel better at least?"

Finally, her arms come to circle my waist. Her head rests against my chest. "I do."

"Good."

WHEN I LEAVE the bedroom hours later, Annetta's asleep in a nest of bedsheets.

Turi had texted back to let me know the girls Annetta risked her life for were already at the airport to head home. I guess Marisol isn't a total piece of shit.

Just outside the bedroom door, Rafa pulls a chair over and sits down. He sets his phone and gun in his lap and glances at me over his glasses.

"You got this?" I ask.

"Yeah." His attention is already back to the door. "Have fun."

I pass by another of Turi's men—Camillo—in the apartment lobby. Mauro's stationed outside on the street. I'm not taking any more risks this time.

In my truck, I call up Turi. He answers on the first ring.

"Dom," he says as a greeting.

I stab the keys into the ignition. "Don't *Dom* me. Is Aceto still at his house?"

"Yes."

"Is he planning to hurt Annetta?"

"Not that I know of. He's upset his son threatened her. He knows we're going to be watching him now."

I roll my eyes. "Alright. What about Lasso? Annetta said he's the fuck that hit her."

"If Lasso has a connection to the Chiarellis, he's better off alive—"

"I don't give a fuck, Turi. Maybe you should have thought of that when your wife put *my* wife's life at risk."

"She can make her own decisions."

It's not clear whose wife he's talking about, but I don't give a shit.

"I'm sick of her life being constantly in danger."

"I understand." And it fucking pisses me off that he does. "I'm working on it."

The bastard's voice barely rises. Salvatore Luporini and his perfect fucking blood pressure.

"By going on double-dates with all the capos to find a sweetheart for your brother?"

Ever since his half-brother Nico moved into town, he's been way too focused on finding him a girlfriend instead of shit that actually matters.

"Securing a marriage between Nico and one of our women gives us more security with the Commission, especially if the Chiarellis move against us."

"I don't give a fuck about the Commission! How many hoops do we have to throw ourselves through for their precious approval? When Marisol was under threat, I helped you to kill our fucking don. When Matteo—"

"*Don't.*"

I'm heaving like I've run a mile.

Matteo. He might not be here, but his memory binds Turi and me together like an invisible net.

"I'm your brother too," I finally say. "And she's my wife."

After a heavy silence, Turi exhales, long and slow. "He's getting drunk at the Pink Palace."

THE BOUNCER at Pink Palace is smart enough to let me in without fuss. The interior of the club is one long room, a single floor with two exits and four stages, and I spot Lasso immediately. He's in a circle of friends while a pair of run-down-looking strippers make out in front of them. Even from here, I can tell he's drunk. That's the problem with these fucking wannabes. They all think this lifestyle is drugs and pussy, but that's the shit that catches up with them the quickest. The smart ones know this lifestyle demands you live like a monk.

I stride up to Lasso's little group of friends. One of them, a man with more neck than chin, spots me first, his eyes growing comically wide. Beer sloshes over his hand as he slaps Lasso's back, who shoves him away to lean in toward the strippers.

I hook Lasso from under the shoulders and drag him over the top of his chair, and the club erupts into chaos. The women scream and run away as the men in Lasso's group turn tail. Not a single one of them lifts a finger for their buddy as he fights and squirms in my hands like a rabbit on a snare.

I haul the idiot kicking and screaming into one of the backrooms. Guess he's getting the VIP experience tonight.

I throw him inside, grab a stained purple chair, and shove it under the door handle. He reaches for a trash can and misses, throwing up on the carpet at my feet.

Fucking great.

"What... the... *fuck*," he says in between retching sounds.

"So you like beating up women?" I walk up and kick him in the dick like I'm launching a soccer ball.

Lasso screams, high-pitched and pathetic. His drunken eyes slide from the ground to me.

"No," he groans. His face is turning all sorts of interesting shades of red and green.

I aim and stomp on his hand. Was it the one he touched Annetta with? I kick his other hand for good measure, and he screams out.

"You like seeing a woman with a bloody nose, is that right?"

He shows his first glimmer of intelligence by covering his face with his broken hands as he shakes his head.

I do the unexpected thing and squat down in front of him.

"You know who Serafina is, don't you?"

He peeks at me through his fingers and shakes his head.

I cock my head and suck in air through my teeth. "I think you do. You know, she named you. Said you were the one who fucked up her face. I happen to like her face just the way it is."

His eyes fill with tears. "Please. I was... I was just following orders. Stefano told me to grab her. His dad told him. She-she's not who she says she is. She's the other twin. The bad one—"

He chokes and scrambles back as I pull out my knife from my leg holster. "That's where you're wrong. Cause you see, my wife? She's a fucking angel."

"WHEN CAN I GO AFTER ACETO?" I ask Turi over the phone.

I drive with the windows down to air out the car after my quick stop at Aceto's house. He's not going to like the little present I left on his front porch. Most of the blood washed right off, but I'll have to take a stain remover to my T-shirt later.

Turi's silent on the other end, which means he's thinking. That, or finger fucking Marisol. Those fucking idiots can't keep their hands off each other.

"Once he gives us something damning about the Chiarellis."

"Or I could just pop down to Florida and kill them all now."

"Don't. I have too much on my plate right now. I'm working with Ottavio," he spits out his dad's name, "to choose a suitable replacement for the Chiarellis. They've kept the peace for now. We need a little more time."

I squeeze the steering wheel. "So we can whack our don for your girl, but I have to wait for mine to get murdered before I'm allowed to raise a finger?"

He sighs, and I imagine him squeezing the bridge of his nose. "Use whatever resources you see fit to keep her safe. I want to try diplomacy first. If that doesn't work, we'll act."

Turi and I both know history repeats itself. If he doesn't act in time to keep my wife safe, he won't be happy with the results.

Instead of saying that, I tell him in a dry voice, "Sure, boss."

25

ANNETTA

Dom wakes me up with a gentle shake of my shoulders. "Let's go, angel."

I blink slowly at his shadowy features. "What time is it?"

"Four in the morning. I got coffee for you. Come on."

I reach out, my fingertips brushing against the fur lining of his coat. "Did you go out?"

The last thing I remember was falling asleep on top of him after we had sex.

He thrusts a pair of jeans into my hands in response.

We're going out of the penthouse? This can't be good, but the possibility of going somewhere new has me slipping into my clothes without argument. Bleary-eyed, I follow Dom as he leads us to the kitchen, presses a warm travel mug of coffee into my hands, and takes us to the parking garage, where the frigid night air snaps my mind into focus.

I have a sneaking suspicion that he went out to hurt Lasso. He might have even killed him. As I start up the SUV, I wait to feel a sense of injustice at what Dom could have done.

Lasso was shitty, but did he deserve to die?

Dom feeds me directions through the nearly empty streets to Lake Shore Drive. The long highway skirts the city's edge, bathed in bright light from skyscrapers along one side, and on the other, a yawning view of the vast, dark lake. The inky depths strum at my awareness as I drive along the scenic route.

Frederico's open mouth.

Lake water rushing inside.

His look of *outrage*, and the deep, sure pleasure at what I'd done all flood through me.

I'm not responsible for what Dom may or may not have done, but I won't fault him if he did it. Sometimes you have to make your own justice in this world.

I've figured out where we're headed well before I see Cousin Red next to the open gates of Graceland Cemetery. Dom nods in his direction as I pull into the entrance and park in the cemetery's tiny, empty parking lot.

"Come with me." Dom grabs his coffee, stepping outside with a blast of cold air, and slamming the door behind him.

The only sounds in the empty cabin are faint metallic pops and pings as the car cools. I don't move from my seat, fixing my gaze on the patch of darkness under the small stone awning for visitors up ahead. Tombstones line the walking path in my peripheral vision just outside the windows.

Whatever relief I felt at getting Maria and Lucia home ices over in this place. Somewhere, Serafina's body is buried in one of those graves.

I take a deep breath in the stuffy, dead air of the car cabin.

The door swings open next to me.

"You coming?" Dom rumbles.

"No." I reach for my mug and sip my coffee, wishing I could be as unaffected as I sound.

He chuckles next to me. "Should I carry you out?"

I clench my jaw. "I don't want you to."

I don't care if he's bigger and stronger than me. He can yank me out of the driver's seat and march me through the cemetery until I stand at my sister's frost-covered grave, but he can't make me do anything I don't want to. I'll stand there in the darkness for hours if I have to.

Everyone seems to think Serafina's soul is there, buried in the dirt, lonely and waiting for visitors, but I already know what I'll find when I go there.

Nothing. She's gone. That's it, and no amount of begging, bargaining, or rage will bring her back. I'm the only person in my world who seems to understand that.

Dom sets his coffee cup on the hood of the SUV with a *clink*. He lowers himself until the heat of him brushes against my face, and pine and smoke fill the air. "You need to forgive her."

I snap my head toward him—our faces are inches apart. His chocolate-colored eyes are too kind in the soft glow of the car's interior lights. I wish he'd be angry. For all his protection, all his promises, all of his rage at the other people who've hurt me, I want him to be *angry* for me, just for this, so I don't have to carry all of it on my own.

"She's *dead*. I can't give forgiveness to a dead person."

I can't make myself like everyone else, who insists her spirit is floating around us, invisible and present as oxygen. She's not here. The emperor isn't wearing clothes. The house is empty, the lights are off.

"It's not about her," Dom murmurs. "It's about you. You're not letting yourself process what happened, and you're getting stuck."

I glare at the shadowed benches covered by the awning. This is the place where people go to rest after they've visited their dead.

"I processed it just fine. My family and I put too much pressure on my sister to be the perfect daughter, and instead of talking to me or any of us, she bottled up all her feelings and turned to drugs and a secret boyfriend for escape. And then she let me get married to Frederico in her place, where I went through hell for three years, while she played Romeo and Juliet with Russell. And in all of our phone calls and my visits home, she lied to me every day, because she didn't trust me enough to tell me the truth. I wasn't important enough for that. I was expendable."

"She loved you."

"Not enough to inconvenience herself. Not more than she loved herself, or *Russell*."

Dom straightens, the hood of the car bisecting his neck so that I lose sight of his face. He sips from his coffee and rests his body against the frame of the car, making it tilt in his direction. "You remember what I told your sister at the stadium? That I wouldn't let any harm come to her? You wanna know what she told me?"

I grit my teeth and squeeze my coffee cup. I don't want to know. I'm sick of picking up the pieces of myself and trying to glue them back together just to get shattered again. I'm not strong enough to keep doing this.

Dom's steady voice continues from just out of sight. "She thought she was getting married to Aldo soon, and she knew that meant she had an expiration date hanging over her head, but instead of telling me thanks or asking me to help get her out of her marriage, she got mad. Or, you know, her version of mad, where she starts box breathing."

I snort despite myself. She was always giving me and

Carlo breathing tips, like if we just breathed in a specific timing or blew pretend bubbles in the air, we could inhale and exhale our way to a perfect life.

"She told me if there was anyone to keep out of harm's way, it was you. She thought she was going to die, and she told me to worry about you instead."

My hold on my coffee cup loosens. "Why would she say that? I never told her anything about Frederico."

"Probably because she was paying attention to you. She loved you."

I scoff bitterly. "Not enough to tell me the truth."

"Sometimes people feel like they have a good reason for lying." Dom sets his cup on the hood of the car and bends down to smirk at the side of my face. "Sometimes, even to people they love."

My breath catches in my throat, and I glance at him. He grins.

I groan and drop my head against the car seat. Tears prick my eyes.

I lied to Dom, didn't I? I told him I was my sister, and I forced him into a marriage that put his life at risk. He didn't ever hold it against me. He trusted me, protected me, *loved* me. And this evening, I left the penthouse without telling him—again—because I didn't trust him to let me go otherwise.

Is Dom's love so true that he can still give me kindness and affection despite my lying and betrayals? Does he forgive me every time I sin against him? Is that love? Forgiving someone, no matter what they do?

No.

That's wrong, I know. Some sins are too big to forgive. But Serafina's?

I blink at the tears in my eyes, blurring everything

around me into dark shapes. I thought I finally had a handle on crying, but that seems to be the one guarantee in my life —always more tears in reserve.

Serafina didn't lie to hurt me. She was just a girl with a broken support system, doing her best to stay afloat.

I don't need to forgive her. There's nothing to forgive. She was looking for relief and love, and she didn't mean to cause any pain.

I know. I just wish I could've done more to make her feel less lonely. I wish I could've taken some of her hurt.

I take a deep, shuddering breath and whisper my confession. "I want to move forward."

"Sometimes you can't move forward without dealing with the past."

I roll my head along the seat to look at him, a bitter smile playing at the corners of my mouth. "You get that off a fortune cookie?"

His grin is as beautiful as the sun. "Nah. Just made a lot of mistakes over the years."

"Like what?"

"Well, for one, letting you get married to another man." He leans closer to me.

My heart thumps in my chest.

He was just a familiar face then. A man I'd shared a single kiss with. I smile, imagining him bursting into my wedding to throw me over his shoulder and ride off into the sunset.

It would've been chaos.

It would've been amazing.

"Do you ever think about that kiss outside your parents' house?" he asks in a low voice.

"All the time."

He huffs a laugh like my answer surprises him. And then

—there it is again, that look he's giving me, the one he's given me before, like he's seeing me as stronger, braver, more loving. Like he's seeing a version of me only he can see.

"I'm sorry for leaving," I whisper, my heart rate spiking.

"You came back," he says easily.

He leans in to kiss me.

When his lips press against mine and my body melts into his, I understand.

Forgiveness isn't love. It's *peace*. And it's not something I give to another person, it's for me, and maybe for Dom, too, the version of myself that he deserves, the one we both deserve.

Maybe I didn't know all Serafina's secrets, but I knew who she was, and I know the love we shared was important and real.

And as I kiss my husband in the empty stillness of the cemetery, I allow myself to let go of some of the pain, and I let myself make room for something new.

26

ANNETTA

A MONTH PASSES QUICKLY. I look out over the black, frost-kissed waters of Lake Michigan. Delicate piano notes trickle out of the *Spirit of Serenity*, broken up by bursts of laughter.

A few partygoers I vaguely recognize from other family events stumble past us, rosy-cheeked from the winter air and huddled together. The men in the group nod respectfully to Dom as they pass onto the massive party yacht.

"We don't have to do this," Dom murmurs.

I break my gaze from the dark waters and turn to him. Tonight, he let me tame his hair into a half-up style, and he's dressed up in an all-black three-piece suit with a light blue pocket square. There are a few buttons undone to reveal a tantalizing window of tattoos and chest hair.

Next to him, I feel like a fraud.

I'm wrapped in a beige wool coat, a pink sheath dress with a modest neckline, and conservative beige heels. My makeup is made to look completely natural, and my nails are long and blush pink. The tip of my nose aches, a lovely winter reminder of my nose job. My hair's beaten into a shimmering, golden waterfall. Only one thing would betray my picture-perfect image if anyone thought to look—the gun I'm carrying in my purse.

"Mom would be upset," I say.

She was very clear that this party would be of utmost importance in convincing the rest of the family that I was Serafina and not a threat to anyone. I've done everything I can to keep up with that ruse, subjecting myself to another "spa day" to look like my sister and perfecting the floral arrangements for their delivery.

He slips his cold fingers into the warmth at the nape of my neck. "You always listen to your Mom?"

"Salvatore would be mad."

Don Salvatore agreed that acceptance from our family would undercut the Chiarellis' beliefs about my identity and paint them as blood-hungry paranoids.

"Fuck Salvatore."

I can't help the smile that creeps across my face as I tuck myself into his arms. "He won't like hearing you say that."

Dom's grin is wide and infectious. "*Fuck. Salvatore.*"

A low voice cuts in. "I'd prefer you didn't."

Dom and I look up from our embrace.

Salvatore watches us from a few feet away without any emotion in his amber eyes, and Marisol smirks at us from his side. She's stunning tonight in a red gown that clings to her curves underneath her thick black coat. Salvatore looks like a mortician next to her in his all-black suit.

Another man, tall and lean with a crop of dark hair, lurks a few steps behind them. He looks so completely out of place with his hoodie, oversized bomber jacket, and ripped jeans that I reach for my purse. He glances toward me with a flicker of interest, his eyes the same intense amber as Don Salvatore's.

"Serafina, this is my half-brother, Nico Matassa," Salvatore says without affection.

"You're late." Dom shifts his body between me and Nico.

Nico smirks.

"We had a small change in plans," Salvatore says.

As if on cue, Marisol reaches out for me. "I heard lemon tarts are on the menu."

Salvatore turns his head to the side to speak to his half-brother. "Go with them."

Nico makes no sign that he heard, but when Marisol takes my hand and pulls me toward the yacht, he trails behind.

"See you inside," I call out to Dom.

He frowns at Marisol's back as we walk away.

She leads me up the steps of the concrete dock to the yacht, her arm hooked around mine, and leans in to murmur in my ear, "They found more women the other night. Another warehouse."

Her gentle tug is the only thing that keeps me from completely stopping in my tracks.

Marisol waves off the pale bald man with a headpiece on the deck. "They're with me," she says smugly and pulls me forward.

Apparently, the man recognizes Marisol by sight, because he lets us and Nico through without a problem.

As I step forward, I look down into the dark gap between the boat and the deck. I can just barely make out the glint of the icy water far below, and for one heart-stopping moment, an intrusive thought—*what if I slip?*—enters my mind before Marisol guides me fully onto the deck.

A server appears from the small crowd of people and extends a tray of champagne to her.

She waves him off. "Just orange juice, please, and a plate of those lemon tarts."

A tendon jumps out in his sharp jaw, but he bows his head respectfully and retreats.

Marisol pulls me under one of the space heaters while Nico watches us from the yacht's edge, leaning carelessly against the railing. Just one push and he'd go tumbling into the water.

I turn away from him. Most of the guests are milling around the inside of the first deck salon, but a few are huddled around the space heaters, smoking cigarettes or cigars.

Behind Marisol, the city twinkles and glitters like thousands of diamonds. She's talking, but it's the lake that takes hold of me, stretching out endlessly into a pitch-black horizon. Is it my imagination, or is it lapping higher against the hull of the boat than I first thought?

"What do you think?" Marisol asks.

I blink a few times, dragging my attention back to her.

The other women they'd found—she wanted to know if I could help them. She said they didn't want plane tickets back home. They want to stay here, but they'll need help finding jobs and housing.

"Why do you want *my* help?"

"Because I trust you," she says with a playful smile.

I can't tell if she's being sarcastic or trying to manipulate me, but in either case, I couldn't possibly accept what she's offering, not when I almost got myself killed trying to help Maria and Lucia.

"I don't think it'd be fair to those women. I don't know what their needs are or how to help them. Don't you have someone more qualified?"

"More qualified? Sure."

The server returns with a flute of orange juice and a small plate of lemon tarts, and she murmurs thanks, sipping from the juice.

She continues. "But I thought you cared about this? Helping others and all that. Without someone like you, they're just going to land back on the streets."

I bite back my immediate response, then realize I don't have a more tactful way to ask. "Why do *you* care?"

She doesn't seem bothered as she shoves an entire tart in her mouth and hums at the taste. "I don't, but we have a bit of a PR problem, and having little pet projects like this goes a long way when we have to rub elbows with certain social circles."

She looks at Salvatore and Dom, who are stepping onto the deck.

"I'll send the details over to you," she says with a wink. "Think about it."

Marisol departs, joining her husband, and Nico detaches from the railing to follow.

The crowd, the boat, and the lake fade around me as Dom and I lock eyes across the deck. In a few quick strides, he wraps me in an embrace so tight it's like we haven't seen each other in weeks. I press my face into his chest, breathing in his scent.

Since we came home from the cemetery, we've been nearly inseparable. I keep waiting for his interest to fade, for him to detach, but instead, our need for each other grows stronger every day.

The desperate, restless way we've been fucking lately has simmered into a gentle and tender lovemaking. It scares me sometimes, how intense it is, and I can't help the feeling that Dom is treating me so sweetly because my life is in danger. Then he texts me photos when he's away from the penthouse of fluffy pigeons on the street, or of him sadly eating a subpar restaurant meal, or flashing me a pair of my stolen panties in his pocket, and I think that's just how he is. Of the rare, lucky people who find great love in their lives, maybe I'm one of them.

Dom unwraps himself from me to kiss my forehead and peppers kisses down the side of my face, making me squeal, until he's kissing my mouth, deep and slow. I drag my nails into the nape of his neck and tug at his hair.

When he pulls away, he has that wild look in his eye like he's thinking about pulling me into an empty room to dip his head beneath my dress. In moments like this, I don't care how little time I might have left—what I have with him is bliss.

He kisses me again, and right as I consider demanding we go find one of those empty rooms, he takes my hand and murmurs, "I want you to stay near me tonight."

Fear drips down my spine, though his presence dulls it. "What did Don Salvatore say?"

"I can't say right now. Can you trust me?"

I squeeze his hand. "Of course."

Elegant piano music washes over us as we step inside the first deck and pass our coats to the attendant by the door. Neil's playing is better than I expected, a small relief. The suit I bought him fits well, and his face splits into a wide grin every time someone passes by and shoves another bill into the already overflowing tip jar on top of his piano.

Waiters weave through the crowd with sizzling flutes of champagne while Chicago's most dangerous citizens dress up in designer clothes and pretend, for one night, to be harmless.

Couples splinter off from the crowd to chat with us, and for once, I'm grateful no one expects much of me. The men try to preserve an air of dignity as they kiss Dom's ass, and the women offer me lavish compliments and saccharine condolences for my loss. I smile, thank them graciously like my sister would, and stand silently at Dom's side until the next person speaks to me.

"Sorry to interrupt," Carlo says as he strolls up to us. "Serafina, could I have a word with you?"

From his sharp-eyed look, I get the uneasy feeling that my brother's completely sober—something he only does out of absolute necessity.

Before I leave, Dom grabs my hand and kisses my cheek before whispering in my ear, "Stay where I can see you."

The council member's wife exclaims something about "Newlyweds!" as Dom turns back to them with a grin.

Carlo doesn't make a single sound of disgust at Dom's kiss, which worries me further. He guides me to the edge of the crowd, near the windows that overlook the dark lake.

"What's going on?" I ask. "Is everyone okay? You're freaking me out."

"Everyone's okay," he whispers. His eyes dart back to the crowd several times. "Have you talked to Russell?"

"Not since Dom beat him up, no."

"He came to see me after that."

I cross my arms. "I'm not going to apologize for what Dom did."

"Geez." Carlo exhales. "He—"

"Champagne?" a sandy-haired server offers. His tattoos peek out from under his shirt sleeve as he extends the tray toward us.

Carlo throws an arm out in front of me and laughs. "No thanks, this one's already had plenty!" he says, making an exaggerated drinking motion.

The server gives him a stiff smile and drifts away.

I shove Carlo. "I haven't had anything to drink. You could've just told him no."

"Okay, whatever. Anyway, Russell comes and finds me at the Velvet Kitty—"

"Gross."

"—and he says he's been in love with Serafina for years. He said he's leaving Chicago because…" Carlo rubs his neck. "Well, he says it's tough for him to see you."

The feeling's mutual.

I guess I hoped Russell would've stayed, and maybe after a few years, we could've spoken about Serafina, but I'm relieved he's leaving. I hope he finds peace wherever he goes.

Carlo leans in. "He said he had to stop by so he could tell you he'd caught wind of Aceto planning something tonight. Something big, but he didn't know what. And I didn't know if he was going crazy from the grief or what, but then I started paying attention. Look at the waiters."

I swivel my head as discreetly as I can to take in the staff snaking through the crowd. Now that he mentions it, most of them are men, and they do have a harsh quality to them. A few have cauliflower ears or facial scars. Most have tattoos. All of them walk with a swaggering confidence that reminds me of many of the men I've grown up with.

I turn back to Carlo, who gives me a knowing look.

"Who are they?" I ask.

He shrugs. "I'm guessing Russians. Maybe Belarusians. Whatever they are, I'm not planning to stick around and find out, and neither should you."

I look back at the party. Dom's still speaking with the council member, but like the connection between us has been tugged, he glances in my direction and flashes me a subtle smile.

Neil's playing the piano in the background, and the rest of my family's here, laughing and chatting. Valeria's here, somewhere. I can't leave all these people to whatever Aceto has planned.

I turn to Carlo. "You go. I'm going to tell Dom, and we'll figure something out."

"If anyone needs to leave, it should be you."

"*Me?*"

"Aceto, the rest. They all want *you*. You wanna protect everyone, then you go."

His comment stings, but I see the truth in it. We already know Aceto's in bed with the Chiarellis, and that his son thought it would be smart to attack me. If the best thing I can do is go back to the penthouse with Dom and let Don Salvatore handle this, then I can do that.

I nod. "Okay. I'm going to tell Valeria, I'll grab Dom, and we'll go."

Carlo shakes his head with a bitter laugh. "You didn't hear? She already left before you arrived."

"It's her dad's party, how could she leave early?"

He glances around before dropping his head near mine and murmuring, "She's probably scared. A little birdie told me her family got a late-night delivery the night you came by for a visit. You know Lasso?"

My stomach drops. I already know where this is headed.

"I heard they opened a box on their front porch, and inside was Lasso's face."

My stomach twists with horror. "What? You mean his head?"

Carlo leans in closer. "No. I mean, the skin peeled from his face, like a mask. They found the rest of him dead at some club."

My blood chills. "Who would do that?"

But I know the answer.

I startle as Dom slides his arm around my waist. "Barbaras! Am I interrupting anything?"

Carlo jerks his head toward Dom as if to say, *your culprit's right there.* "Not at all! We were just talking about you."

"All bad things, I hope."

Carlo laughs. "You know it. You two have fun. I'm gonna go find Mom and take her home. I saw her talking with Nonna earlier, and she usually dips into the hard liquor after that."

As Carlo vanishes into the crowd, I level a severe look at Dom.

His eyes light up, and he leans in to whisper huskily, "You keep looking at me like that, we might have to go find a private corner for ourselves."

"Carlo told me about Lasso." I study his face, waiting for him to lie or deny it, but he doesn't hesitate.

Dom barks out a laugh. "Good. I want every bastard here to know what happens if they touch you."

I should get mad at him, tell him he didn't have to do that.

But I already had an idea of what he was going to do to Lasso, and I didn't stop him, even though I could have.

The fear of what's going to happen tonight, of Carlo's warning, fades away under the harsh, bright light of my husband's brilliant smile. I don't have to be afraid of anything. Dom's here, and he's *mine.*

I cup my hands along his beard and graze my fingertips into his cheeks. "You're a good husband."

Dom's smile widens. "Only for you, angel." He sneaks a kiss against my fingertips. "We'd better head to the upper deck. Salvatore's waiting for us."

"Carlo said we should leave. He said Aceto's planning something tonight."

Dom laughs. "Don't worry. We know, and we got a little something planned for him, too."

He leads me outside where Dad's waiting for us, puffing at a cigar at the foot of the stairs in the half-light from the windows. He pushes himself up to standing as we approach and follows us to the upper deck.

It's quieter up here, the flooring muffling the party underneath us. I can barely make out the distant waves breaking against the pier, and I'm unafraid as we pass into the enclosed salon.

In the next hour, the rest of the party will migrate here to eat, but for now, only Salvatore, Marisol, and Nico sit in the center of a sea of white tables, each headed by one of my floral arrangements—a perfectly balanced mixture of dusty green cedar branches supporting pinecones and white roses as they build to a crescendo of show-stopping dark burgundy dahlias.

At the penthouse, I'd been so concerned with making each individual display perfect, that I'd lost sight of the effect as a whole.

Now, looking across all arrangements, and tasting the faintest floral aroma on my tongue? It's striking and dramatic and uniquely me, and it floods me with pride and the smallest measure of bittersweetness. For all the hard work I did to realize this vision, my sister's artistic influence quietly and undeniably shines through.

It feels, impossibly, like a collaboration.

Dad pats my shoulder. "You did good, kid," he says gruffly and takes a swig of his whiskey. "She'd be proud."

For Dad and me, this is more than just flowers.

I swallow past the lump of emotion in my throat. "Thanks, Dad."

Together, we make our way to the main table.

Once Dom drags my chair next to his and we're seated, the salon doors swing open.

Aceto and a flank of five tall, strong waiters enter the room, all bearing trays of entrees and drinks. The far-off sound of the party below mutes to complete silence as the doors click closed behind him.

"I'm so glad you all could make it," Aceto shouts jovially, excess champagne spilling over the side of his flute. He's the spitting image of his son, with his perfectly pressed suit and coiffed hair. Only his mustache and the greys at his temples set him apart. I bite the inside of my cheek so I don't scowl at him.

Was he the one who gave Valeria her black eye?

The waiters circle our table, placing steaming dishes of lobster and pasta in front of each person.

I move my heavy purse to my lap when one of the waiters sets my plate down. Dom squeezes my knee.

I don't understand how everyone at the table can be so completely at ease. Dad watches Aceto through half-lidded eyes and his hands propped on his belly like he might doze off. Nico's cleaning under his fingernails with one of the steak knives. Marisol giggles softly as Don Salvatore whispers something into her ear.

The waiters step back, and in perfect unison, pull out guns and point them at us.

My breath catches in my throat.

No one at the table reacts. Nico flashes one of the waiters a smirk. Dad's gaze rolls to me, completely calm. Is their plan to shoot at the waiters? Is there another group on standby? Or are they bluffing?

I slip my fingertips into my purse, grazing the warm metal of my gun, until Dom slides his hand over mine and squeezes it.

Okay. I have to trust him now.

My heart's beating like a snare drum. I squeeze his hand back and force myself to lean into my chair.

"What's going on?" Aceto asks, and even to my ear, it sounds fake.

In the corner of my eye, Salvatore gives the barest, most imperceptible nod, and the waiters swivel their guns at Aceto.

Aceto's face pales. He reaches behind him, but one of the waiters shouts, "*Nyet.*"

Aceto's hand freezes, his jaw tightening as he scans the waiters' faces. "What the fuck is this?"

"Business," the same waiter answers.

Salvatore picks up one of the steak knives and rises from the table in a smooth movement.

"On your knees," he says in a low voice as he approaches Aceto.

In a silent battle of wills that lasts seconds, Aceto drops to his knees with a heavy thud. "I've been nothing but loyal to you, Don Salvatore. I don't—"

Salvatore cuts in quietly. "You've been trying to undermine me." Everyone is completely silent, and I get the feeling we're all holding our collective breaths. I glance over at Marisol, expecting a solemn expression. Instead, she's smiling hungrily at her husband.

A shiver rolls through me.

Salvatore lifts the knife.

Instead of bringing it down on Aceto's neck, he lets it drop to the carpet and walks back to the table, where he sits and waits expectantly. His arm rests over the back of Marisol's chair, his fingertips skating along her shoulder.

Aceto whips his head around like a desperate animal. His gaze falls on me, and Dom scrapes his chair back to protect me from Aceto's view.

"Don Salvatore, you have a rat," he shouts. It feels like a stab to the chest when he points a finger in my direction. "That girl isn't Serafina—that's Annetta, the Chiarelli widow. She's going to get us all killed!"

Salvatore taps against the back of Marisol's chair impatiently. "Don't waste my time."

Aceto bows forward, fists and jaw clenched, and screams through gritted teeth. Inches away, the knife waits for him.

He turns his head toward it and, with a tremor I can see from here, takes it into his hand. His face is a mottled red, and he doesn't make a sound as he raises it.

I realize with a choked gasp—Salvatore is making Aceto kill himself.

Dom turns toward me and presses my face to his chest. "Don't look."

"Stop."

At first, I don't recognize who's talking. I've never heard his voice before, but I place the speaker—Nico.

I peek around Dom to see Aceto watching Nico with hope glimmering in his eyes.

Salvatore raises an eyebrow at his half-brother. Nico rises from his chair with an easy athletic grace and makes his way to Salvatore's side, where he leans forward and whispers in his ear. Even though we're at the same table, I can't hear what he says. It must be shocking because both of Salvatore's eyebrows lift and then come crashing down.

"Are you sure?" Salvatore asks.

Nico stands and places a hand over his heart, but his

loose posture makes it clear he's being unserious. "With every fiber of my being."

Salvatore sighs. "Looks like it's your lucky day, Aceto. You're going to come with me instead. Stand up."

Aceto's eyes widen, and he scrambles for the steak knife he'd just dropped. Nico's faster, striking out with almost inhuman speed to knock the knife from his hand. With a cruel smile on his lips, he grabs Aceto by the back of his neck and drags him kicking and screaming toward Salvatore.

Marisol casually reaches into her purse like there isn't a man fighting for his life within arm's reach and pulls out her phone. When she reads the message, the relaxed smile falls from her face. She shows the phone to Salvatore, and his eyes flick to Dom.

"Dom, take Barbara and Annetta to Knossos hospital," he says. "Rafa's been shot."

27

DOM

By the time we get to the hospital, Rafa's in the operating room.

Barbara bounces his knee in the corner of the waiting room while Debbie paces back and forth with a rosary in her hands. Carlo's tucked into his chair, sucking constantly from his vape until Debbie snaps at him to stop.

Annetta is pale, her arms trembling under my touch. She's dropping hard from the adrenaline of that fucking bullshit with Aceto. I've rubbed her hands between mine to keep them warm, but she barely seems to register anything that's going on around her.

I trace a fingertip along her face, tucking her silky hair behind her ear. She doesn't react.

"Everything's going to be okay," I tell her gently.

Her eyes are dull as she glances toward me, and a stone drops into my stomach.

"I can't lose another family member," she says in a thin voice.

I press her against me so I don't have to look at that face, the one I've seen countless times before.

It's the way a person looks before they do something they'll regret.

After hours of waiting, a short doctor in her fifties steps out. "Raffaele's alive. He's in stable condition now, but he'll be disoriented and tired from the effects of the pain medication he's on." The efficient, professional look about her slips for a fraction of a second. "He was shot in the side of the knee. We removed the bullet, and your primary doctor will discuss options with you, but it's likely he will need substantial physical treatment after today. He may not walk without an aid ever again. You all can see him now."

Debbie cries out, "Thank God!" and throws herself behind the doctor.

Carlo pulls his vape out of his pocket and waves us off. "You go first. I'll come after."

Barbara doesn't say anything, but he looks suspiciously close to crying. I politely ignore him as I help Annetta up and walk us down the long white hallway to Rafa's room.

Silent tears track down Debbie's face as she stands at the side of her broken son, who is rigged up to a half-dozen machines with medical bandages wrapped around his leg and chest. Despite what the doctor said, he's alert, staring forward without any expression until Annetta and I enter the room

He catches my eye.

"How are you feeling?" Annetta asks tentatively as she moves to his other side, opposite to her mother.

"Alive," he answers in a croaking voice. He stares at me. "I saw his face. He told me who it was for."

"*No.*" Debbie stands to her full height, giving us a firm look. "No, not now."

He ignores her as he holds my gaze. "They said it was for Frederico Chiarelli."

Debbie gulps her protest and cups her hands to her mouth. Annetta gasps softly.

I nod to Rafa.

He sighs, leaning his head back against the pillow with his eyes closed.

I'm done with this. The Chiarellis have overstepped for the last time.

Annetta stumbles out of her chair, waving me off from catching her.

"I'll be with Carlo," she chokes out and dashes out of the room.

I give it as long as it takes to type out a message to Turi asking for the address to the Chiarelli homes before I follow her. It's too risky to leave her alone right now. Once she's calmed down and is ready to go home, I'll take her to Turi's. He'll keep her safe until I get back from Florida.

If I get back.

My chest burns. I'll call in a couple of favors. I'll make it back. And if not?

She'll be protected. She won't need to get married again —she'll have all the money she'd want from my will. She'll have Turi's and her family's support. She'll survive. She's strong.

My phone buzzes.

It's the address for Marco Chiarelli and Giulia Chiarelli's homes.

TURI

What should I tell your wife when you leave
her a widow?

I storm out of the room and jerk to a stop outside the door, my chest heaving.

A patient walking past takes one look at me and scurries in the opposite direction.

Fuck. I can't leave her alone. She's got her family, but would anyone protect her like me? And Turi's a brother to me, but he'll let Marisol use my wife if it benefits them.

At the end of the hallway, Barbara takes slow, measured steps toward me as my thoughts crash into each other.

Barbara stops before me. He exhales.

We never spoke about the change in command from Aldo to Turi. I always knew where his loyalty was, and him killing his old don proved it. Barbara will always put his wife and kids first, and so long as Turi understands that, Barbara will be loyal to him, too. It's the same reason Barbara sponsored me as some young, angry wannabe all those years ago.

I've always put his family first.

Rage and worthlessness war inside me as I meet his eye.

"Gonna do something stupid?"

Not for the first time, he impresses me with his perception. I know his sleepy old man act is mostly a ruse, and still, I underestimate him like everyone else.

"You know me, Barbara." I chuckle bitterly. "The paragon of good choices."

"Do you remember the promise you made to me?"

You protect mine. And I'll protect yours.

"You gonna take care of my daughter?" Barbara asks.

Everything around me stills.

I can't do it.

I can't go on this suicide mission to keep Annetta safe. I can't be the rusty blade that cuts through her enemies—I need precision. I need to make a better decision. She deserves better than what I intend to do. I have to be a good husband.

"Yeah. I'll take care of her."

Barbara grabs the back of my neck and pulls me down until our foreheads touch briefly.

"Good," he says and walks to his son's hospital room.

For a moment, I'm blinded by the glaring white lights in the hallway as I stare straight up. I gather myself and stride toward the waiting room.

Carlo sits alone.

"Where's your sister?" I ask harshly, covering the distance between us in a few long steps.

Carlo jerks upright. "You told her to get something from the car."

It hits us both at the same time.

She ran.

28

ANNETTA

I KILLED MY EX-HUSBAND. I did the hard thing. I made the difficult choice.

But his fucking ghost won't stop haunting me.

A drizzle of rain drums against the windshield, broken up every few seconds by the wipers.

I bought a black T-shirt and gym shorts at the last gas station, but I'll have to make another stop soon for better shoes. My heels won't do. Under the passenger seat, I found a hunting knife and another handgun. Both rest in the cup holders next to me as I drive.

Over my new clothes, I'm still wearing my big wool coat. No matter how much I crank up the heat, I can't stop shivering.

I called Marisol once I was on the road. I thought she'd demand I come back, that she'd tell me how angry the don was. Instead, she gave me all the information I asked for.

The Chiarellis are leaving for France tomorrow. While my brother's in the hospital, they're going on vacation.

Marisol told me to find the tiny GPS tracker under Dom's SUV seat and throw it out the window along with my phone. I don't know if she's treating my decision with respect or if she's letting me go to Florida as a lamb to slaughter, but I suspect she's being an opportunist—if I kill them or they kill me, one of her problems will disappear.

I glance at my rearview mirror again.

After eight hours of driving, I'm not even halfway there, but a black sedan already clings to my car's shadow. At first, I thought it was one of the Chiarelli mercenaries, but the grey morning sunlight shining through the windshield tells me a different story.

It's my husband.

He's coming for me.

My gas tank burns a glowing red *E* into the corner of my vision. I have to stop, but I can't—he's going to take me home. He'll tuck me into a corner of his penthouse, guarded by strange men—or worse, hand me off to Don Salvatore or my parents.

He's going to tell me to wait. To be patient.

Tears track down my face.

I'm so fucking sick of being patient.

They took my sister.

They tried to take my brother.

The Chiarellis want me so badly? They can have me, but I'm not waiting anymore. If I can take Marco or their mom with me, that's one less person to go after the people I love.

The wheel locks. Power steering is engaged.

I'm out of time.

I push the car as far as I can, as if, through sheer force of will, I could drag it through the last leg of the trip. But my will must not be strong enough, because slowly, the SUV grinds to a stop. I guide it to the shoulder of the road at the last possible second and lean my head back against the back of the driver's seat.

When the front door opens, letting in a rush of cool air and misty rain, I don't react. I let my eyes fall shut. Exhaustion weighs down my shoulders. "You caught me."

"I'll always catch you, *reginetta*." It feels like I haven't been called that name in years.

"I was going ten over the speed limit."

"I was going twenty."

I blow out a stream of air and blink my eyes open.

Dom is wearing the same black suit from the party, but his hair is bound tightly in a bun. Even now, with a deep sense of unfairness sweeping through me, I itch to pull out his ponytail and bury my face in his hair. The suit strains against his broad, muscled chest as he shifts to lean one arm along the hood of the car.

"How far you plan to go with this?" His gaze flicks to the gun and knife in the cupholders before returning to me.

"As far as I could."

He makes a *tsk* sound. "Then this is it. It's time to come home."

I don't move. "I'm just going to try again."

I can't keep waiting in the penthouse for someone to kill me or hurt my family. I have to do *something*.

Dom cups my cheek and guides my face toward him with his big, rough hands. "I thought we were supposed to kiss before one of us leaves."

My lower lip trembles. "I told Marisol to tell you—"

"Marisol isn't my fucking wife. You were supposed to tell me. I thought we were supposed to trust each other. You know, at the hospital, I was planning on doing the same thing you're doing now."

Wild panic thrashes in my chest. Dom's never been to the Chiarelli homes. He doesn't know where the guards will be, where the secret hiding places are. He'd get himself killed."

He must see it in my face because he laughs. "Not so fun, is it? Imagining your partner dying under horrific torture because you didn't sacrifice yourself first. You want to know why I didn't? Because of you. I thought I needed to stay because I knew no one would protect you or take care of you like I would. I thought I was making the right choice, but you'd already left."

A lump of emotion wedges in my throat as I meet his gaze. "I can't keep putting my safety above my family's. I'm just one—"

His eyes flash with anger. "You are not *just* anything. You are Annetta fucking Lombardi. You are my fucking wife. And you don't get to decide to get yourself killed for anyone."

"I'm not any more important than—"

Dom snatches my shoulder and shakes me. "You are more important than *everyone!*"

He dives into the car, grabbing the back of my head, and presses our foreheads together. "If you'd done this, I would've killed everyone. The Chiarellis, your family, Salvatore." His breath burns against my lips. "They'd have to put me down like a rabid dog. No one would've been safe. Don't you ever forget the level of petty, ruthless cruelty I'm capable of."

I suck in a breath and, at the same time, he crushes a kiss to my lips, lashing his tongue against mine. I wrap my arms around his neck and drive my nails into his scalp and let my anger pour into him.

When he finally pulls away, we're both heaving.

A car drives past us with a whoosh of air.

"I'm taking you home," he says. "*Now.*"

"They're going on a plane tomorrow morning. If I don't go now, I'll lose this chance."

"Then we wait here until I have one of Turi's men come pick you up, and I go. Alone." Some of the frustration fades from his face. He exhales. "Go home, Annetta. Your family needs you. Let your husband do your dirty work."

I touch his chest, his arms. I stroke my nails along his neck—touching that place where I bit him. Dom's fingers flex against my back.

"No one knows the Chiarellis like I do. Last night, Marco was sleeping off a hangover at his mistress's apartment. His mom slept in her bed on the second floor, first door to the right. Tonight, they'll have the housekeepers pack their suitcases. Marco will eat dinner at Giulia's house. He'll go home to play cards with Mario and snort cocaine. Giulia will spend time in the garden, and her guard Tommy will walk the perimeter, but he has a bad knee, so he'll rest against a tree—"

"Marisol told you all that—"

"No. This is what I know after spending the last three years of my life stuck there. If I go back home, back to your penthouse, or to my parents' home, or even to Salvatore's, I'll be a sitting duck again. They'll pick off my family one by one, until they get to me, and they'll do to me what they did to Matteo."

Everyone in the family knows what happened to Matteo, how he was tortured and cut up into a hundred pieces. And everyone knows what Salvatore and Dom did to seek justice after.

"Don't say shit like that."

I take his big, heavy hands in mine, hands he uses for unspeakable violence but have only ever been used to love me. I press my cheek against the back of his hand and drop my voice to a whisper. "I need this to end."

When he steps back, he fills up my entire vision. This man, I realize, has never lied to me. He's been the one constant in my life. He's the only man I've ever loved.

He steps away. "Come on."

I inhale suddenly, unaware I'd been holding my breath, and follow my husband.

IN HIS CAR, Dom makes me swear a hundred times over that I won't leave the vehicle.

He's driving now, a light touch on the steering wheel. He pushed his SUV further onto the side of the road, texted Salvatore to get it towed, and tossed a backpack full of practical, dark clothes for me into my lap.

"What if they take me?" he asks.

"I'll drive away."

"And if I take too long?"

"I'll drive away."

"What do you do if you see someone approaching your car?"

"I'll drive away."

He quizzes me for hours.

How many bullets does your gun hold? Nineteen.

Where are the extra bullets? Show me how you replace the magazine. Pull your knife out of the holster. Again. Braid your hair. Tuck it away. Tuck your shoelaces. Tuck your shirt.

He drives for hours. For once, he doesn't have the radio playing, and we sit in tense silence, broken only by another clipped command or question as he thinks of them.

He encourages me to sleep, and I do, contorted across the center console, hugging my body against his arm. After fading in and out of a restless sleep, I wake up to the sight of a river in front of us.

I reach for my gun.

"Where are we?" I ask groggily, jerking my head around.

"Shh... We're going to sleep as much as we can, and we'll do the last leg. I don't want to get there while there's light out."

I take a moment to steady my racing heart and lie back down against him.

He cups my waist with his hand.

"What happens after this?" I ask.

He leans his chair back and blows out a sigh. "We head home. I beg for Turi's forgiveness. You go to therapy, and we live happily ever after."

"You think we will? Live happily ever after?"

He kisses my temple. "I know it, angel."

29

ANNETTA

THE CLOSER WE GET, the more relaxed Dom seems to become.

Hours ago, he turned on the radio to a low volume, humming along with the music in a deep baritone as he toys with my fingers. If I concentrate, I can pretend we're going to a cabin in the woods for a relaxing vacation.

But as I start to recognize the streets and buildings where I spent the last few years of my life, the fantasy dissolves into reality.

We're going to Marco's house first.

Even this close to midnight, the neighborhood is brightly lit, and Dom weaves through the streets until he finds a slice of road that cloaks us in darkness.

He turns off the radio and faces me. "Get in the driver's seat."

Gone is the man who serves me in the bedroom, and the woman I become with him. I follow his order without question.

We step out of the car. Mild night air brushes against my exposed skin, and I inhale the familiar saltwater scent of the bay as I walk to the driver's side. This late at night, almost all of the lavish, two-story homes are dark and silent.

I've visited a few of the families in this neighborhood. If any of them recognized me on this empty street, they'd invite me into their homes with bright smiles as they reported me to Marco or Giulia.

Dom's adjusting the bulletproof vest under his clothes, the gun at his waist, and the knife at his calf. I remember our wedding when I thought him a warlord. Now, the only difference is I've tasted the truth of it.

When he looks at me, the teasing, playful smile he usually wears is nonexistent. He's businesslike as he moves, tugging at the Velcro of my bulletproof vest and speaking in a firm tone.

"Stay alert. If you see anyone approach the car—man, woman, or child—drive away. We'll meet at the neighborhood entrance. If I take longer than thirty minutes, drive away. Use the burner in the glove box to call Salvatore. Keep your gun out and ready to use."

I hang on to every word, nodding.

His hands pause on my waist as his gaze skates over my face like he's memorizing my features. Then he wraps me in a tight hug, the bulk of our vests making the movement stiff and awkward.

"Stay safe," he whispers against the top of my head.

I swallow. "You too."

He waits until I jump into the car and lock the doors, and he's gone, jogging down the street through the backyard of the nearest house.

I wait.

Without Dom at my side, I'm hyperaware of how exposed I am, parked in the middle of the neighborhood with great big houses looming over me on every side. No one's out this late at night, and judging by the lights in the windows, only the house across from me has someone still awake.

To keep myself alert, I check my radius every minute, circling my head hundreds of times. Only one other car passes me with a young woman inside, seemingly oblivious to the gun I had pointed in her direction as she headed home.

After twenty minutes, a figure limps from the shadows of a nearby hedge.

Dom.

My intuition screams that something's wrong. He's favoring his left leg and clutching his neck. As he steps under a streetlight, the form his body suggests cuts into sharp definition. Blood. Blood on his hand, his neck. He's pale and gritting his teeth.

My breath seizes.

I lean over to open the car door as he approaches, and groaning, he hauls himself inside.

"Drive," he wheezes.

I don't question him, I just start driving and glance into the rear view mirror for anyone that might be following him.

"Dom, what's going on?" I take every effort to smother the panic in my voice.

He's covered in so much blood. It's streaming through his fingers onto his chest.

He laughs, but it's a frail-sounding thing. "I kicked the hornet's nest, and I got stung. They had a couple of guards I had to take out first. Marco had extra friends over for poker, and I spent too long fucking with the last one. Marco snuck up on me and shot me. Bastard got me right in the fucking shoulder."

Dom wheezes a chuckle as he pulls out medical tape from the glove box and wraps it around the bloody meat of his shoulder, right where I bit him a lifetime ago. "Don't worry. I got him back. He's dead. Drive to Giulia's house."

I swipe at the tears welling in my eyes. "You need a hospital."

"Drive to Giulia's house," he grits out. "That's a fucking order."

I could disobey him.

I should.

Instead, I maneuver his car through the labyrinth of million-dollar homes, toward my ex-mother-in-law's house. There's no safety, no peace for any of us until this is finished. My former family knows that, and it's taken me all this time to understand it as intimately as they do.

I strangle the steering wheel and pray to a god I've forsaken a hundred times over to please keep my husband safe. Take anyone, take *me*, but please don't let Dom die. And like always, He is silent.

The edge of Giulia's property slices into view. I press down on the gas pedal. We're almost done.

CRUNCH.

The airbag explodes into my face like a grenade and smashes me against my seat.

What was that?

My ears ring. I can't hear anything else.

The airbag hangs from the center of the steering wheel like an empty pillowcase. Acrid gunpowder smoke stings my nose.

"Drive," Dom shouts.

I don't think—I slam on the pedal. Our car revs, but something has it hooked—it won't move.

We're stuck.

Bullets punch into the glass of the back window. Dom's hand slams onto my head, jerking me down. He lets loose a slew of curses.

"I get out. Then you run."

"No, Dom—"

"That's a *fucking* order. Now run!"

He jumps out of the car, his gun popping off at the car behind us—at Marco—*he survived?*

I scramble to unbuckle myself and dive out of the car. When my feet hit the street, I bolt straight for Giulia's house.

To my left, a porch light flicks on. Our crash woke up the neighborhood. We don't have much time.

Instead of running toward Giulia's front door, I race for the back. I know the family. I know their habits and their hobbies and their sins.

It's a Saturday night, and Giulia has insomnia.

She'll be in the garden.

My lungs burn, but I force myself to keep sprinting. The pain is a sweet reminder that I haven't failed yet.

I'm alive.

I put on another burst of speed.

I have to finish this.

I can't go back for Dom. I have to trust him. No one will hurt him—he's *Dom*.

My body is not my own—it's a machine, the muscles of my thighs and arms working in perfect, practiced synchronicity to propel me forward like a freight train toward Giulia's sprawling backyard. And when I see her guard walking the perimeter of her house—Tommy, the one who always ate my desserts and played cards with me—I don't think. I pull out my gun, jerk to a stop, aim, and shoot.

He crumples to the ground in a soundless heap. I keep running until I meet the border of the dark green hedges that wrap around the perimeter of her yard. I force myself through a narrow gap between the branches and leaves. The wood claws at me as if obeying the will of their mistress, but tonight, my will is stronger. When I burst onto the other side, we see each other in the moonlight.

Giulia Chiarelli, matriarch of the Chiarelli mob, aims her gun directly at me.

She doesn't hesitate.

But neither do I.

She cries out when my bullet tears through her shoulder —right where her bastard son shot my husband. Her gun goes flying.

Her bullet hits the plate armor of my bulletproof vest, and I don't make a sound.

She crumbles to the ground, but she doesn't waste a moment searching for her fallen gun in the dark grass.

I spot the dark gleam of metal first and sprint to kick it far away.

When I turn back to her, she's grimacing at me, her bloody hand clutched to her shoulder and her knees in the dirt.

"I always told my son you were a dumb whore," she spits at me, in English for once. She must be in unbelievable pain as she grasps the arm hanging loosely from its socket. Blood pours out between the fingertips of her left hand.

"Your son was a pedophile."

The vicious look on her face is completely unrepentant.

"Your other son, he's going to die by my husband's hand. Tonight. Do you think my Butcher will be lenient with baby Marco?"

A new emotion flashes across her features—fear— although she smothers it with arrogance. "What do you want, *fottuta puttana*?"

This is the woman who's haunted me for months, who's responsible for the death of my sister, who raised her sons to be vile men.

Who attacked my brother, me, and my husband.

There's no forgiveness for this woman.

When I raise the gun again, my round-faced, soft-spoken former mother-in-law chokes out a laugh. "I'm so happy your sister died first."

I shoot.

I waste only one breath, staring down at her dead body. I shoot her three more times in the head and the chest like Dom taught me, and I run after my husband.

The vehicles are still smashed together in the middle of the street, but the drivers are nowhere to be found. A few neighbors stand outside, wrapped in winter coats over their pajamas, phones pressed to their ears. One of them shouts after me, but I don't stop to listen.

Gun in hand, I creep from house to house, looking for Dom's unmistakable shape and praying I don't find it on the ground.

If Marco took him, his death won't be as quick as his mom's, and I don't give a damn if the police are on their way.

I find them, almost completely swallowed by the shadow of a towering, pale house. Two formless shapes merge into one dark horror.

"Dom," I call out as I approach, gun raised in my hand.

The larger shadow moves.

"Don't make a sound," Dom murmurs to the man underneath him. When he looks to me, I can barely make out his eyes in the darkness.

"It's over now," I say. "She's dead."

I recognize Marco's voice as he cries out in anguish.

"I have to take you to the hospital now. We have to go."

Dom's laugh is fragile. He turns to the man. "You hear that? Your mom's in hell. Now, why don't you go join her?"

Dom slashes his arm to the side and staggers to his feet, leaning heavily against the side of the house. His knife, bathed in blood, shines darkly from one of the streetlights. Dom sheathes it and turns to me, stumbling forward and nearly crushing me to the ground under his weight.

I've always loved how big he is, how much larger than life he feels, but right now, I hate it. I can barely keep him upright, and that's with him supporting most of his own weight. I don't know what I'll do if he faints.

"Lost a lot of blood," he says dreamily. "I love you. Don't know if I said that yet. Thinking it a lot."

My heart wrenches. He wasn't supposed to get hurt. He's *Dom*—he's invincible.

A tear slips down my cheek. "Dom, I love you too. I love you so much. Stay awake, okay? I still need you. I have to set you down right now. I'm going to get the car."

"Don't leave me, *reginetta*," he whispers against my hair. "Stay with me."

"I have to. I'll be right back, I swear."

I do my best to ease him to the ground, but he's too big, and I drop him with a heavy thud into the grass.

"Don't go," he calls weakly after me as I sprint back to the cars.

"Are you okay?" an old man shouts at me from the sidewalk. I ignore him. In the distance, there's a wail of an ambulance and police sirens.

I stop before the vehicles. Our car is hooked onto Marco's, and the front of his is almost completely smashed in. I don't know if either will work. I try ours first, diving in and yanking the gear stick to drive.

It revs uselessly for several long seconds until, in desperation, I scream through gritted teeth and swing the steering wheel to the side. It jerks free and slams into someone's mailbox.

I tear through a patch of flowers and nearly crash into the side of the house where Dom is.

"Hey!" someone shouts from the street.

I stumble out of the car, and a bald man in a bathrobe marches up to me.

"What the fuck, lady! Are you fucking drunk—"

I swing my gun at him.

The man stills. Distantly, a woman screams.

"Get back in the house," I tell him. "Lock the door."

He scrambles back, tripping over his robe to get to his front door.

I spin to Dom and kneel at his side.

And my heart stops in my chest.

He's dead—no, no, *wait*, he's breathing. He's unconscious. *God, please.* Blood soaks his shirt. Whose blood?

I can't—I won't be able to get him into the car. He's too heavy, and I'm not strong enough.

I try anyway, tears streaming down my face as I drag him along the ground to the passenger seat as the ambulance circles closer. I might as well be hauling an entire fridge into the air as I shove his upper half against the car body. His blood is hot, sticky, and slippery.

I can't lift him inside. I can't lift his whole body into the car.

"Dom," I cry urgently. "Dom, please. Please wake up."

He rolls his head. His eyelashes flutter.

"Just stand a little, and I'll handle the rest. I need you to get inside, please."

He wheezes. I bite my lip so hard I taste blood. Then I slap him—*hard.*

"Stand!"

With monumental effort, he brings his legs underneath him and pushes. Together, we heave him into the passenger seat.

"Don't you dare fucking die on me," I say as I dive into the driver's seat.

I'm not sure if I imagine it, but I think I hear him laugh a little.

I break a hundred traffic laws on my way to the nearest hospital.

30

DOM

I'm in heaven.

An angel hovers over me, a thoughtful look etched into her beautiful face.

The first thing I do is laugh.

The angel frowns.

Heaven? Me? Saint Peter must be a shitty sort of clerk to let an undeserving bastard like me in. Good things really do happen to bad people.

With honey blonde hair brushing against her shoulders, the angel floats to my side.

She looks exhausted. A twinge of worry touches me.

Maybe this is hell.

"Dom?" she asks uncertainly.

My memories come crashing into me with the force of a semi-truck.

"You have to get out of here, now," I croak, sitting up. "The cops, they—"

"Look who's awake," a quiet voice says.

I take in my surroundings. I'm on a flimsy bed with thin

cotton sheets. Beeping monitors circle me. How did I get into a hospital?

In his winter coat, Salvatore Luporini looks like a great black bat that fell into the armchair opposite my bed. He rakes a hand through his hair and blows out a sigh.

"Where are we?" I ask.

Turi doesn't bother standing from his chair, the lazy bastard. He waves a hand. "The hospital, obviously."

Jackass.

"That little wife of yours somehow got you to the ER. Set off about a hundred different alerts of mine. I paid a small fortune to have men go out and do a discreet cleaning of the huge fucking mess you made," he says without heat. He stifles a yawn. "I had you sent to Chicago after you were stable. Doctors said you barely made it."

I glance out the window of my room's door and spot the back of Eduardo's head. Then to Turi and Annetta.

"So, I'm not in trouble?"

Turi scoffs. "If by 'not in trouble' you mean I'm going to have you do the most disgusting grunt work imaginable until I feel better about the mess you made, then yes."

I set that aside. Turi thinks touching a public doorknob is disgusting, so we have vastly different ideas on the subject. "What about the Chiarellis?"

"Dead. All of them."

"And the Commission just accepted that?"

Turi frowns. "I had to pull quite a few strings. Nico and Valeria will be married immediately—"

"Valeria?" Annetta blurts out.

Turi's gaze cuts to her.

"I... I didn't think they even knew each other."

"Yes, well, somehow seeing Aceto on the verge of death stoked the flames of Nico's desire for his absent daughter."

He pauses, as though waiting for Annetta to object, but she chews on the news in silence. "Nico's marriage will be good for our relations with New York. We're also in negotiations to marry off Carlo. And the old Chiarelli don in jail—he's been taken care of." He sighs. "The Commission was happy enough to promote one of the Florida capos as the new, loyal leadership in place of the Chiarellis. One who will happily lick their boots and won't encourage the skin trade like the old dynasty."

I lean back in my shitty hospital bed, feeling lighter than I have in months. I reach for Annetta's slender hand and rub my thumb along her knuckles. She smiles at me, even as exhaustion lines her young face and ages her ten years. In different conditions, it'd suit her, but right now, I'm aching to get her home and in bed so she can take a well-earned rest.

Turi stands. "Marisol is expecting me for dinner. You can leave after the doctor does her final check-up, and Eduardo will help you get back to the house. And, Annetta, we've explained the mix-up to the family. You can go by your real name now."

Annetta sighs with relief.

"Turi," I say. A dozen forms of gratitude cross my mind, but Turi appreciates efficiency above all else, so I just say, "Thank you."

A rare smile pulls at his mouth. "Next time you pull a stunt like that, I'll have you cut off your own finger."

And with that lovely thought, he leaves.

I turn back to Annetta. She glances at the door. "Was he...?"

"Don't worry about it," I say, grinning roguishly at her. "Come here, angel."

She shakes her head, tears filling her eyes, and touches

her fingertips to her lips. "Dom," she says in a choked voice, "I'm *so* sorry."

"Angel, don't cry."

"I thought I'd lost you. It's all my fault. I'm sorry I left. You were right. I never should've gone without telling you." She laughs bitterly, rubbing her face into her palms. "I thought I was protecting everyone by leaving, and I almost got you killed."

"It'd take a hell of a lot more than a few bullets to kill me." Or to kill Marco, apparently. I shot the bastard three times, and he still had enough strength to come after us. I wish I could've dragged him to Turi's basement for risking Annetta's life, but he wouldn't have survived the trip, and knowing he died in emotional agony is a good-enough compromise.

Annetta's lower lip quivers. "You were lying in a pool of your own blood."

"Hey. Most of it was the other guy's."

"I couldn't lift you up! I thought..." A few tears escape and trail down her cheeks. "I'm sorry."

"It's not all your fault. You might have had a chance if I hadn't put on so much damn weight since you moved in."

She laughs through her tears, and I grin. She looks so beautiful when she laughs, like her face is reflecting pure sunshine.

"Dom, could you ever forgive me?"

Why is she still talking about forgiveness when I'm in bed, and she's all the way over there? I reach for her wrist. "Already forgiven. Now get under these sheets and on top of me."

She slaps my hands away. "Dom! You almost died."

"Exactly. Let's celebrate life."

"You told me you loved me."

I slow, looking up into her dark, teary eyes. Strands of her hair catch the harsh, fluorescent lights and transform them into gold against her rosy cheeks and her elegant neck.

Maybe this *is* heaven.

"Of course I love you."

She sucks in a tiny gasp and touches her fingers over her heart. I cup a hand on her hip. I'd better get it all out so she knows how I feel, and we can get to the good stuff.

"Annetta, I fucked this all up too. I did everything wrong in that church and made plenty of mistakes after, and you still treated me like the sweetest, most loving wife alive. You're loyal, kind, and strong. And a great cook. And a fucking bombshell in bed. And everything a man like me doesn't deserve but is going to hold onto anyway. I'm going to cherish you for the rest of my life. And if that ending comes sooner rather than later, you already know my final thoughts will be of you."

I want to kiss the tears streaming down her cheeks. She's beautiful when she laughs, and she's beautiful when she cries.

I never stood a chance.

I need her to stop crying so far away from me and come lie on top of me, or better yet, boss me around a little as she takes me inside her, so we can both feel better.

I clutch her waist and heave her to my side.

"I love you too!" she bursts out with wet cheeks and a wide smile as I tow her toward me. "I love you, I love you so much. I don't know how I got so lucky to find a man like you, but I'm so happy I did. I'll never let you go, Domenico Lombardi. I love you."

I cup her cheek. "Oh, angel. I know. It's why all your cooking tastes so fucking good. Now get over here."

She laughs and kisses my fingertips. "You barely fit on

that bed by yourself, you big idiot. There's no way we can both fit."

I laugh. "We'll make it fit."

EPILOGUE

ANNETTA

5 Months Later

A YOUNG DEER walks into Dom's view.

Half of it is hidden behind dark tree bark, and the other half is bisected by a shaft of sunlight filtered green by the tree leaves.

I hold my breath, waiting to see if Dom will take the shot.

He presses the shutter.

The deer flicks its head in our direction and bounds away into the underbrush.

Dom and I release an exhale at the same time.

"Did you get it?"

"Did I fucking get it?" Dom repeats, flipping the camera monitor in my direction with a cocky grin. "Of course I fucking got it."

I snatch it from his hands. "*Wow*, this turned out even better than I expected. I love the way you caught the light here. The composition is fantastic."

Next to me, Dom rolls onto his back in the grass and dirt,

so much like Coco or Bunny that I stifle a grin. The newest additions to our household like getting dirty almost as much as they hate baths. When we dropped off our little Dobermann puppies at my parents' house before our trip, I fully expected Mom to make them wipe their paws before they came into the house, but she surprised us all by bringing them an entire chicken breast each and new, pink collars. It's still a little awkward between us, but I think she's accepting that kids aren't in the picture for Dom and me, and it helps that she has Coco and Bunny to dote on.

I also thought Dom would oppose a camping trip just for fishing and photography, but he jumped at the opportunity. We've spent the past few weeks picking out all the perfect accessories for this trip. Now, looking at his breathtaking photo and the others he's taken, I'm struck by his natural eye. In another life, he might've been an artist.

"I knew you'd make a good shooting partner." I turn toward him and freeze at the thoughtful look in his eye, like he's been watching me the whole time as I admired his photo.

"I used to think the same about you and hunting," he says with a private smile.

Behind him, dark grey storm clouds float above the tree line, the electricity in the air so strong, I can practically taste it. We'll have to leave soon to get back to the tent before we get rained on, but for now, I gingerly set his camera down and roll my belly onto his chest.

"You know I don't hunt," I murmur as I stroke my fingers through his hair.

If it's uncomfortable to lie on a bed of rocks and sticks, he doesn't complain. A little green leaf sticks out of his hair like it sprouted from his head, and dirt streaks his temple. I stroke my fingers through his salt-and-pepper beard, admiring his square jawline, his gentle eyes. How does he manage to get more beautiful every day?

Even though I've gained some weight and I don't wear makeup anymore—for once, I get to enjoy my face as my own, and no one else's—every day, he says I'm beautiful too.

"But you're so good at it," he says, hooking his leg under mine so I'm straddling him.

We've barely made it out of the tent the past few days, spending most of our time completely naked and soaking in each other's presence. At night, we lie together in the hammock as Dom points out the stars and constellations to me, and I rest my cheek against his chest and doze off to the low rumble of his voice.

"I'm good at lots of things." I grin, stroking my hand over his chest and sitting up so I grind against his growing erection. "And anyway, I prefer my prey to be a lot bigger and *harder* to catch."

"You keep moving like that, it'll be plenty hard." He stretches out long underneath me and reaches for me with his dirty hands.

I shriek and smack them away. "Not when you've been digging in the dirt. Hands over your head."

Grinning, he takes his sweet time to obey, shifting his hips and watching me with half-lidded eyes while he arranges his hands loosely over his head in the dirt.

"*Good* job."

He grins wider at the praise. I swear if he had a tail, he'd be wagging it. God, he has such a nice smile—bright and honest. I can't help but smile back.

He lifts his hips for me as I tug his gym shorts down to his knees.

I turn away from him and catch sight of the flickering

storm clouds looming over us. I inhale deeply. The air smells like change.

Trusting in the isolated location, I step my heels together, hinge at the waist, and take my time shimmying my leggings and panties to my ankles, giving Dom a generous view as I do.

When I turn, he's wearing a feral expression—like he's starving, and I'm the only food for miles.

"No, no, bring that up here first," he says as I start to lower over his hips.

I glance up at him with a raised eyebrow. "We've been hiking for miles today."

"I don't give a fuck. Come on, *reginetta*. Just a taste."

I love when he gets like this—all rough and needy, but his hands are unmoved like my demands are ironclad.

"Okay, but just a taste."

It takes a bit of maneuvering with my ankles bound by my leggings, but I manage to get myself up to his face, making sure not to put any weight on his newly healed shoulder, and lower myself onto his mouth. His fingers twitch over his head like he wants to grab for my thighs, probably to push my full weight onto him, how he likes it, but only let the wet heat of his tongue stroke through me a few times, before I rise again, setting off a round of complaints.

"Come on, *reginetta*. I was just getting started, just one more lick."

I shift back down to his hips, ignoring his pleading, and press him to my entrance. He stops talking, and his body goes tense underneath me. Thunder crackles in the distance.

Slowly, I feed his length inside me until I'm gasping and seated. As good as he looks right now with his biceps straining next to his face and his broad hands flexing overhead, I'd rather he be touching me.

"Grab my hips, please."

His palms snap to my hips right as I find a rhythm. We work in sync—me grinding my clit against his pelvis and rubbing him against an especially delicious spot inside me as he forces my hips down to give me even more friction. It doesn't take long for me to throw my head back, my spine arching as I moan into the open air. A few raindrops kiss my face, and a slow, sweeping heat builds and crashes into me as I gasp for air and cling to Dom's wrists.

Dom finishes right as I'm coming down, the pulsing of his release prolonging my orgasm by a few extra seconds. The moment we both come down, we scramble to jerk our clothes back on and shield the camera in Dom's backpack from the building rain.

Right as we stumble back onto the trail, a sleet of rain comes crashing down. The storm drums against the canopy as we race back to camp, laughing at the rain soaking through our clothes and chilling us. By the time we get to the tent, I'm wet and shivering but grinning ear-to-ear. We strip down, crawl onto the mattress, and press our naked bodies together for warmth while the rain creates a symphony above our heads.

THE NEXT MORNING, we wake up to birds chittering beyond the tent. We make love again and dress to go on one last hike before we have to pack our supplies and head back home. This has been the honeymoon of my dreams, but I miss my new work with Marisol, my family, our penthouse, and our puppies.

"I found this spot a few years back." Dom takes a swig from the water bottle and passes it to me. "It's right around the bend."

The rain gave way to a hot, muggy day, and between that and the hike, I've never been more looking forward to modern-day plumbing back at the penthouse.

He buries the bottle in his backpack and points ahead on the trail. "Right there."

We stumble upon a wildflower meadow. Pink, yellow, and lavender flowers brush through the landscape, their rich colors amplified by the rain. A cooling breeze whispers past us to rustle through the long grass, and the blossoms sway in a gentle dance.

Dom steps behind me, circling his arm around my waist as tears sting my eyes.

I half-turn to him. "Dom, it's so beautiful."

Since Dom and I came back from Florida, I've visited Serafina's grave with Mom and Carlo, but it was as empty as I expected. She wasn't there—but here, in this place full of life and color and gentle things? Places like these are where I find my sister.

"I thought you might like it." He squeezes me tighter and rests his head on top of mine.

"I love it," I whisper through a choked voice. "I love *you*."

He kisses the crown of my head. "And I love you."

We soak in the scenery and the warmth of each other's closeness before I say a quiet goodbye, we turn back on the trail, and we go home.

ALSO BY EVE CIRIC

Sacred Vows Series:

Mask (Novella)

The Devil's Wife

The Butcher's Wife

ABOUT THE AUTHOR

Eve Ciric writes mafia romances with dark, twisty suspense and panty-melting dirty talk that will have you staying up late just to see what happens next.

She lives with her husband and her two black cats on the East Coast between the mountains and the sea. She loves running outside, practicing her Spanish, baking slightly undercooked chocolate chip cookies, and HUGE... cups of coffee.

Stick around and sign up for the newsletter for updates, fan art, bonus short stories, and more.

www.eveciric.com